SACRED SINS

ELUDING DESTINY
BOOK SEVEN

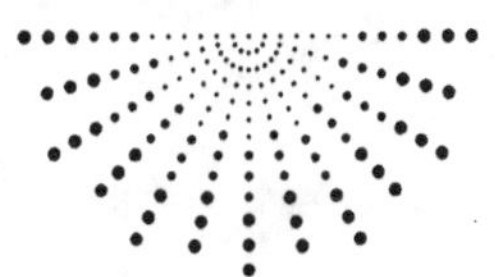

CHARLIE NOTTINGHAM

LIQUID MIND PUBLISHING

CONTENT WARNING

This one's for my pops, the best grandpa in the universe.
You showed me what it means to be a good man.
Whenever I say "I hate all men," you are always the exception.
I love you so much, Pops.

What is good?
Life? Justice? Obedience?
What is bad?
Death? Murder? Defiance?
Is there a finite line to differentiate between the two?
If it does exist,
What happens when that line begins to blur?

CHAPTER ONE

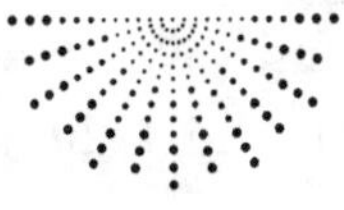

JEREMY

My head rested against the messy, dust and blood covered hair hanging from my son's neck. All I could hear was the pounding of my heartbeat in my ears and Laila's relieved, yet tense, uneven breaths beside me. Micah stunk so bad, like a combination of urine, feces, and dirt. But Jesus Christ, he was alive, and that was all that mattered.

We did it. Three god forsaken years later, and we finally brought our son home.

"Is everyone okay?" Hannah asked from the breakfast nook.

I pulled back and looked between Laila and Micah. Stars in the royal blue sky twinkled around his head before the glass patio doors. This wasn't how I envisioned my son looking when I met him for the first time. Still dripping crimson, muddy, cheeks hollowed. But somehow, that view of him standing in front of the glass window was the most beautiful thing I'd ever seen.

I cupped his bloody cheek, and a smile came to my lips. "You're okay, right?"

He smiled and bobbed his little head in a nod.

Chris turned to me and Laila. He smiled, eyes filling with tears. "Yeah, I think everyone's okay."

Eyes. His *eyes* filled with tears.

He had eyes again.

How the fuck did he have his eyes back? How did Micah do that?

"Mommy," Micah said. His hand lifted to Laila's face. She looked at him in awe, or maybe disbelief, as salty water flowed down her cheeks. "Mommy, why awe your cwying?"

She let out a quiet laugh and wiped her cheeks. "I'm just so happy."

"Everybody's hungry, right?" Leah rubbed her watery eyes and smiled between the four of us. "We—me and Hannah, I mean. We made cookies this afternoon, and I think there's still pizza on the stove."

"What time is it?" Chris glanced around. "McDonald's isn't open, is it?"

"Yeah, you'll have to wait on that Big Mac." Laila smiled.

"Pizza 'll do then." He smiled at her. He looked at Leah. "Do you have Sprite?"

She helped him to his feet. "We have Sprite, and Jeremy brought you some clothes over before they left. We'll all get something to eat, and then you guys can all get cleaned up."

"Should we do that?" Brody asked. "The cops are going to be involved soon; we can't have him wearing Jeremy's clothes."

"We can't really show up in these either." Chris looked down at his ruined scrubs. "Where did this come from anyway?"

"You don't remember?" I asked.

He shook his head.

Well, at least that crossed one thing of the list of things we had to worry about. Chris didn't remember slitting his own throat. That meant that Micah probably didn't either.

Laila blew out a sigh. Her gaze shifted over Micah before sliding back to Chris. "We'll talk about it later."

Leah put some pizza into the microwave. Hannah tossed Laila a pair of pants. "Might want to put some clothes on, lady."

"Oh, shit." She looked down at the hoodie covering her torso, tele-ported the sweats over her legs, and started to her feet.

She lifted Micah with her, his legs tightening around her hips. He smiled at me over her shoulder. I smiled back and put my hand on his arm. He was half her size in height; they looked a little silly like that. But it was still the most perfect sight I'd ever beheld.

My wife, holding my son. It was a dream come true. Even if we were all covered in blood and smelled like shit.

"You guys can get cleaned up and take a breath of fresh air for a while," Laila said. "Everybody can get something to eat, get cleaned up, and breathe for a minute. Then we'll get some clothes from the hospital everyone was taken to after the first compound. You guys can change, and then we'll... we'll figure out a way to involve the police and get you guys back onto the radar."

I looked at Chris and back to Micah. "How did you do that, buddy?"

"My eyes?" Chris asked.

I nodded.

Micah moved his shoulders in a slow shrug. "I just did."

"He did it before." Chris cleared his throat. Leah handed him a cookie. He smiled at her before looking back to me. "We can talk about that another time, okay? Let's just... Let's just catch up."

If he'd done it before, that meant that Peterson had cut out my brother's eyes not once, but twice. He didn't have to relive that memory to me. I was dying to know how my son could've done it, but they didn't call him the savior for nothing. It must've just been one of his many, many abilities.

I summoned a smile.

Christ turned and gazed over the small crowd with a smile. "I know you guys; you haven't changed much." He looked between Leah and Adam at the other end of the granite island. He turned to Brody and Hannah. "And I think that you're my little brother and sister, but you don't look so little anymore."

Hannah grinned. "You look a lot like you did then."

"You look a lot better than you did the last time I saw you." Brody smirked.

"That was you," Chris said. "I thought so, but I wasn't sure. Puberty changed your voice a lot."

Brody was quiet for a moment. "Yeah. Yeah, that was me."

"And who are you guys again?" He turned to Celena and Kai.

"This is my little sister, Celena." Laila gestured between them at the breakfast nook to my right. Milly was in Celena's arms, wide eyes shifting between us all. "And this is my twin brother, Kai."

"You're the one who's dating Hannah, right?"

Hannah grinned, lifting her ringed finger toward him. "Engaged, actually."

"Aye." Kai stood and wrapped an arm around her waist. He kissed the top of her head, extending his hand toward Chris. "I've heard only good things."

"Yeah, likewise." Chris smiled and shook his palm.

"You remember Wyatt, right?" Hannah asked. Chris nodded, and she said, "Celena is Wyatt's par animo."

He knitted his brows, glancing at Celena. "No shit."

Huh. I thought that Laila told him that when they were in captivity together. Then again, he probably hadn't believed that the par animarum even existed then.

"Well, that's pretty crazy," he muttered. "I'm sorry, how old are you?"

"Twenty-one," Celena said.

"Where's Helena?" Laila looked around.

"She fainted when she saw Micah grow Chris's eyes back." Adam chuckled. "I took her to the couch."

I laughed. I walked toward Celena and lifted Milly from her arms. "You don't want to get cleaned up first?"

Hell no. I'd just seen four of the people I loved most in the world die and come back to life. I wanted to hold my baby girl.

I squeezed her into my chest. She tightened her legs around my ribs. Her always big green eyes were a bit wider than usual, but she gripped my shirt so tight. I walked to Laila and Micah with a smile. "You wanted to meet your little sister, right?"

A big grin pulled at his lips as he reached out to touch her hand. His dirty fingers grazed hers, and those wide eyes softened. She smiled back.

It wasn't one of those 'bring the new baby home from the hospital and introduce her to her big brother' sort of things. But in a way, it was much more beautiful. He'd been anticipating meeting her just as much as he would have if he'd have seen Laila's belly slowly grow to the size of a basketball. She didn't really understand what was happening, but it was still a wonderful moment.

"What's her name?" Chris asked.

"Milly," Laila said

"Like Mom?"

I smiled. "Like Mom."

"Your other nephew's sleeping with his mom upstairs," Adam said.

Chris's face said he wasn't sure he believed that. "You've got a kid too?"

Adam smiled. "Luka."

"Sorry. We didn't have much time to fill you in," Laila said.

Chris smiled and bit into a piece of pizza. "God, this is better than an orgasm."

I heard them all talking, but it wasn't really registering. All I was thinking of was my son. How happy I was to have him home. That sweetness in his eyes as Milly wrapped her fingers around his thumb and bashfully buried her head into my chest.

And how frail he looked.

His clavicle practically broke the skin of his neck beneath his mess of black waves. The cheeks that reminded me so much of Laila in the astral reality we'd visited him in now hollowed into his mouth. His scrubs hung loosely on his bony shoulders—just as Daniel's had all those years ago.

Why was he so thin? Why was he treated the way that he was? When we'd found the last compound, and the one before that, he had an entire nursery fit for any normal child in the world. What changed?

"Are you hungry, Micah?" I put a hand on his shoulder. "Do you want something to eat?"

He smiled and looked up from his sister. "I'm stawving."

I chuckled and ran my hand over his messy black hair. "Let's get you something to eat, okay?"

He grinned and gave a nod.

I kept Milly on my hip and started to the pizza on the counter. But Chris caught my hand and awkwardly cleared his throat. Then his voice lowered. "He... he's not going to be able to eat that."

My brows fell with confusion.

"He doesn't really know how to chew."

He'd be three in two months. And he didn't know how to chew.

Why? What the fuck had he been eating then?

"That's okay," Leah said. "That's okay, we have other stuff. There's leftover mashed potatoes in the fridge. And bananas. A banana would be okay, right?"

"A banana should work," Chris said.

"No, I got this." Adam brushed past me to the fridge. He pulled out the freezer drawer and grabbed a tub of chocolate ice cream. He turned to Laila and Micah with a grin. "Have you ever had chocolate, buddy?"

Micah shook his head from Laila's lap at the breakfast nook. I was still holding the piece of cold pizza. She and I exchanged a look of grief before she pushed a smile.

He's home. And we get to be with him for all the best firsts, she said into her mind.

She was right. At least he was home. He'd be with us for the rest of forever.

But he still should've been able to eat that damn piece of pizza.

CHAPTER TWO

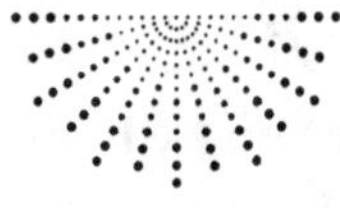

LAILA

"This is so good." Micah shoved his spoon into the tub of chocolate ice cream on the table before us. I forced a smile as he raised the spoon to me. "Do you want some, Mommy?"

I kissed the top of his head. The knot in my throat swelled, and I swallowed it back down. "No, that's okay. It's all yours, kiddo."

My stomach danced with butterflies over holding my son for the first time. His warmth and purity on my lap was the best feeling I ever had. But I hated that looking at him made my stomach churn with guilt. I had to clench my hands together to keep sparks from leaving my fingers when I saw his feeble hand struggle ice cream from the tub.

This whole thing was fucking bullshit. I wanted to grab one of those knives from the butcher block, run downstairs, and slit the throat of bastard responsible for it. My baby, my sweet little baby, should have never been where he was. He should have always been right here on my lap with his father beside me.

But Micah just smiled and turned back to the container.

I let that feeling wash away.

He was home. He hadn't been, but he was now.

Jeremy caressed my bicep. I turned to meet his gaze. He smiled and

"

reached out to cup my neck in his hand. "We should go to the house and get cleaned up soon."

"After he eats." I twined my fingers through his. "Micah and Chris can go first, then you. I'm not too bad. The fire kind of charred everything."

"I'll come with." Chris glanced at Micah and gave a smile. "Might help with the adjustment a bit."

"Sure." Jeremy smiled. "Sure, thank you."

He smiled and dipped his head in a gentle nod. "Where are you guys living? Did you get a little house in town?"

Jeremy laughed.

Leah smiled. "They're living in the cabin."

"The cabin," Chris said. "Dad's little hunting cabin? The one I was conceived in?"

"What's conceive?" Micah asked.

Jeremy laughed. "Ask me that again in, like, twelve years."

Micah turned back to his ice cream.

Smiling, I raised a shoulder. "We renovated a bit."

"A bit." Kai scoffed. "All the bloody hours ye had me breaking my back. And ye say a *bit*."

I laughed and looked at Chris. "We basically built a new house around the fireplace."

"It's beautiful," Leah said.

"Ya know, we were actually talking." I looked from Jeremy to Chris. "We're all on the same property and everything. But we set up a bed in the guest room beside Micah's. If you want, maybe you could stay with us for a while. We're here a lot anyway but..." I glanced at the basement door.

He turned toward it and cleared his throat. "He's down there."

"He is," Brody said.

Chris was quiet for a moment. His fingers around the glass of Sprite trembled. I wasn't sure if in fury or fear, but he set it down and turned back to us. "Yeah. Yeah, I'll stay with you guys. It'll be nice for Micah and everything too."

"Who?" Micah looked up at me and Jeremy. "Who's down thewe?"

I cleared my throat and tried to speak, but I found myself sitting there with my mouth open.

"Don't worry about it, kiddo." Chris smiled. "Just grown-up stuff."

"Oh." Micah took another bite of ice cream. "Mommy, can I have some watew?"

"How about some juice?" Leah asked from the counter.

"What's juice?" Micah asked.

"You'll like it." Chris smiled and turned to Leah. "He'll need a bottle."

I clenched my jaw and looked down at the messy little boy in my lap. The sweet, innocent child who did no harm to anyone yet had been treated like a prisoner of war since his birth. A prisoner to his parents' war, I suppose.

He deserved so much better than he'd been given. By three years old, he should have been long off a bottle. He should have known how to chew. He was smarter than any three-year-old I ever met. But he was so far behind where he should have been in almost every other milestone.

"Maybe we should walk down to the house," Jeremy said. "It's dark, but we could all probably use some fresh air. Huh, Chris?"

He smiled wide. "I'd love a walk in the moonlight right now."

"My belly huwts a little," Micah muttered with a hand on his stomach.

"Well, that's what happens when you eat a lot of ice cream." Jeremy grinned and poked his tummy.

Micah giggled, and I blinked hard at the water forming against my irises.

Another thing I hadn't considered. Micah had never been full before he ate that half tub of ice cream. He'd never eaten a real meal. He'd only had the bare minimum to survive.

After discovering the second compound and then seeing him through our astral communication, I believed they treated Micah well. Like a child. Far from normal, but decent. Lydia wasn't malnourished when we found her. She was odd, but cared for. In that last compound, Micah had a room with painted blue walls and fluffy white clouds, framed photos of his mother, and a crib with a real mattress.

And it dawned on me.

We'd found them. We'd found their cushy, renovated torture chamber. And then they had to hide.

They moved fast and frequent because they knew we'd find them if they stayed in one place for too long. As they travelled, they threw my son and his uncle into little sheds, basements, and God only knew what else. Anything small.

Smaller confines are easier to cast complex perimeter spells around. The smaller they kept their prison, the better they could fortify it. And the harder it made it for us to break.

"I like that big white dog." Micah pointed out the patio door. Tinkerbell lay on the porch, panting as she gazed out over the blue, moon lit field. "What's hew name again?"

"Tinkerbell." Jeremy smiled. "But we call her Tink."

"Tink," Micah murmured. A smile spread across his lips, and he giggled. "She's funny."

I raised a brow. "What do you mean, kiddo?"

"She's just funny."

Chris laughed too. "Micah does this thing you guys should probably know about."

"What's that?" Jeremy asked.

"I talk to aminals," Micah said.

An odd laugh left me. "And do they talk to you?"

"Not weally."

"They communicate some way or another," Chris said. "We had this little mouse at the last place, huh, bud?"

Micah nodded and grinned up at me. "I called him Stew."

"I actually called him Stewart. Ya know, like Stewart Little." Chris smiled. "And Micah couldn't say Stewart. So. Stew."

This kid was Fae alright. And I couldn't think of a worse way to torture a person with a deep connection to animals and nature than to lock them in a place with access to neither.

Fucking Christ, why? Why do this to him? Peterson couldn't have found him a stray cat to care for? Or a hamster? He couldn't have given his supposed savior one source of happiness in there?

"Well, you'll really like playing out in the woods here then." Jeremy gave a playful grin. "We've got all kinds of little critters out there. Once we figure things out, we'll go down to the creek and catch frogs. Might even be able to find a mouse or two."

"What's a fog do again?" Micah asked.

Chris opened his mouth to answer, but I beat him to it with a croaking, "Rib-bit."

Chris sent me a sad, almost apologetic smile. Neither of us could say it. But I resented him so much at that time. I was eternally grateful and forever in his debt. Still, I found myself more jealous of him than I'd ever been of anyone in my entire life.

CHAPTER THREE

JEREMY

I wrapped a blanket around Micah's shoulders at Laila's hips with one hand and lifted Milly higher up mine with the other. "We'll get you a coat first thing in the morning."

Micah smiled and tightened the blanket at his chest. As he did, something in the way he moved his shoulders looked just like Laila. Something in the turn of his lips, maybe something with the hair falling in his face. But something. I smiled back and pushed messy, matted curls from his face.

As Leah opened the door and the cool spring air touched our skin, the scent of dew and early spring blooms dancing into our noses, I watched Chris's shoulders loosen. He released a small, calming breath as tears coursed from his eyes. It was exactly how Laila looked the day that she woke up in the hospital after she escaped. An expression of the purest form of relief.

But Micah clenched tighter to Laila. "It's so dawk."

"That's okay." She swiveled him on her hip and pulled a licking violet flame to her hand. "We have light. And nothing out here can hurt you anyway. We have a very special spell around this place."

"Like the one Nastya had?" Chris asked.

"Kind of the opposite," I said. "That necklace I put on you when we grabbed you, it allows you to come in. Take it off, and you're going to appear outside the border. Walking seems more effective though."

He looked between the three of us, forehead crunched down. "But you guys aren't wearing one."

"We're a part of the spell. We can add you to it so you don't have to wear a necklace." Leah took a step outside with a smile. "Micah's their kid so he doesn't need one."

"Huh," Chris muttered. "So it doesn't keep things in. It keeps everything else out."

"That's the idea," I said.

"Can I walk, Mommy?" Micah asked, big blue eyes flittering between hers.

I glanced at his bare feet and instinctively wanted to say no. But then it occurred to me that he probably never wore a pair of shoes in his life.

Fae tended to enjoy walking barefoot anyway. Laila did the same all summer long.

Laila smiled wide. "Do you want to race me to the tree line?"

"What's that?" he asked.

Every single thing that came out of my son's mouth made me want to tell them to walk back to the house without me. Micah knew nothing of what being a child meant because of Peterson. He knew what sounds animals made, he could count to ten, he was smart. But that was only because Chris had done the best he could to give him a sense of normalcy in there. Micah didn't know how to be a kid. He hadn't gotten to because of that piece of shit I finally had the opportunity to beat to hell and back.

But we only had a couple hours with him before we had to turn Micah and Chris over to Tina and act like we didn't save them. My wife and son's kidnapper was tied up in our basement; we had to cover our asses. We couldn't turn him over because he could tell them anything.

And he didn't deserve a trial. He deserved what he had done to my son, wife, and brother. He was gonna get it. But ten fucking fold.

Laila and Micah spoke for a moment before they took off running down the driveway. Leah laughed and tailed close behind as Tink bolted out the door and nearly knocked me over. But Chris stood still.

I placed my hand on his shoulder and smiled. "You're out, man."

He turned back to me with watery eyes. His lip trembled and his head shook a bit. "It's just so much prettier than I remember it. I thought maybe I built up these memories, ya know?" He wiped his eyes. "I thought I imagined it being this beautiful. It's weird when you can't see but you could before. Memories kind of fade into your imagination. I guess isolation does that too but..."

"We have a number of earth connected Fae here now. They keep the gardens looking pretty good." I held my smile. "Not as dreary as it used to be. We were never great with the landscaping."

He cleared his throat, wiping his eyes. "Not just that but this." His gaze shifted to Milly in my arms. He glanced at Laila and Micah running with Tink toward the tree line. "You guys did it. You made lives for yourselves. When I met Laila, I just... She told me her fiancé would find her. And I told her he wouldn't."

I laughed. "Yeah. Well, she helped me find her. Helped us find you."

"And the others." A smile came to his lips. "You got the others too, right? How's Haley?"

"Her and Leah just had a pretty nasty breakup so don't say her name in her presence," I muttered.

"Damn." His eyes widened a bit. "A lot's changed in three years."

"Yeah." I glanced down at Milly. "Yeah. Once we get you settled in, we'll sit down and talk about everything."

"Yeah, maybe we could get a beer or something." Chris grinned. "That's what guys our age do, right? We're old enough to do that now."

The dreaded topic.

My big brother was my hero growing up. I loved him with my whole heart. But he'd always lingered on the judgmental side of things. And I wasn't looking forward to telling him that I was a recovering heroin addict.

I scratched my head. "I don't really drink. But I mean, I'll tag along."

The wheels cranked behind his eyes for a moment. "I really have missed a lot, huh?"

"Ten years is a long time," I said. "But we've got the rest of our lives to catch up now. This is over. You're home, man."

CHAPTER FOUR

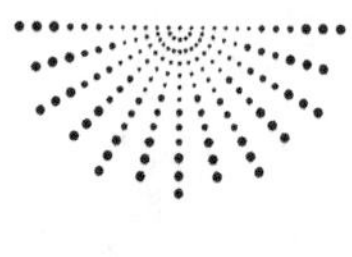

LAILA

Opening that front door with my toddler by my side and my baby in her daddy's arms behind me filled me with a sense of freedom I'd never felt in this life. When I flicked on the light, and Micah gasped in amazement, I had to battle tears.

I loved this house so much. Every detail. The wall of windows, the gorgeous fireplace, the big kitchen island, the intricately carved handrail to the massive steps. I loved every detail. But it'd only felt half full until that moment.

Now, with my son, and my daughter, my husband, and our dog, it felt complete.

"Woah. It's so big." Micah's eyes widened as he spun in a circle around the couch. "And it smells *soo* good."

I laughed. As we walked down the drive, he kept saying that everything smelled good. And I bet it did, because he smelled like he'd just crawled out of a sewer. The mom in me was screaming to get his little butt in the tub and clean him up.

Jeremy passed Milly to me, hand sliding over my back. He kissed my head.

"You really did build the whole house around the fireplace." Chris laughed. "Dad would be so amazed, dude."

Jeremy sucked his teeth and forced a smile. "How about I give you the tour and get you some towels? You can take a shower real quick in the upstairs bathroom. I really want to show you the balcony too."

"Yeah, that sounds great." Chris turned to Leah. "Do you want to catch up when I'm done?"

"I'm not going anywhere." Leah laughed. "I'll put some tea on."

He smiled. He and Jeremy started upstairs.

"Do you want to get a bath too, kiddo?" I asked Micah.

"Yeah, in a minute, Mommy." He meandered toward the fireplace. His fingertips coasted along the back of the couch. He turned to me with a grin. "Evewything's so soft."

I smiled and looked at Leah. "Can you watch Mills 'til Jeremy comes down?"

Leah smiled back. "Yeah, of course."

"Mommy." Micah gasped at Jeremy's guitar on the wall. "Mommy, mommy, look!"

I fought the tears that welled in my eyes as I lowered myself to the ground beside him. "How about we all get cleaned up, then Daddy can play you a song."

His eyes widened, a grin tugging at his lips. "Weally?"

"I mean, you'll have to ask him, but I think he'd be happy to." I smiled and pushed hair from his face. "But I really want to help you get this knot out of your hair first."

I mentally prepared myself a long time before that night to see his scars. I knew he wouldn't have the lashes on his back because Lydia would have told me. But I expected him to be healthier than he looked.

Jeremy and I were always very light-skinned. But Micah appeared utterly colorless as the mud and dust washed into the bubbles beneath him. His shoulders were even more narrow than Daniel's had been all those years ago. His stomach sunk inward, slightly below his thin ribs.

But he smiled so wide when I showed him the bathtub crayons. He giggled as I squeezed soap onto a rag, rubbed it in, and blew bubbles out the other side. He laughed the sweetest baby laugh when I swayed the water away from his eyes while rinsing the shampoo from his hair.

One thing I could thank Peterson for was letting his hair grow. I didn't know why they cut Chris's and not his, but I was glad all the same. It reminded me so much of Jeremy's.

As I watched him splash in those warm bubbles, when he commented on how good the soap smelled, while that blood washed down the drain, I finally felt the resolution I'd been waiting more than three years for.

I had my son back. He was safe, he was home, and he was beautiful. We had a long road ahead of us. But the worst of the heartache passed.

After all of this time, I've lived countless awful things. Some, worse than one would dream. But still, nothing hurt as bad as losing my son.

And nothing felt better than bringing him home.

"Mommy," Micah said with a look around. "Why's youw bafwoom so big?"

I laughed. "I don't know. Because I wanted a tub and a shower, I guess."

"I like the tub." He gazed around some more, then splashed his hands into the bubbles. "I like the watew."

"Me too." I smiled. "I'm still gonna take you to the beach one day soon, okay?"

He smiled and gave a fast nod.

"But, buddy." I paused and cupped his cheek in my hand. "Remember what I told you before? How we have to pretend we don't really know each other when we talk to the police?"

He drooped his head. "Is it gonna be a long time 'til I see you again?"

"Maybe a few hours. I hope not any longer than that. But Uncle Chris will be with you; you won't be alone. I'm going to be there at any chance I get as long as the police let me."

He turned his gaze toward the bubbles floating in the water. "I not going back thewe, am I?" He looked up at me and wiped his watering blue eyes. "Cause I don't want to. I like it hewe."

I smiled and shook my head. "You'll never be in a box like that again, buddy. I promise. I won't let anyone hurt you."

He looked up with a sad smile and wiped his eyes. "I'm kind of seepy."

I grabbed his towel. "Are you ready to get dressed and let me comb that messy hair?"

He grinned. He stood up and took a step into the fabric, commenting on how soft it was against his skin.

Although thin, he still seemed bigger than most kids his age. Tall. Jeremy stood a good bit over six foot, it made sense for Micah to be tall too. He clearly had a lot of those Skoulda genes.

As I helped him pull some teddy bear pajamas over his arms, a quiet knock sounded at the door. "Hey, you." Jeremy smiled.

"Hewe, look." Micah extended his hand to his dad. "See how good I smell."

Jeremy laughed and walked toward us. His hand lifted Micah's toward his nose. He smiled wide. "You smell a lot better, that's for sure." He pulled his hand away and smiled. "Can I talk to your mommy for just one second outside, buddy?"

"But can you play a song when you'we done?"

Jeremy gave a gentle a nod, still smiling. "That sounds like a plan to me."

CHAPTER FIVE

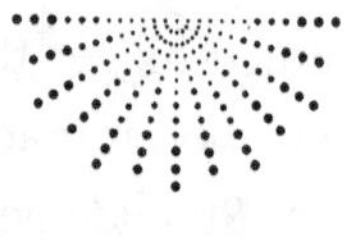

JEREMY

"So if these are too loose, let me know and I'll run to Walmart and grab you something else. Micah needs a pair of shoes and a coat anyway." I laid the clothes on the bathroom sink and turned to Chris. "There's a few patio chairs on the balcony if you ever want to go outside. There's an entrance in the hall and another in Micah's room, but we keep them locked if we're not out there because our dog knows how to pull the handle. She got stuck up there for a few hours while I was at work once, and I felt really bad so it's kind of a house rule now."

Chris laughed, gaze moving over the tree covered lawn out the window of the guest room. "She does seem like a weird little dog."

"She has her quirks." I stepped into the room and sat at the desk. "We all do. If you hear Laila scream in the middle of the night, don't come running in worried someone's killing her."

"Try and do the same for me." He exhaled a long sigh and turned to meet my gaze. "So this necklace. I've got to keep it on while I shower."

"If you don't want to end up naked in the woods a few hundred acres away."

He laughed and looked up to meet my gaze. "So, Peterson. To be in the basement, he's got to be wearing one of these too." I thought of that reality for a moment. "If he ripped it off, he'd be out of here."

"Wyatt's with him right now. We made it pretty clear that roughing him up was encouraged. He's probably out cold at the moment," I said. "But yeah. In theory."

His jaw tightened. "You know what you've got to do, right? I'd love to, but I don't think I could without killing him. Laila probably couldn't either."

I glanced at the scar at his neck and then back to his eyes. It wasn't gonna be fun. But he was right. It had to happen. "Yeah. I know."

"You should do it soon. Then have someone heal the skin so he can't pull it out." Chris clenched his jaw. "I don't think Micah and I should leave until you do. How long do we have until we have to turn ourselves over to the feds, anyway?"

"We agreed on noon unless Tina tells us they have a lead they have to follow. But yeah, I've been looking for a reason to hurt the guy since you told me this was the second time Micah grew your eyes back."

Chris turned his gaze to the floor and ran his hand over his mouth. He cleared his throat. "I... That's one of the things I don't think I'm ready to talk about just yet if you don't mind. I understand why you want to know, but... Just, please don't ask me talk about that."

Ah, fuck.

Maybe I shouldn't have said that. It kind of just slipped out. I hadn't brought it up to pick at the scab, I just remembered Chris as being a very blunt guy. But it made sense that certain topics were not open for conversation now.

"You don't have to tell me anything, man. You don't owe me shit. You helped me get my kid back. You took care of him when I thought that he was dead. I owe you my life, Chris."

He turned back to the dawning sky and released a huff of a laugh. "He's kind of been my reason to live for the past three years."

I looked down. "Kind of the reason I *didn't* want to live for a couple. Or at least, that bastard in the basement is."

"You said something like that before in the astral reality. About you having Peterson in the basement before?"

"Not exactly. He was in a guard's head," I said. "Do you want to get into all of this right now? Because it's pretty complex. We can go over all of it later. You should relax and spend some time with Leah. She's driven herself crazy looking for you."

"Yeah, I'll get in the shower now. But..." He rubbed his mouth. "This is going to be a little harder for you than it is for Laila."

I turned my head to the side a bit. "With Micah?"

He nodded. "He loves you; he does. But Peterson... I know you know how he feels about her, but you don't understand what he made her out to be in your son's eyes. He idolizes her, Jeremy. That's not necessarily a bad thing in this situation, I guess. But I think that means you're gonna have to try really hard for him to see you the same way. He's got a lot of expectation built up in you too. And I... I don't want something to happen and that expectation not get lived up to."

My jaw involuntarily clenched when I realized what he was getting at.

He was worried I wouldn't be a good enough father for my kids. That Micah expected me to be a superhero and might get stuck with a failure. Don't get me wrong, I was far from the ideal role model. But if I was good at one thing, it was being a dad. Milly loved me as much as she loved Laila. Not to be conceited, but some days, she seemed to prefer me to Laila. We were great parents.

I cleared my throat. "I'm a good dad, Chris. I'm not perfect. But me and Laila... We've got a nice life going for our kids. It's not like we're loaded or anything, but we have money to take some time off and get used to Micah being here. We own a diner in town, we can take the kids with us any time we need to. Adam lives upstairs so we have family pretty much everywhere that we go. We have a network of safety while still leading simple, happy, human lives. He's going to have a happy, normal childhood. And nobody's asking you to leave, man. We know how much you guys mean to each other."

"I can see that you're a good dad," Chris muttered. "I saw the way your daughter looks at you. I just meant... I don't know. He... he saw Amy's body, Jeremy. And he... he thought that he did it."

That was not my proudest moment. I hated that it went down the way it did back there. But there was no other option. We had to kill that bitch. And the only way to do that was through Micah.

I cleared my throat and turned my gaze to the ground. "That was actually Laila's idea. But she's going to take that memory from him."

He pressed his lips together. "Yeah, that's probably best."

I stood as he started into the bathroom. But as I did, the weight of his words fell heavy on my shoulders. I wasn't always proud of the person I was, but since my daughter was conceived, I busted my ass to become the man that stood before him that day. He was right about how we killed Amy, but it was a last resort. I wouldn't have put Micah through that if I had another choice. And I knew Chris would see that in time. But I had to say it anyway.

"I am, Chris. I'm a good dad."

"I believe you. I do. I'm just... Look, I know he's your kid. But I've been with him since he was an infant, man. And I love him. I'm going to have to learn to keep my opinions to myself, I know that. But it's... it's going to be an adjustment for me too. I would have done things differently and—"

"We had to get her out of there, Chris. We figured if we got Amy from the inside—"

"But we died anyway." He gestured to his shirt. "That's what this is, right? They sacrificed us?"

I ran my tongue along my teeth.

I teleported downstairs to wash Laila's long-dried blood from my palms. Leah sat on the couch beside Milly. She was curled between a pillow and her aunt, sleeping peacefully. But Chris's words still lingered in my mind. I was at a year and half sober now. Then again, maybe I wasn't anymore. Peterson had shot me up with that heroin cocktail. Did that wash away my sobriety? Was I failing as a father already?

"Laila's giving Micah a bath. I gave Mills a quick one in the sink, changed her into some PJs, fed her a bottle, and she's out."

"Thanks." I smiled, scrubbing up my arms. "I really appreciate it."

"Are you kidding?" She grinned. "This little thing is nothing compared to what you and Laila did. I know things didn't go exactly as planned, but you did it. They're home."

I watched the maroon water move down the drain. A thought dawned on me then. Legally, returning Micah to us would be a process. Then Chris's words echoed through my mind, and my heart skipped a beat.

I looked up and cleared my throat. "Hey, do you think you can ask Ray for some piss when you get back to the house?"

"What? Why?"

"Well, when they get Micah and Chris to the hospital, they'll remove the implants. But that won't take long and since they're both of sound mind, they'll be released pretty quick. I hope, anyway. But they aren't giving us Micah if they see the heroin in my system."

Her mouth fell open. "What?"

"Peterson." I dried my hands on the towel. "It made the beating pretty painless though. Either way, I'm gonna need clean piss."

"Jeremy," Leah murmured.

"My clean date hasn't changed since I didn't really have a choice, right?" I asked. "I mean, technically, I had a choice. I could have let Chris slit Micah's throat. But it seemed like the right choice. Right?"

She stood and started toward me with a concerned gaze. "Are you okay?"

I was. I was genuinely better than I'd been in a very long time. But I was scared too. I couldn't have gone through all of this just to lose my son for having to choose between shooting up and letting him die. "Yeah. Yeah, I'm good. I am, but... I didn't relapse, right?"

"No." Leah frowned. "No. You didn't."

"I didn't think so," I muttered. I summoned a smile to my lips. "I'm gonna get changed and help Laila get Micah to bed. But then, I have to go take care of something with Peterson. You're going to stay here, right?"

"Yeah, I'll be here. Do whatever you have to do."

"I'm going to shower at your house when I'm done."

"Don't drip blood all over. I just mopped."

CHAPTER SIX

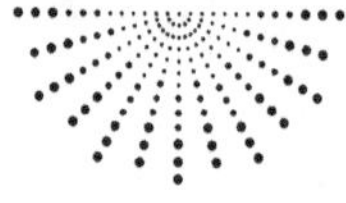

LAILA

"How is he?" Jeremy asked, eyes moving over Micah on the bathroom floor with a toy boat.

"He's good." I smiled with a glance at him then back to Jeremy. "He doesn't want to leave, but he's good. He's happy to be here."

He smiled, gazing at him a moment longer. "What song should I play him?"

"Something timeless. The Beatles maybe?"

He held his smile. "Yeah, I think I've got it. But he looks tired. He'll probably fall asleep soon, huh?"

"I think so."

"When he does, I have to go take care of something with Peterson," he murmured. "I won't be gone long, but Chris made a good point. It wouldn't take much for him to rip that necklace off and slam outside of the perimeter."

Was I against Peterson being tortured? No. Was I against him having a rock jammed into his flesh like he'd done to all of us? Hell no. I wanted that bastard to feel the worst pains imaginable.

But I wanted this moment more.

I wanted to embrace every millisecond I had with my baby before we had to give him back. I wanted to ride this high, this win. I wanted to soak up every second.

I didn't want to think about the horrors of how we came to this beautiful resolution. "Very true. I... I don't think I'm ready for that yet. Do what needs done, but Micah's all that matters to me right now. I can't think about him."

"I know." He twined his fingers through mine and brought them to his lips. "I won't be long. But it'll be messy so I'm going to shower at Leah's."

"We'll be waiting," I said.

He kissed my forehead. He brushed past me into the bathroom. "What do you have there, kiddo?"

"Mommy says it's a boat," Micah said.

"That is a boat. But do you want to see something cooler than a boat?" He looked up at Jeremy with a smile. "Do you want hear a real-life guitar?"

Micah's face lit up, eyes glistening with joy. He gave a quick nod. Jeremy laughed and leaned forward to touch his hair. "Maybe we should take care of this first."

"I can brush it while you play." I smiled. "Let's go relax for a minute."

Jeremy played *Simple Man* by Lynyrd Skynyrd that night. He didn't really sing, he hummed more than anything. He carefully focused on the chords, smiling as Micah watched his fingers lift up and down off of the strings.

Milly slept in the crevice of my arm and Micah dozed off with his head against my chest. When they both fell asleep, the sun started to rise in from the wall of windows. Jeremy played a minute or two longer after the kids fell asleep. I think he waited to see if I would fall asleep too.

I was exhausted. I really needed a full eight hours after my death and resurrection. But I needed this moment more.

Both of my children with washed, lavender-scented hair, wearing clean, soft pajamas, dreaming calmly, curved against my chest as their dad played his guitar on the armchair a few feet away.

I waited lifetimes for this moment.

I couldn't have wasted it sleeping.

Instead, I smiled as Jeremy set his guitar down, grabbed the snowflake fleece blanket from the couch, and laid it over the three of us. He looked over both of them with a gaze similar to mine. His fingers ran along Micah's damp hair. He looked up at me with a smile. "I'll be back soon."

"We'll be here." I smiled back.

As those words left my lips, I watched his shoulders fall in a gentle sigh. He leaned down, kissed me, and smiled once more.

And he disappeared.

In that moment, I didn't care about anything but the two lives my arms held. I thought that I'd want to beat and torture Peterson the way that he did to me. I thought I'd be ready to take my revenge.

But that didn't matter. I'd get there, but not that morning.

That morning, I only felt and thought of love.

CHAPTER SEVEN

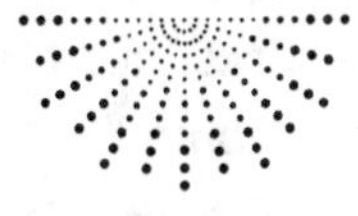

JEREMY

The familiar scent of warm apples touched my nose. The scent was usually so comfortable, but a chill stretched down my spine at what I was about to do. My muddy Chucks squeaked against the brown ceramic tile as I walked. I glanced around the kitchen, scanning the breakfast nook and large granite island.

"Kai, Celena," I called. "Where are you guys?"

"Over here," Kai said from the couch in the living room. "I think Celena's downstairs with Wyatt."

"Even better," I muttered. I started toward the basement door and peeked into the living room. Hannah's long black hair laid against his lap, his fingers running through it. "Thanks, I got it from here. Just, don't open this door, alright?"

Kai swallowed hard and lowered his head in a nod. I spun to the basement door, turned the handle, and started down the steps.

I heard Celena and Wyatt's hushed conversation as each step creaked beneath my feet. As what I was about to do dawned me, I'm ashamed to admit that I felt accomplishment. Maybe I was even a little happy.

Only momentarily though. I was glad that we had him. I was glad that this was going to be over. I was glad we were going to get justice for the pain he'd caused us and all the others he'd tortured.

But I wasn't a sadist. Couldn't call myself a pacifist, but this sort of thing always grossed me out. I never minded a hand-to-hand fight. Hurting someone that was tied down though... Not my thing.

"Hey." Wyatt wiped his tired eyes and met my gaze. "Our shift all done down here?"

I noted Peterson's head slumped against his chest. My gaze shifted to the once white crystal now tainted red that hung from his neck. "No, I need you guys to help me with something real quick."

Celena glanced at me and then at Peterson. "Don't you want to spend some time with Micah?"

"This won't take long." I walked to the armoire near the landing and pulled it open.

The knife looked more like what he deserved, but less precise. I couldn't kill him; we needed to know what he knew and what the fuck they did to my son. The kill was Laila's anyway. So I settled on a scalpel.

"What are you doing?" Celena asked.

"Celena." Wyatt shot her a look.

"I don't have the time to torture him right now, if that's what you're asking." I turned. "But that necklace he's wearing is the only thing keeping him in our hands. Meaning if he manages to knock that chair over and get that little piece of rope hooked on something, all he's got to do is jerk his head to the side and he's free."

"Oh," Celena murmured.

"I'm going to need you to heal it. He's a doctor, he could figure out a way to pull stitches," I said. "If you could help me hold him down too."

Wyatt said, "Just tell me where you want me."

"I'm kinda hungry though. Mind if I drink him when you're done?" Celena asked.

"Do whatever you want with him. Just don't let it be a pleasant experience."

She smiled and arched a brow. "Can do. Then I'll heal him so you guys have a blank canvas."

"Just make sure to clean up the mess. We might have to move him once the feds get involved. Probably not but just in case." I turned to Peterson. "We both know you're not sleeping."

He kept his head turned toward the ground, but his legs started to tremble.

"So now you're quiet." I took a few steps toward him. "Had a lot to say yesterday, though."

I grabbed his hair and turned his head to face me. His lip was busted, but he didn't have any bruises. He hadn't been hit that hard.

"Open your eyes," I said. When he squeezed them tighter shut, I lifted the scalpel to his neck. "Open your fucking eyes or I'll cut them out."

He clenched his jaw and slowly peeled them open. His lip quivered, water pearling from his bloodshot gaze.

In that instant, he looked so helpless. I almost felt guilty. I remembered who he was and what he did to the people who mattered most to me.

"Are you going to be a little bitch when I put this rock in your back or are you going to cooperate?"

He tightened his jaw but stayed quiet.

"Alright then. When I untie this rope, I highly recommend that you don't try to fight me. If I kill you, I'll just have to bring you back so Laila can kill you again."

He panted out slow, calculated breaths and remained silent.

I released his hair and lowered myself to the tight rope at the back of the chair. When they were too hard to untie, I began cutting at it with the scalpel.

"You're going to dull the metal." He broke the silence.

I turned to him with furrowed brows. "Do you think I give a shit about how smooth the cut is?"

His jaw hardened, more tears rushing down his cheeks.

I rolled my eyes and finished cutting the rope. As his hands hung loose, he quickly reached up for the necklace. I teleported to my feet, grabbed a hold of his throat, and teleported him to his back on the cement. He reached for my hand on his throat, but I lifted his head and slammed it to the concrete. Just like he'd done to me a few hours prior. His eyes widened in agony, and my hand tightened at his throat.

"Jeremy," Wyatt said. "You've gotta let him breathe."

I released my hand and looked between his eyes. Deep breaths drew in and out of my nostrils as it all flickered through my memories.

The slashes across Daniel's back. His terrified scream when I hit him with the Forester. The way he devoured a plate of bacon and eggs the morning after we got him. The terror he must have felt when they ripped him from that car and held a blade to his throat.

Laila's screams in my ears when he put the implants in her. Her pleas when he shackled her to that table and forced himself inside of her. That ache in her tongue she had to keep in place when she had to hide the birth of our son in that room.

All the years I'd missed out on with my brother. The fact that he lost that free ride to Columbia. How he hadn't held a guitar or a paintbrush in a decade.

My son. His begging cries when they cut him open like a frog in a high school lab. The fact that I'd missed so much of his life because of this piece of garbage whose life I now held in my hand.

Jesus fuck, I'd never hated someone so much in my life. There was nothing I wanted more than to kill him. I hated the waiting of torture.

But the kill wasn't mine. It was Laila's.

"You're not getting out of here." I pushed my hand into his shoulder. "I don't mind beating you every time you try to escape, but it'll get old pretty quick where you're sitting."

He tightened his teeth to a line and continued to look between my eyes.

I grabbed his shoulder and rolled his scrawny body until he laid face first against the cement. He groaned as his head slammed to the ground. I pushed my knee into his back and looked at Wyatt and Celena.

"Wyatt, you hold his legs. Celena, I need you to get his arms. When you go to heal him, I'll take his arms."

They brought themselves to the ground.

His body quaked with sobs as I raised the scalpel to cut through his shirt. I didn't care how scared he felt, not really. Not until I ripped the fabric and saw the scars covering his back.

They weren't like Laila's or Daniel's. They were inflicted by a whip of some kind, but there weren't nearly as many. But it stopped me in my tracks.

I pondered if a younger version of himself was his own victim. I wondered if that's why he idolized Laila the way that he had, because she was his hero, and he didn't realize until he was much older that he was her villain.

But the timeline didn't add up. The book we wrote in the future was published in 2060-something and was clearly old to him even then. And he was in his forties, at least. That meant to be his own victim, he would have had to be much older. But since time travel came into play, I couldn't be certain of any of it.

"Where did you get these?" I asked.

"Not myself, if that's what you're thinking," he snapped. "We all have our own horrors that create us, Jeremy."

I was still kinda curious. But fuck it. Maybe he'd had a fucked up life. Maybe he'd been tortured. But that didn't magically make me see him as some victim I needed to pity.

We make our own decisions. We decide what type of person we want to be, and he chose to be the enemy of the most powerful family that ever walked this little blue rock.

He deserved everything that was coming his way.

With that thought from my mind, I raised the blade to his scapula and stabbed it into his flesh. He groaned and pushed up against me, but I applied more weight to my knee. I pulled back on the blade.

He screamed, his blood rolling past my fingertips. I grabbed the gem from my pocket and pushed it into the bleeding wound. I grasped ahold of his wrist with my free hand as Celena moved hers over the oozing cut.

His screams echoed louder, writhing against Celena's bright white energy.

I waited for the skin to heal. Once it did, I turned to Wyatt and Celena. "I know you don't get to play with your food often so have fun. Eat the flesh off him if you want to. Just keep him alive."

Celena grinned, and Wyatt raised a brow with a half-smile. "Normally don't *like* to play with my food," Celena said. "But I got a feeling I will this time."

I teleported to my old bathroom. I pulled off my clothes and set them in a pile on the floor, noting to burn them when I finished with my shower. I turned on the water, stepped inside, and began washing all of the blood from my skin.

Fuck, I hated this part of what we did. Killing, I didn't mind. Killing is quick. But torture was never my thing. I was good at it. But I hated it.

I tried not to hear his screams echo from the basement as I watched a mixture of so many people's blood slip down that drain.

Once he started being a smart mouth again, I wouldn't mind it so much. But it's really hard to beat a silent man. No matter how much I hated him.

When I finished, I stepped from the shower and rubbed my hair between the towel.

A wavy lock fell in my face, and my face screwed up in confusion.

I lifted the piece of hair upward to the light, and I had to rub my eyes to make sure they weren't fooling me. I hadn't noticed earlier; my hair had been matted in dried blood. It wasn't quite as noticeable wet, but I could see it now.

My hair had always been such a dark shade of brown that it looked bluish in some light. But now, it was salt and pepper colored.

Overnight, I'd gone gray.

The longer I looked at it, the more I thought back to the white light.

Chris was right. When they died, something big happened.

CHAPTER EIGHT

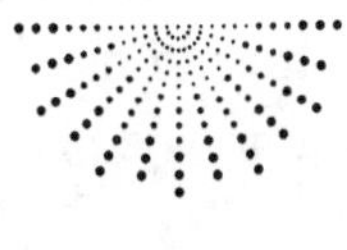

LAILA

"Hey." Jeremy kissed the top of my head from behind the couch.

I glanced up with a smile. Water dripped from his hair to my shoulders. "Hey."

"Where're Chris and Leah?" he asked.

"Out on the patio last I saw." I turned to Micah curled against my ribs. "Haven't really moved since you left."

I turned up to him. And my head cocked to the side. The once jet-black hair that hung around his face now had thin streaks of gray throughout. "That wasn't there yesterday, was it?"

He pulled the hair in front of his face. "No. It was not."

"People don't normally go gray in a day, do they?" I asked.

"I'm thinking it was when that light went off. But I don't want to worry about that right now. I just wanna enjoy this."

I smiled. "Kinda sexy though. Very silver fox."

He laughed. His eyes slid to our kids sleeping soundly. "It's a little surreal, isn't it?"

I smiled and kissed Micah's forehead. "Little bit."

"You don't want to go take a shower, do you?" he asked. "I can sit out here with them."

"I'm not very dirty. My hair kind of smells like smoke, but it's okay. Micah should probably smell like smoke when they pick him up anyway. I'll shower while we wait to hear from the FBI that they found my son. We'll have to set up flights to California and everything. I'll have some time to get cleaned up then."

"Good idea." He walked around the couch and lowered himself beside Micah. He touched his sleeping hand, thumb sliding against his knuckles. A slow, joyous breath of relief left him. A smile edged up his cheeks, looking between the three of us. He met my gaze. "My grandparents have a timeshare for a private plane. I could call them; they'd probably let us use it."

I did like the idea of not blowing our savings on plane rides back and forth from California until this was over. But I was not a fan of anyone on the Chambers. Jeremy's grandparents were especially not fans of mine.

"Don't they hate me?" I raised a brow. "Don't they look at our kids as abominations?"

"Just my grandpa. But that was before you built the name that you have. The Chambers have been trying to get a meeting with you for months. Maybe we could take a favor and pay one. We'll be back and forth from here and California for a week at least, and the cops are going to be watching us. It's a good idea to use the resources we have available here."

I blew out a deep breath "Yeah, I'd rather not drain our savings on flights if we don't have to. A meeting's just a meeting."

"They'll want to help Chris anyway. He was always kind of the golden boy in their eyes. They'll probably want to set up a trust fund for him. I'm not sure what happened to the one he was supposed to get when he graduated, but I'm sure they'll have something for him. And since we don't know what the hell happened when Nastya did the sacrifice, there's a good chance he's going to want to cash that money in for tanzanite and gold."

A lump stiffened in my throat.

The goal in saving our son hadn't *just* been to save our son. It'd also been to prevent the sacrifice that Peterson claimed would initiate the apocalypse. And Jeremy had brought him back from the dead; he was here, and he was alive, but we hadn't prevented the sacrifice.

The sky hadn't fallen just yet though. The world seemed just as it'd been before we left. There were no stars raining onto earth, there was no great serpent rising from the center of the planet. Everything seemed okay.

But I knew that didn't mean that it was.

If the full-on biblical apocalypse started going down, we'd planned to escape to the Fae Realm and start a life on that plane. It did seem just—especially now that we knew that thousands of years ago, we were the gods that created that dimension.

However, that's also what made it feel wrong. If we were just people like anyone else, sure, running from the apocalypse was the right thing to do. But... if we were gods... didn't that make it our responsibility to keep the people of this world safe?

"Maybe."

"But I'll call them after we hear from Tina. What's the plan there? How do you think we should do it? We can't really put them in the shed."

"There were cars outside. I'm sure one of them has doors that only open from the outside. I'll sit in there with them until I see Tina pull up."

"But they're going to wonder why Peterson locked them up and left."

"To get them off his tail," I said. "It makes sense. You're tired of running, you give the cops what they're looking for and go on with your two trusty sidekicks."

"They're gone, right?" Jeremy asked. "Nothing identifiable?"

"Couldn't identify the ash at the other compounds. We should be okay."

"What about our DNA in that cell?" he asked.

"I teleported in and set a fire from the inside while you took Micah and Chris home. There's nothing for them to find."

"Looks like we've got a pretty solid plan then."

That it was. But I wasn't ready for this moment to end. I'd spent so long looking for my baby, I wanted him to stay right there in my arms. With his little sister at his side and our dog on the floor beside us. This was where he was meant to be. I didn't want him to be locked up in a hospital again.

I barely whispered, "I don't want to let him go again."

"It's only going to be a few hours." Jeremy sent me a hopeful smile. "We might be living out of a hotel for a week or two until they let us take him home, but we'll get to be there. They'll let us visit him in the hospital and everything."

I was quiet for another moment. Looking for a subject change, I said, "After they take him, will you run to town and grab Micah a few things? I don't know what the weather's going to be like when we get to take him home, but I want him to have a couple thing. And I want to take him to the beach before we leave California."

"We might have to fly." He smiled. "Shasta's pretty far from the ocean."

"That's okay." I squeezed Micah a little tighter. "We can always stay the night out there or something. It might be kind of nice. I'll call Max once we figure out how long this is going to take and see when he's coming home to take care of the diner. But I don't care, we can shut the doors until he gets back if we have to."

He nodded with a smile. We fell quiet for a moment, gazing between each other and the little lives we created.

It was so peaceful, yet so surreal. We'd waited for this moment for far too long. Now it was finally here, and it was hard to tell if it was even reality.

"Pancakes get pretty soft after syrup, right?" Jeremy asked. "I gave Milly a piece of one a week or two ago and she did okay."

I smiled, studying his concerned gaze. "Yeah, I think pancakes will work."

CHAPTER NINE

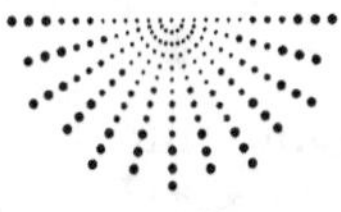

JEREMY

We lay on that couch for five hours and watched our kids sleep. Neither of us wanted to join them, despite our apparent exhaustion. We just lay there and whispered quietly as our son and daughter dreamed in our arms.

By ten, Laila and I were starving. When I stood, Milly woke, but Micah tightened his head into Laila's chest. I got Milly dressed and sat her in the highchair, I started breakfast. Shortly after, Micah woke up too. But he was quiet in the mornings. Milly excitedly screamed and bounced with glee, but Micah quietly rubbed his eyes and murmured pleases and thank yous for drinks and help finding the 'bafwoom.'

Laila sat between Micah and Milly as I flipped pancakes at the stove. Tink was at their feet picking up scraps of berries Milly tossed to the ground. My brother and sister were on the porch with blankets wrapped around their shoulders, laughing as they looked out over the dewy fields. Laila and I drank a cup of coffee and the world felt right.

For once in our fucking lives, the world felt right.

"Daddy." Micah looked up from the mashed bananas on his plate.

"Micah." I smiled.

His big blue eyes grew serious, face showing virtually no emotion.

Whatever he was about to say, he meant business. "Did you weally get me a sasophone?"

I laughed. "I really did. It's upstairs in your room. I can show it to you after breakfast, how's that sound?"

A big smile heightened at his lips. He nodded fast.

"You haven't even gotten to see your room in real life yet." Laila smiled. "Just wait until you see it."

Suddenly wide awake, his eyes shot open. "Can I see it now?"

"Let's eat first," I said.

"It do smell good," Micah murmured.

"We have whipped cream, right?" Laila asked.

"Pretty sure we do," I said.

Just as she started to her feet, the damn phone rang.

As that specific ringtone sounded, my chest tightened. Tina.

Laila tightened her jaw and reached for the phone. But I grabbed it first and sent her a smile. "Watch these for a minute for me, alright?"

As I slid the green bar, I started toward the back patio. "Knew it wouldn't be long."

"You're back." She breathed out a relieved laugh. "Thank god. Oh, thank you, God. That means you have Micah then, right?"

"And Chris." I leaned against the handrail, looking over Laila and the kids in the kitchen. "How much time do we have?"

"Forty-five minutes, maybe an hour," Tina said. "Maybe a little sooner."

"Great." I gazed at Micah's big smile. "We'll rush through breakfast then."

"I'll give you a five-minute warning," she muttered. "But listen, Jeremy, we figured this out tracking those plates."

My heart thumped. "Someone drove out of there?"

"Yeah, some middle-aged woman. She won't talk to us. But she... she gave us something. A video. From Peterson. I couldn't get rid of it; it wasn't given to me personally."

"What's on it? Is it—"

"Not like the last one, no. But... Well, there were two. The first one though... Well, you don't want to know. But the second one's a confession. He doesn't mention your world, he doesn't call any of you out for what you are. But he says that if we find Micah, that means Laila found him."

I licked my teeth, eyes shifting over her at the kitchen island. She laughed as she sat a plate in front of Micah. Her fingertips slid through his hair before she wrapped her arms around his chest from behind and kissed his hair.

That fucking prick. He couldn't just accept his fate. He was going to try to take this from her too.

"You have to make sure your alibi's concrete, alright?" Tina asked. "Make sure you have a story lined up for where you've been the past few days, round up people who can testify to your whereabouts, and whatever you do, don't teleport here, Jeremy. There's an agent working this case with me and he's..." She paused. "He's kind of a conspiracist. And he's got a lot of theories about this case. Quite a few about your wife."

Well, not like I blamed him. Her case definitely screamed paranormal. The lies we'd told to cover our asses were far from concrete. Even Tina figured out that something wasn't right.

I blew out a slow, even breath. "Alright. Well, I'm going to go have breakfast with my son, show him his bedroom, and then put him back into the shitty scrubs he's been wearing for three years."

She fell silent. After a moment, she said, "I wish this was easier for you, kid."

"Yeah, me too," I said. "But I'll see you soon, I'm sure. Thanks for everything, Tina."

"Happy to help. But just for the record, we never had this conversation."

"Or any others. I know."

Another sigh. "I'll see you soon, Jeremy."

"Bye, Tina."

I started inside and stowed the phone into my back pocket. I turned to Micah and smiled. "Do you like the pancakes?"

"They is so good." Micah sipped orange juice from one of Milly's bottles.

"He really liked the chocolate chips." Laila smiled. "He asked if he could just have those without the mushy stuff next time."

"He's got a little bit of you in there after all." I grinned.

She chuckled and gestured toward the phone in my pocket. "How much time do we have?"

"Little more than a half hour." I slid my gaze to Micah. "How about me and Mommy go show you your bedroom and I play you a quick song on your saxophone?"

"I thought you said you wasn't vewy good," Micah muttered.

"Well, I can wail out some *Hot Crossed Buns*." I smiled and extended my hand to him. "Might not be Charlie Parker, but I'll get better as I teach you."

He smiled and took my hand. I smiled back. I gestured outside to Leah and Chris on the porch. My gaze met Laila's. "We should fill them in."

She lifted Milly from the highchair. Her lips pulled into a smile. "I'll be up in a minute. You can show him his saxophone on the balcony."

I grinned and looked down at Micah. "You want to race me?"

He hopped down with a grin and took off running.

Laila laughed. "Look at you, teaching him to run in the house like a little hoodlum."

"There's room to run here," I said. She gave a sad smile. But I leaned forward and pressed my lips to hers.

Now wasn't the time to be sad. We'd done plenty of that over the last three years. Now was the time to be the happiest we'd ever been.

"Daddy, awen't you coming?" Micah called.

I smiled and pulled away. I teleported in front of him. He looked over his shoulder to where I stood in the kitchen a moment before. "Boo." I grinned.

He jumped, turned up to me, and laughed. "You's allowed to do that?"

I fought the frown that pulled at my smiling lips. "Yeah, buddy. We're allowed to use our powers as much as we want as long as we don't hurt anyone else."

He smiled. "I like that wule."

I smiled back and pushed hair behind his ear. "At home, anyway. Out in the real world, you can't really use your powers until you're a little older. Just because it's easy to accidentally hurt someone when you can do the things that we can do. But we can talk about that later. Let's go check out that saxophone."

CHAPTER TEN

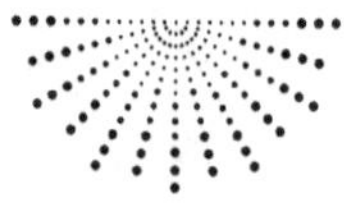

LAILA

Cool, spring air drifted around me. I tightened Milly at my hip, gently shutting the patio door. The smell of dew and early morning flowers touched my nose.

"Hey, guys. Sorry to interrupt." I gave Chris and Leah a smile. "We just heard from Tina. We need those clothes from the hospital."

"Brody has them back at the house." Leah stood and rubbed her tired eyes. "I'll go call him. He can bring them down. Is there coffee?"

"Always." As she started past me, I turned to Chris with a smile.

It was such a surreal moment. Since they'd been back, Micah had been the center of my attention. But I'd been dying for this one too. It'd been three years since I met Chris. And he'd only seen me in dreams ever since. Until a little over a year ago, he had no idea what I looked like. And I knew him as looking far different than he did now. Those big blue eyes really did make him look like a Skoulda.

"Hey, Chris."

"Hey, Laila." He stood and looked over me, laughing. "Kind of weird to finally meet you in the flesh."

"Kind of nice." I grinned.

"I really thought you'd be blonde."

"Just for a couple months in high school. Kind of washed me out though." I lifted Milly's hand and made her wave at him. "Did you get to say hi to your niece yet?"

"Not formally." He smiled as his gaze shifted to Milly. His fingertips reached out to graze hers. "She looks nothing like our side of the family."

"That's not true, she's got Jeremy's butt," I said.

"You can tell this early?"

"Well, it's too bubbly to be my butt." I laughed. "Do you want to hold her?"

He smiled, looking between her eyes. "Does she like new people?"

"She gets tossed around like a hot potato." I smiled, scooped my hands under her armpits, and held her out in front of him. "She won't mind."

He laughed and reached out to take her. He spoke softly to her for a minute. She giggled, reaching out to touch his cheek.

Seeing him like that, holding my other baby, it made this feel a little better. And it also made sense.

This was why Peterson had made us cellmates. So that when I lost my son in there, Micah would still have his uncle. I hated that bastard so much, but he made sure my baby had a piece of his family in there, and for that, I was remotely grateful.

I cleared my throat and met his gaze. "Thank you. For everything you did for my son, I mean. Thank you."

Chris turned to me and smiled. "Wish I could've done more."

"I wish you wouldn't have had to do anything at all," I muttered. "I wish I never would have gotten in that van."

"Wouldn't have found me if you didn't. You don't owe me anything."

That wasn't true. I owed him my life. Even if he hadn't been able to keep Micah safe from everything, he kept the concept alive to him. He told Micah about his dad in a place where the man holding him captive was filling his head with lies about him. He made certain that my son knew how much we loved him.

I owed Chris everything.

He cleared his throat. "After Micah entered the picture, they stopped doing the stress tests on me so that was nice. And Micah kind of... he made life worth living, ya know? Getting to be there for him? Having family around again and everything."

I managed a smile. "Yeah. Yeah, I guess."

He turned back to Milly. "So when I talk to the cops, Leah said to be incredibly vague. Tell them nothing, right? He drugged us, I never saw his face, never heard them talk. She said that's what all the other survivors did."

"Yeah, that's the best way to go about it. Micah knows that, right?"

"Yeah, he does. I told him to tell me what he wants to say if they ask anything about Peterson, or Amy, or Nastya. They'll just crack it up to being a shell-shocked little kid who only trusts the person that's taken care of him since he was a baby." He paused, eyes on mine for a moment. "I told him that he can tell the cops he knows you're his mom. Peterson kind of worshipped you, he's heard stories about you his whole life."

Worshipped me.

That was the problem with religion. I was a goddess once; I knew that now. But there was a reason I'd been an atheist before I learned about the supernatural races.

People do fucked up shit when they believe they're acting for the cause of a higher power. And Peterson loved me so much that he destroyed countless lives in my name. That was never what I wanted. I didn't want praise, or sacrifice. Regardless of the life, I knew that wasn't the person that I was.

Still, the day had to go on. And I'd rather not spend it thinking about what that man thought of me.

I tried to smile. "I'm sorry you guys can't stay. But we'll make sure everything's set up before you come back. We'll get you guys' sizes, and we'll make sure you have clothes and shoes and everything. Jeremy's going to call your grandparents to see if we can use their plane to get back and forth until they let you come home. He's going to see how to get your trust fund set up, too."

"That sounds great. And it's alright. Can't wait to get these things out of me anyway." He gestured to his scars.

"Getting those out was the best thing I've ever felt," I said. "Besides meeting my son last night and that little lady last year."

He looked up from Milly and gave a gentle smile. "Yeah, I bet. Hey, at least you were right though. We're both out of there by our birthdays."

"That's true. We're gonna throw some big ass parties to celebrate." I smiled. "But I'm going to go spend some time with Micah before it's time to go. Go ahead and grab something to eat."

"Look, Mommy!" Micah yelled from the balcony doorway. "Look how pwetty it is!"

I smiled and set Milly on the floor. "I knew you'd like it out there."

Jeremy smiled, turning to meet my gaze. He rubbed the top of Micah's head. "You want to look out here for a minute while I talk to Mommy?"

Micah nodded, placed his arms on the railing, and gazed out over the backyard. Jeremy smiled and took a step inside. Milly crawled her way toward him, reaching her arms out. He picked her up and started to me.

"I think I should take them," Jeremy whispered.

My face screwed up in confusion. "Why?"

"Peterson sent some videos with someone else that was working for him. Apparently, she isn't talking, but she's playing messenger for him."

My heart picked up speed in my chest. "What were the videos?"

"He said that if they find Micah, that means you found him." Jeremy raked hair from his face. "You need to stay here, somewhere out in the open. Go out and get coffee, or spend some time at the diner, I don't know. But you need to have a solid alibi."

That little fucking bastard. How many times did he say he knew I'd get him one day? Why hadn't he accepted his fate? Why did he want to try to take me down with him?

But fuck it. I wasn't stupid. I'd come up with a concrete story to explain my whereabouts over the last few days. No one was locking me up for this.

I fell into thought for a moment. "I'll take Milly to the doctor and say she's been sick all week. That'll be a good reason for you to not be at work the past two days and for me to not have left the house. And Adam can lie and say you were in the office all day today."

"That should do," he murmured. "We don't have long now. We should get him dressed and say our goodbyes."

CHAPTER ELEVEN

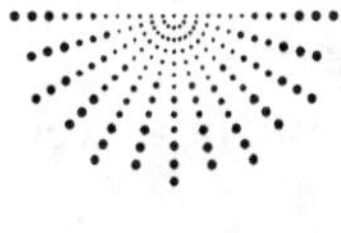

JEREMY

"But I don't want to go, Mommy," Micah murmured with watery eyes. He rubbed his balled fists against them and bit his quivering lip. "I want to stay with you."

"I don't want you to go either, buddy." She fought the tears I felt sting across her eyes. "But as soon as that police officer calls, me and your dad and your sister are going to be on the first airplane to come see you, okay? As soon as they tell me I can."

He continued rubbing his eyes, looking between hers. "You pwomise?"

"I promise." Laila smiled with a hand on his cheek. "But you've got to go with Daddy and Uncle Chris now, okay? And I'll see you again real soon."

He gave a sad, slow nod. He reached out and wrapped his arms around her. She locked hers around his back and closed her eyes against his shoulder. "I promise I'll see you again real soon, okay?"

My chest was tight, heart shattering in my chest. Fuck, I didn't want him to feel like we were abandoning him. But this was the only way. We had to get him back the right way—through the legal system. It sucked, and I hated it, but this was the only way we could get him back for good.

He pulled back and looked at me. "Can you cawwy me, Daddy?"

I smiled, and my arms opened. He took a step forward, and I lifted him to my torso. Laila brought herself back to her feet wiping her eyes. She fought back angry tears, clearing her throat.

"I'll be back soon." I smiled. "Milly's lying down in her swing, why don't you go get a shower?"

She forced a smile. "Yeah, I've got to call my mom first, but I will."

I smiled back and tightened my arms around Micah. I looked at Chris. "You all set?"

"Not really," he said. "But might as well get it over with."

Neither was I, but exactly.

I placed my hand on his shoulder.

Laila tightened her trembling jaw, and I forced my smile wider across my lips. "This is the last time we have to say goodbye. This is all going to be over soon."

Micah's arms tightened at my neck.

I closed my eyes and teleported back to the still smoking building.

"So this is it," Chris muttered with a look around. His jaw stiffened. "We're getting in a car, you said?"

I looked at the field where a white mobile office van sat beside a BMW and a Mercedes. "Van's probably the way to go."

Chris sighed, giving a nod.

I tightened my arms around Micah. I teleported again and landed just outside the van. I pulled my jacket sleeve down over my palm so I wouldn't leave prints on the door. The handle was locked, as I figured. I turned to Chris. "I'm not going to leave until I see them pulling up. You won't be trapped in here."

He formed a gentle smile and nodded again.

I teleported inside. We lowered ourselves to crouch in the ambulance styled vehicle. I sat with Micah still wrapped around my chest as I looked out the small glass window to the driveway in the distance. "Check the doors, make sure they don't open from the inside."

"Yeah, we're locked in." Chris lowered himself to the plastic flooring.

"Daddy," Micah nearly whispered.

"Yeah, kiddo?" I asked.

"I just have to *pwetend* that I don't know you, wight?" he asked. "You wemembew me, don't you?"

I laughed and kissed his hair. "Yeah, I remember you, buddy. But the police will know that I know you; you just have to pretend that you don't know me."

"But you know I do, wight?" he asked.

I smiled, looking out the window to the driveway ahead. "Yeah, buddy. I know."

"Good," he muttered. "When you leave, can you stay close for a little? Until the peace offews get us?"

I laughed and took a glance at Chris. He smiled too. "You mean the police officers?"

"I said that," he said.

I laughed again. "Yeah, buddy. I'll stay in the woods right over there until they get you guys into their car. I'm friends with one of the police officers, her name's Tina. She's really nice; I think you'll like her."

He tightened his arms at my neck.

I enjoyed it for a moment. Just sitting there, holding my son. It was the first time I really got to do that. I'd roughed up his hair, I'd touched his hand. But I was actually holding him. For the first time in his entire life.

And it felt so right.

But it also made me furious.

This moment should've come and passed almost three years ago. He should've been at the age where he didn't want us to hug and hold him anymore. I was glad that he did, and I was glad that he loved me, but it wasn't the way that it was supposed to be.

We had a long road ahead of us.

Sirens began to hum in the distance. My eyes closed, and I squeezed him a little closer into me. Chris released a long, shaking sigh. When I opened my eyes, red and blue lights flashed through the tree line.

I grabbed Micah's shoulders and tugged him back to look at me.

"I'll be right over there in those trees, okay?" He bit his quivering lip and raised his balled fist to his eyes. "Go sit with Uncle Chris for a little bit longer. Me and Mommy will see you soon. And then you'll be with us every single day, okay?"

He climbed over to his uncle. I looked at the two of them for a second, then I forced a smile. "Won't be long now."

"We'll see you soon." Chris smiled back.

I roughed up Micah's hair with a grin. And I landed in the tree line a few hundred yards away.

I watched as ten or maybe close to fifteen marked and unmarked police vehicles raced up that gravel path. They parked as close to the building as possible, jumping from their cars and SUVs with guns drawn. They darted like ants in every direction, some approaching the burning building and others starting to the cars.

When I saw Tina climb out of a black SUV, a tinge of relief washed over me. I trusted her. She'd keep her eyes on my son every moment that I couldn't.

She said something to another cop before they started toward the vehicles. I heard the quiet echoes of Chris banging on the van.

Tina jogged toward it with a man I couldn't describe from the distance. I nearly held my breath as they raised their guns to the back of that van. She shot at the handle. Jesus Christ, I hoped that they were far enough back that they didn't get hurt.

She ripped the door open. Tina's shoulders fell in relief. Then the other cop lowered his gun.

A second or two later, Chris stepped from the vehicle with Micah wrapped around his chest. As they stood outside, Micah looked for me over Chris's shoulder.

I'm right here, kiddo, I said into his mind.

His gaze found mine through the brush. He smiled. I smiled back. Then a cop put a thermal blanket around their shoulders.

Tina carefully ushered them to the SUV she just jumped from and loaded into the vehicle. As they started down the gravel path with two other cruisers, all flashing their lights, I expelled a long, trembling breath.

I teleported back to the living room.

Laila sat on the couch with her hand cupped over her mouth and closed eyes. "Tina's got them," I said. "Go get a shower, baby. I'm gonna call my grandparents."

She looked up and wiped her eyes. "How long will it be for the plane?"

"Probably a few hours. We'll have to drive to an airport too. I'll pack a bag for me and Mills while you shower. We can get a nap on the flight."

Gazing at the ground, she started to the bedroom. But I caught her hand and brushed some hair from her face. "It won't be long now, alright?"

"I know. I know, it's just hard, ya know?"

That it was. But it was almost over. Everything was gonna be better soon. He'd be home, really home, and we could put all of this behind us.

I kissed her cheek.

As she walked past me, I reached for my phone in my pocket. I went into my contacts and dialed a number I'd only dialed one other time in my adult life.

After a moment, Mèmè's soft voice spoke into the speaker. "So which one of my grandchildren is this?"

I laughed and lowered myself to the couch. "It's Jeremy."

She laughed quietly. "Oh, is it now? Finally decided to accept an invitation to come visit your old grandmère, hmm?"

"Maybe." I chuckled. "Maybe, but I'm actually calling you because I have some good news."

A quiet gasp echoed from the line. "You found your brother, didn't you?"

"And my son. Yeah, we found them." I cleared my throat and rubbed my mouth. "Look, I'm actually calling to ask a favor too. The government's involved in this so we can't teleport back and forth from here to where they're keeping Chris and Micah. Laila and I have some money but not like you guys have. We were hoping you'd let us use a plane for a week or two until they release them to us."

"If it were my choice, I'd say of course. But you know your grand-père, Jeremy. There's going to be strings attached."

"Laila and I will meet with you guys." I rubbed my temples. "Not until we get Micah settled in, but we will. We'll take a meeting."

"That should do then. Maybe you and your family can stay in the guest house for a night or two. Give me a chance to finally meet that little girl of yours and her brother at the same time."

"Yeah, maybe, Mèmè. But you'll talk to Papy?"

"Yes, I will. I'll send over some details once we speak."

"Thank you. Thank you so much."

CHAPTER TWELVE

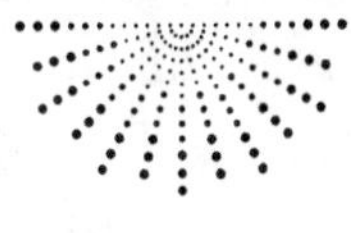

LAILA

I stared at my phone on the coffee table, teeth angrily chomping on the edges of my fingernails as Milly crawled around at my feet. Once Jeremy got back, he went to Walmart, and I took to Milly to the closest urgent care where I lied and said she'd been sick for the past few days for an alibi. I'd stopped at Starbuck's and gone inside, making sure to be visible on the building's security cameras. I'd expected to have gotten the call by now, but we were still waiting.

"It's been three hours, don't you think they should have called by now? Because if we don't hear something soon—"

"It's been two." Jeremy placed a hand on my back. "It's been two, and I saw them get in the car with Tina. They probably just got to the hospital. The doctors are probably examining Chris and Micah, and she hasn't been able to get somewhere private to call us. It's okay, Laila. I'm still bound to Micah; I'd know if something was wrong."

"Right."

He kissed my forehead. "Any minute now."

Almost simultaneously, the phone rang. Of course, that conversation had already repeated itself a good thirty times before that phone rang so it wasn't exactly poetic.

I slid the green bar to the private number and lifted the phone to my ear. "Hello?"

"Hello, is this Laila... Laila Call—I—die?"

"Laila Callidy? Yeah, that's me. Who is this?"

"Uh, yeah, that's it. This is Agent Russel Ward with the Federal Bureau of Investigation. Do you have a moment, miss?"

"Sure." I looked at Jeremy. "Sure, what's this about?"

"You were informed in 2020 by Agent Tina Davis that your son may still be out there somewhere, according to my records here."

"Yeah. Yeah, well actually, I heard it from one of the survivors first. But yeah, that's what I've been told. Have you—Did you find something?" I asked.

"We think we found your son, ma'am," the man said. His voice was flat, neither gentle nor excited. He could have been placing a lunch order for all I knew. "We'll have to run some tests to be sure, but he looks just like the pictures Tina's shown me of your husband. I think this is him."

"Really?" I said, not even having to pretend to sound excited. "Where? Where is he? My husband and I will get on the next flight."

"Northern California. I'll send you a text message with the address to the hospital. He's being seen and observed right now, but he's okay. No injuries or anything, no one's hurt. He seems like a really sweet kid. Very quiet though. Sweet but quiet. But look, there's something you should know before you meet him. He's... he's got some scars, miss."

"Like mine?"

"Not on the back. But he's got those things in him like the rest of you did. I just wanted you to be prepared. We're waiting to remove them until DNA is established so the proper papers can get signed. But we'd like to get that over with sooner rather than later. So the soonest you can get here, the better off we'll be."

"Yeah, of course. Of course, we'll pack a quick bag and be on our way. Thank you. Thank you so much. Is— Did you find his uncle too?"

"We did. We did, he says that the boy's you and his brother's son. Right now, they're both being held in protective custody in the hospital because we haven't found their kidnapper. But I assure you, we're still looking high and low, Miss Callidy."

Jeremy tightened his jaw as he met my gaze.

"Good," I muttered. "Good, I can't wait to see him. Thank you so much, Agent."

"Course. We'll see you soon, miss."

As the phone cut to silence, I met Jeremy's gaze. "I don't like the way he said that."

"I have an alibi; they can't touch me." I brought myself to my feet. "It's going to be fine."

He fought a frown. "I know. I just want to make sure we keep a teleporter back at the main house in case we have to move Peterson last minute."

"Let Leah know. I'm going to get Milly ready to go and loaded up in the car."

CHAPTER THIRTEEN

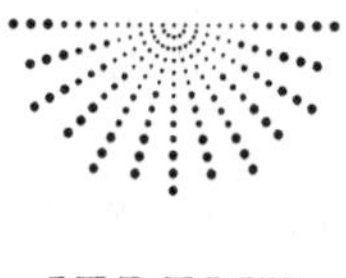

JEREMY

"Puis-je vous apporter quelque chose à boire, monsieur?" *Can I get you anything to drink, mister?* the stewardess asked with a smile.

"Non, merci." I smiled, shaking my head. I looked over Laila sleeping with my jacket draped over her shoulders. "Mais pourriez-vous me procurer une couverture pour me femme?" *But could you get me a blanket for my wife?*

"Oui." She smiled.

"Merci, merci beaucoup." I smiled back, then glanced down at Milly napping in her car seat.

"Une equ s'il vous plait," *One water please,* Leah said.

"Oui," the stewardess said.

"Can't believe we're finally here." Leah grinned, gazing out the small window across from me. "Almost can't believe we found them, ya know?"

"Yeah, took us long enough," I muttered. "We're not in the clear yet. Laila's a suspect in Peterson's disappearance. We all might be."

"Then we brainwash the shit out of him and turn him over if we have to. Or we have him kill himself somewhere out in the open where no one can accuse us of being responsible."

"No, if he's leaving our custody, it's going to be in a body bag. He doesn't get to walk out of this. He doesn't get a trial."

"Couldn't agree more. Especially after all the shit Chris told me." Her jaw tightened, stare still out the window.

I wondered what that entailed for a moment. I decided I wasn't going to push the subject. Curiosity wasn't worth killing the cat. But I did need to know what his attitude toward my parenting style was about. "You guys talked a lot last night, right?"

"All night long." She shifted from the window to meet my gaze. "Why?"

"Did he tell you why he doesn't like me?"

Her head tilted. "He loves you, what are you talking about?"

"Something he said last night. He's mad we didn't get to them sooner, I think. But you know how hard we tried, Leah. We were fighting like hell for years. And I know that we lost them, but we got them back."

Leah frowned. "I don't think it's that, Jeremy. He knows how hard you've worked and he's grateful. But... Well, he didn't say this. But I think he's jealous of you."

My forehead wrinkled. "Why? Because Laila came into some money and paid to have us a nice house built for our family? It's not like he can't do the same, he'll have a trust fund and—"

"No, not that. Well, maybe in part. But no, I think it has more to do with Micah."

"What do you mean?"

"Think about this from his shoes, alright? He was eighteen when he was taken. That was a decade ago. And three years ago, Laila shows up in that place pregnant with your baby. She gives him hope again, she tells him she's going to get him out of there. She tells him that we didn't give up on him.

"But she loses the baby. And she tries to set everyone free, Chris included, but a guard grabs ahold of him in the chaos. He gets carted off onto a plane, and they hand him the baby he believed was dead. Laila got shot that night; he thought she died. Peterson told him you killed yourself a moment later. And because of the bond, he believed it.

Then the bastard told him he has to take care of this baby because he has no one else. Of course, he's going to take that opportunity."

"Which I'm eternally grateful for, but I'm not dead." My brows were deep in my eyes. "I'm here, and I've been looking for my son since before he was born."

"I know that." Her green eyes were gentle. "And he knows that too. But he's taken beatings for Micah, Jeremy. He lost his eyes for him. And then Micah meets you and *you're* the one he sees as a hero."

Yeah, I supposed I understood. But what was I supposed to do? Be a dick to my kid? Be a bad father so that Chris could take my place?

I huffed and looked away. My head shook a bit. "Am I supposed to feel guilty for my son liking me?"

"No. No, of course not," Leah said. "But that doesn't mean it doesn't hurt."

"We're not trying to kick him to the curb. We set him up a bedroom, we're getting him clothes, we're trying to make this transition easy for everyone."

"He knows that. And he appreciates it. This is just going to be hard. No matter what, this is going to be hard. You remember how hard it was for Laila, and she was only in there for a couple months. He was there for a third of his life. It's normal for him to be a little angry right now."

I thought back to Laila's state when she got out of captivity. "Yeah. Yeah, I guess."

"But you guys will find a balance. It's just gonna take some time.

I looked out the window at the clouds drifting by. "Just sucks, ya know? I wasn't just excited to get my son. I was excited to get my brother back too."

"Well, he was really happy that you guys asked him to stay with you." Leah smiled. "So you'll have plenty of time to catch up. He said something about making s'mores in the fireplace when they let him come home."

A quiet laugh left my lips. "Yeah, me and Laila already talked about that."

"It's going to be nice. Just hard at first, ya know? Remember me and Lai when she got back? That big fight we got into?"

It wasn't an easy thing to forget. "Yeah. Yeah, you're right."

CHAPTER FOURTEEN

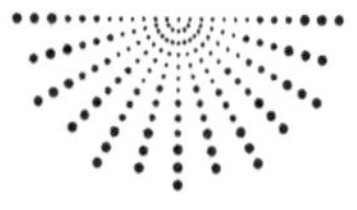

LAILA

"You must be Laila Callidy, and you've got to be Jeremy Skoulda." The middle-aged man with short gray hair and glasses smiled as he shook my hand. He looked how I imagined he looked. Short, chubby, balding. Unhappy. "That family resemblance is undeniable."

I forced a smile as he shook Jeremy's hand. "That's us."

"And I'm sorry, what's your name?" he asked Leah.

"Leah. Leah Boucher, I'm Chris and Jeremy's adopted sister." She smiled and extended her hand out to him.

"Nice to meet you, Leah Boucher." He smiled back. "Well, my colleague will be ushering the two of you to a private room upstairs. But I'd actually like to talk with you before we introduce you to your son, Miss Callidy."

I adjusted Milly on my hip as warm summer wind fluttered hair into my face, trying to appear casual. "I'm sorry, what do you mean?"

"There's some things we were hoping you could help us clear up first."

"I'll answer whatever questions you want, but can I maybe do it tonight? Like after he turns in for the night? I just, I've been looking forward to this day for so long and—"

"No, I'm sorry. We're going to have to talk first." His ice blue eyes cut into mine.

Ah, fuck.

Not that I was happy about it, but whatever. I knew how to lie to cops. One way or the other, I was going to see my kid before the day was over.

Jeremy tightened his hand at my hip. "About what?"

"I'm sure she'll tell you all about it."

"Are you charging her with something?" he asked, gaze somewhere between defensive and pissed.

"I could." He looked between Jeremy's eyes. "The murder and or kidnapping of Robert Peterson. Maybe the murder of Moses Baker, too."

Rationally, I knew he could only try. None of those charges would stick. I had an alibi for both. Unless he was going to appoint a human judge at that very moment and tell them I was a teleporting murderer, he could not arrest me. If Jeremy or I made a scene, he might have the grounds to make an arrest, but he couldn't press murder charges. There wasn't enough evidence to call for an arrest warrant, let alone a conviction.

Jeremy laughed and rubbed his mouth. "You're kidding, right?"

He looked at me. "What's it going to be, Laila? Are you going to come in for questioning, or am I going to have to arrest you?"

I forced a smile. "Well, sir, I have nothing to hide. Not really sure what you would arrest me *for*, but I will absolutely answer a few questions for you. But when we're done, I get to come back here and spend some time with my son until it's time for him to go to bed, right?"

He smiled back. "Of course."

"Alright then." I passed Milly to Jeremy and rolled onto my tiptoes. I pressed my lips to his and smiled. "You tell our son how excited I am to meet him."

He forced a smile and kissed me again. *Watch every word you say. He's looking for a gap in your story. If they charge you, you tell me right away and we'll get a plan together. If we have to run to Mexico, then we'll run to Mexico.*

I smiled back as I pulled away. I turned my gaze to Milly and tickled her sides. She giggled, pushing her head into Jeremy's chest. "I'll see you in a little bit." I turned back to the agent. "Are we going down to the station?"

"We are. I won't put you in cuffs, but you do have to sit in the back."

I gestured to the parking lot. "Well. Lead the way, agent."

"Well, it is nice to formally meet your acquaintance," Agent Ward said. "I've heard your name so many times, I was starting to think you were some sort of urban legend."

"Oh, yeah?" I sent him a friendly smile. "What am I famous for?"

"All those people you saved." He set a cup of coffee in front of me. "They do call you the savior, don't they?"

"Huh," I muttered. "I couldn't say. Doesn't ring a bell to me."

He chuckled. "Surprisingly good coffee for a police station, you should try it."

I wasn't an idiot; I knew what he was doing there too. But I huffed and took a sip. "You could have just asked for my DNA, and I would have given it to you. I'm giving it to you already to prove I'm my kid's mother anyway."

"That's a paternity test for social services. I'd have to get a warrant." He smiled and took the cup back to his end of the table. "But I'm glad to see you're cooperating."

"I'm playing your game." I sat forward. "We both know you have nothing on me. I was in Pennsylvania until three hours ago. I have no idea what happened to that bastard. But I'm pretty disappointed you guys don't have him. That is what you were supposed to do, right? Capture the bad guy?"

The breath he released came out as more of a scoff. He took another sip of his coffee. "I'm pretty disappointed too."

I crossed my arms.

"Ya know why I'm questioning you right now, Miss Callidy?"

"It's actually Missus. But no, sir. I don't. I know you think that I have something to do with whatever it is that happened to Peterson for him to not be in your custody. But no, I don't know why you're pointing fingers at the person who's been at home with her sick baby all week."

He flipped open the laptop on the desk and typed for a moment. He clicked a few times before he turned the screen to face me.

Peterson's face stared back at the screen with a friendly smile. My jaw involuntarily clenched. Agent Ward clicked play.

"Hello, Agent Ward. I assume that's who's watching this anyway. We have not met, and this is probably the first time you've seen my face. But my name is Doctor Robert Peterson." He stood and flipped the camera. Micah lay on a metal table unconscious with gauze taped to his neck, wrists, upper arms, legs, and feet. I closed my eyes and turned away. "And this is Micah Skoulda, son of Laila Callidy and Jeremy Skoulda." His voice paused, sounds shuffling. I opened my eyes and struggled to look back to the screen. It was facing Peterson again. "I'm making this video tonight in case something should happen to me. And I'm not saying I don't deserve whatever comes my way, regardless of who dishes it to me. But what I am saying is this. If this little boy is in your hands, it's because Laila got me. She might have killed me already; she might be trying to get information out of me first. Regardless, I'm telling you with absolute certainty that if you have this child, and you don't have me, she does or she did.

"The matter is a very complicated one to divulge. I don't have the time to explain all of this..."

That fucking asshole. Why? Why do this? Why tell the cops that I was going to take him? He'd said many times that he'd accepted his fate. That he knew I was going to kill him, and that he was okay with it. So why turn me into the police? Did he truly want to live that badly?

"Please turn that off." I looked away and pressed my lips together.

"It starts to get good right about—"

I had to keep my eyes shut to keep them from glowing. "Please turn it the fuck off."

He fell silent and clicked a button. After a moment, he said, "At that point in the video, Peterson goes on to talk about how he deserves justice for what he's done. More specifically, he says that you deserve vengeance for what he's done to you. But that he has information we want. He wants to tell us what his purpose was in all of this, Laila."

"Great. Find him and figure it out," I snapped.

He got quiet again, gaze narrowing at mine.

"Tell me, Laila. When he did that to you." He gestured to my scars. "When he took your baby from your supposed dying arms. How did you find the strength to get out? And to open over two hundred other cell doors along the way? All while avoiding a bomb and only being a few weeks postpartum. My daughter just had a little girl too, you know. Took her three weeks to even walk normally again."

I forced a smile before gritted teeth. "Well, I've been told I have an ideal birth canal. They just slip right on out."

He huffed. "How'd you get all those people off the island, Laila?"

"Couldn't tell ya," I said. "I remember getting out of my room. I remember opening my two cellmate's doors. But I'm not exaggerating when I say that everything else is a blacked-out blur. I don't know how we got out of there. I don't know how I survived, although I'm told I barely did. Maybe that's why I remember so little. I can't say for sure, agent."

He squinted me over. "Something doesn't add up with your story, miss."

I clenched my jaw. "Well, that's my story. Take it or leave it."

Agent Ward leaned back in his seat. He crossed his arms against his chest. "You're right about one thing. You have been in Pennsylvania the past few days. But I started doing a little digging when I got this video. And I couldn't help but wonder what happened to the eight hundred thousand dollars that was in your bank account a little over a year ago. Really odd how you only have a little over a hundred grand left in there."

Huh. Didn't that require a warrant? Whatever, it didn't matter. I had the paperwork to prove where every dime had gone.

Ah, shit. Helena. Well, fuck it. Her business is on the books. Witch-

craft and psychics aren't illegal. The most anyone could say was that I was stupid for believing she could help.

I laughed and arched a brow. "Are you trying to suggest I hired a hit man to take out Peterson?"

"Stranger things have happened," he said.

"If you must know, over two hundred thousand of that was used to build my home. You'd have to ask my husband for the exact amount after we paid all of our friends and family for helping, but if I'm not mistaken, it was somewhere around two and a half hundred thousand. We have the receipts to prove it. The rest of it is in a safe in my basement, give or take a couple thousand we've used for bills and basic necessities."

He made a face. "Why?"

"Because we don't trust banks. We lived at a diner before, but when we built our house, we got a heavy duty safe put in. Pretty advanced security system, more trustworthy than a bank if you ask me."

He studied me hard for a minute. "Could you prove that?"

"If you want to fly back to Pittsburgh with me, then yes. Can't really do it from in here."

Agent Ward paused for a moment. "You know what, Laila. I've got another question for you."

I leaned back in my chair.

"How did you *not* know that your son was alive?" he asked. My jaw tightened, and my breaths grew short. "How did that happen? How did you give birth to this child and then believe that he died without getting to see his body?"

My jaw squeezed tighter. I turned my gaze to the metal tabletop.

I didn't know. At the time, I still pondered it. Even to myself, it made no sense. I didn't believe anything else that came out of that man's mouth, so why did I believe my son was dead when I'd never seen a body?

"Ooh, struck a nerve there, huh?" he asked. "Yeah, guess you were telling the truth about that part. But walk me through it. Walk me through how you gave birth to your son and immediately fainted before even seeing him."

"No."

"I'm sorry?" He lifted a brow.

"That was the worst experience of my life, and I'm not talking about it."

Agent Ward grew quiet for a moment. "The worst experience of your life. What's the second worst then, Laila?"

I turned away.

Agent Ward huffed again, turning the laptop to face himself. He clicked around for a moment.

I heard my own voice coming from the speakers.

"You have no idea what I'm going to do to you when I get out of here." My head shot up as he turned the screen to face me. "You evil piece of shit. I can't wait until I get to fucking kill you. Because I will, Peterson, I'm going to fucking kill you."

She looked so helpless. Me. *I* looked so helpless.

Bolted to that metal table, big wad of gauze taped to my thigh, greasy dark hair laying over my oversized hospital gown, basketball sized belly standing up beneath it. I fought against those restraints, angrily peering up at him.

My fingertips rubbed against the phantom pain in my legs as my jaw clenched.

"Turn this off," I said. "Turn this off right now."

"This wasn't the worst experience of your life, Laila?"

My heart hammered against my ribs, and my hands started to shake.

I get why he showed it to me. I made a valid threat about murdering the man. But to let it keep playing as he spoke, to force me to relive that conversation, it took everything not to catch that damn laptop on fire.

Everything blurred as Agent Ward continued to talk, nearly yelling now that I killed Peterson. Trying to force a confession out of me by making me relive the worst trauma I ever felt. The only one that could still send me into an instant panic.

My head shook, tears whisking down my face. I wanted to lean across the table and punch him for making me hear the sound of my cries as I begged Peterson to get off of me. I wanted him to hurt this fucker way that he made me hurt in that moment, but he was human, and my entire foreseeable future was riding on him.

As I heard myself on that video, it brought me back to that moment. I could smell his breath against mine as he bit my lip. I could hear his pants louder than I heard my own screams. I could feel my insides aching with each thrust. I echoed myself, begging that man to turn the video off and make it stop.

But he wouldn't. He just kept screaming at me. I couldn't make it stop. And my body went into a massive anxiety attack.

My breaths grew short, water rained from my eyes, my tight limbs shook, and gasps heaved into my chest. Still, Agent Ward continued yelling, insisting that I was a liar. That I knew exactly what happened to Robert Peterson. Not like he was wrong, but it was still pretty insensitive.

"What the hell are you doing?" a man's voice said at the door. "Is that—" He gasped, eyes catching the laptop on the table. I didn't even look at him as he rushed across the room and slammed the screen shut. "Are you out of your god damned mind?"

"This is my investigation, and I'll run it how I see—"

"Not anymore. And I hope she sues you," the man snapped. "Laila. Laila Callidy, right?"

I stared at my shaking hands on my lap. He placed his palm on my shoulder. I quickly pushed it away. "Please don't touch me."

"Sure," he murmured. "Of course, I'm sorry. My name's Connor Taylor. I recently acquired your son's case. I was hoping I'd get word to Agent Ward before he questioned you, but I see that I'm a little late."

"On whose orders?" Agent Ward asked.

"Check your phone. You should have gotten the memo by now."

"What department are you in? This is my case; I've been working it for—"

"This is out of the FBI's hands, agent. Now that's enough. If you have a problem, take it up with your superior." He lowered himself to the chair beside me and tried to meet my gaze. "Laila, do you want to go see your son?"

CHAPTER FIFTEEN

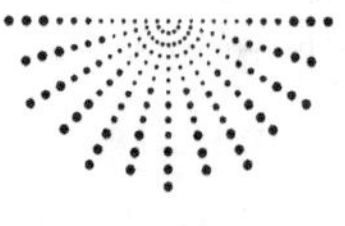

JEREMY

After Laila walked into the unmarked SUV with that FBI agent, I turned to Leah and fought the urge to run after her. She sent me a smile as if to say Laila could handle just about anything, with or without me. And she was right, but I still didn't like it.

I tightened my arms around Milly and followed the other FBI agents through the elevator. Leah made small talk about the weather as I anxiously bounced my daughter against my hip. I just wanted to see my kid, and all of this red tape was making me a nervous wreck. I told him I'd see him soon; this needed to move faster.

We met with a child psychologist. She told us to let Micah and Chris take the reins, not to usher the conversation to what we want to talk about, and to let them feel accepted. I explained that my wife and I had already gone through a lot of therapy to prepare for today, but she kept rambling for about forty-five minutes.

Leah and I continued giving smiles and nods until she finally gave us the okay. When that door opened, Micah and Chris turned to us with wide smiles. Chris started to his feet and began with introductions. But Micah cleared the distance between us and threw his arms around me. He whispered some sweet little comment into my thoughts about how he knew I'd be back.

For the next couple hours, we pretended to get to know each other over chocolate milk while *Paw Patrol* played on the TV from the corner of the room.

Tina sat with us, making little notes in a handbook as we waited to hear from Laila. About an hour or so later, she came to the doorway with red eyes and blotchy cheeks. I asked her if everything was okay, but she said we'd talk about it later.

Laila and Micah pretended to meet for the first time. But her tears were as genuine as ever when they spilled down her cheeks to the shoulder of Micah's hospital gown.

Both mine and Laila's mouths were swabbed shortly after. When we asked how long it would take to get the results, and they told us a week, we asked if we could pay to expedite the process. It cost us a couple grand, but they found a facility that could confirm our results within twenty-four hours. Laila signed the check quicker than any of us could argue. She figured if we proved paternity sooner, they'd release Micah to us sooner. While she was right, we still had a number of grueling days ahead of us before they let us take our son home.

Micah smiled wider than ever as he showed Laila and I the special fuzzy slippers one of the nurses found for him. He laughed as we shared Twinkies and Hohos from the vending machine. He happily showed us around his little hospital room just as we had shown him the house earlier that day.

It wasn't as great as being at home with him. But at least we got to see him. We got to be with him. We got the process started.

The goodbyes weren't easy on any of us. Micah begged us to stay, but the nurses insisted that visiting hours were over. Chris tried to soothe him, but he erupted in violent sobs and wouldn't let Laila go. I could see that it took everything in her not to do the same.

After nearly an hour of persuasion, I finally got him to lie down and sang to him until he fell asleep. When he did, we snuck out of the room and started to the lobby. Laila muttered something about how we were having lunch with some agents while Micah got his implants removed the following day but didn't say much else throughout the Uber back to the hotel. I tried to ask what happened with the FBI guy, but she said she'd tell me about it later.

Once we got back to the hotel, Leah and Laila got a cup of tea in the lobby while I set up the basinet for Milly. She fell asleep in her car seat on the way home, so I teleported her into the basinet and grabbed a quick shower. Then Laila came in, got a shower, and silently sat on the bed beside me.

I looked up from my phone and smiled. "Hey, beautiful." She met my gaze with a quivering lip. I leaned forward and pushed damp hair behind her ear. "Hey, what's wrong?"

"Peterson. He—He sent them..." She pressed her trembling lips together and raised her shaking hand to cover her mouth. "He sent them a video of the night that he... that he... after I was shot and he..."

A spin turned in the pit of my stomach. The day after she was shot was the day that he raped her. And that sick fuck recorded it.

That's what Tina meant when she said I didn't want to know what the other video was.

My gaze softened.

Her hands raised to wipe the tears that escaped her eyes. "He showed it to me."

"What do you mean?"

She blew out slow, calculated breaths. When she answered, her voice moved fast, almost too fast to follow. "Before Peterson did that to me, I was yelling at him. I kept saying I was going to kill him, and even a few times while he was doing it. And I think—I think Agent Ward thought he'd get me to confess, but I didn't. I didn't tell him anything but—But I'm... I'm having a hard time." Her teeth chattered as water trickled from her sad green eyes. "I-I'm having a really h-hard time."

"Baby." My expression softened again as I thumbed away her tears. "What can I do?"

"Can you just hold me?" she whispered.

I gave a sympathetic smile, nodding. "Get over here."

She smiled, wiped her eyes, and trudged beside me up the bed.

We climbed beneath the sheets, and I twisted my arms around her waist. She rolled over to meet my gaze, still wiping her eyes.

"That can't be legal. I can check with Hannah, but I don't think he can do that. What you said in a moment like that can't be used against you in court, that isn't fair," I said.

"It won't make it to court." She wiped her running nose. "All that they have on me is that my story's weird. Most of it can only be explained by supernatural intervention. They wouldn't believe the truth if we told them every detail. That's why he wanted a confession, so they could finally have a human explanation to all of this."

I gave a slow nod. "We need to have a plan in place in case they do try to build a case against you. I'm not losing you, Lai."

"We go to the Fae Realm," she murmured. "No government agency's finding me there."

Frowning, I said, "But we kill that bastard first."

She gritted her teeth and dropped her head to my chest. "Another cop came in and interrupted my interview with Ward. His name's Connor. He said he worked for the CIA."

I leaned back. "The CIA?"

She nodded and twisted up to meet my gaze. "That's literally the only conversation we had. He came in while the video was playing, yelled at Ward, and asked me if I wanted to go see Micah. I asked him who he was on the car ride back to the hospital. He said he worked for the CIA. Said not to worry about anything for tonight, just enjoy spending some time with Micah. He said we could have lunch at the café next to the hospital while Micah has his procedure tomorrow. He'll be out for a few hours and lunch will only take an hour. Seemed like a better option than getting hauled off to the police department again."

"CIA," I murmured.

I hated the Chambers, the Elders, and the Council. Especially considering how little they did to help us bring our son home, even more when I realized that my entire life had been shit because of the god they worked for. But I did know one thing about the Chambers.

They secretly worked hand in hand with all the significant governing authorities worldwide.

"How much do you wanna bet they know exactly who Peterson is and what he's done?"

"Wouldn't surprise me," Laila said. "But that would mean they know about us."

"Oh, yeah. I'm betting on it. The Chambers have links in governments all over the world. I wouldn't be surprised if this is who we have to thank for keeping you guys out of the press. When you were found, there were like one or two reports put out but when you first went missing, your name was everywhere."

"Yeah, I guess. I always just assumed it was because the other survivors kept their mouths shut to hide our secrets. Tina did say a bunch of files were redacted though, remember? Even files she wrote?"

I cocked my head to the side. "So were they just covering up our world? Or were they trying to cover Peterson's tracks?"

Her breaths picked up in pace, eyes widening. "You're still bound to Micah, right?"

"Yeah, he's sleeping. And I didn't feel any power at the hospital, did you?"

"No, everything felt human to me." Her brows creased slightly, thinking hard. "And the CIA guy seemed really nice. Almost too nice, but I didn't feel any power coming from him either. That doesn't necessarily mean anything though. There are ways to disguise abilities."

I paused. "What do you mean too nice? Like creepy nice?"

"No, not creepy," she murmured, head shaking. "Just... I don't know. Remember when we met Avery and Asher? How they almost felt familiar?"

"Huh." I thought back to that odd queen of the Open Lands. "I guess we'll see tomorrow. We should try and get some sleep though. We're both exhausted and there's free breakfast in the morning. If we get up early enough, we get first pick of the yogurts."

She laughed and leaned her head into my chest. "I love you."

I kissed her hair and tightened my hands at her waist. "I love you too."

CHAPTER SIXTEEN

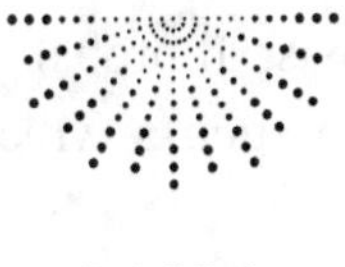

LAILA

Each time I woke up in a pool of sweat, and Jeremy gently told me that it was a dream, and everything was okay, I contemplated teleporting to that basement and beating Peterson's face in with a baseball bat. Or pouring gasoline on it, catching it on fire, healing him, and doing it again.

I'd had a lot of time to think of all the ways I wanted to torture that man, but unfortunately, my creative mind always proved a bit more volatile than my conscious.

Instead, I snuck off to the bathroom, cried, and went back to bed. By the third time, I woke Milly, and she refused to lie down again. So, I lifted her from the basinet, got her changed, and took her for a walk with me. Jeremy rolled over and said he'd get up too, but I insisted he get some more sleep. I slept on the plane the day before, but he hadn't slept since Peterson beat the fuck out of him. He needed a full night's rest. I did too, but that wasn't happening any time soon.

I strolled Milly along the gardens outside the hotel. We watched the sun rise in the distance, listening to the passing cars fly by. I wondered how long it would be until I got to watch the sun rise with both of my kids.

After a while, we went back inside, and I got a cup of coffee. While I sat there, I tried to enjoy the feel of travel the way that I used to. Watching the people in the city I'd never seen before, taking in the new smells, noting all of the little different types of flowers that bloomed outside and the different bugs fluttering about.

I wondered why I couldn't appreciate it as I had all those times before. I questioned if it was because I now knew that my soul played a part in picking each species for each environment. Maybe that's why it always fascinated me in the past. It probably would have fascinated me that day too if I hadn't been such a wreck over everything the past three days had entailed.

I suppose sitting in that hotel lobby with Milly on my lap was the first time the last seventy-two hours started to register in my mind. I knew what had happened. I knew that we finally made it to the home stretch. But it all hit me at once.

Since he brought us back, I hadn't even thought about Jeremy's newfound ability of resurrecting the dead. I hadn't thought about how he used my abilities or what that meant. None of that even crossed my mind until I took a sip from my coffee and gazed at the morning glories blooming outside of the window.

As always, so much happened in too short of a timespan for me to absorb it. More memories from the past few days washed over me in slow waves, but one was front in center before the others. Perhaps watching that video was what brought it back. Regardless of why, it came back, and with it came confusion.

Standing in that cell with my skirt pulled up my body as Peterson held my husband's blade to my neck. At first, the smell of his breath stuck out the clearest. But after a moment, the memory of his hand reaching toward my underwear sent a painful swirl to the pit of my stomach.

Then the sound of that whir. Or maybe roar. I can't quite describe it, but I knew it wasn't human.

I replayed pieces of Jeremy's conversation with him as I struggled to stay alive in his arms. Somebody told Peterson to do those things.

Somebody told him that he was a part of this story. And he'd mentioned being a part of the story before, but I thought it was metaphoric. But it couldn't have been. Somebody helped him pull that shit off. And whoever they were, they agreed with torture. But apparently not rape.

The person responsible for the twenty-four-year curse had clearly been another god. Heylel's father, the big guy above the Angels. But in a way, what Peterson had done helped us break that curse. He made sure my baby lived when he was born. He took him from me, yes, but he played some part in breaking that curse.

Surely, they couldn't be the same person. The person who made the curse couldn't be the same one that told Peterson to help us break it.

Could he?

Leah yawned, tickled Milly's armpit, and sat beside me. "You're up early."

"Couldn't sleep," I muttered.

"I passed out early as shit. Jet lagged or whatever." She stifled another yawn. "But I slept like a baby, I need to know what type of pillows they use."

"Just take one and let them bill you for it," I said. "Just check it for bed bugs first. I'll kill you if I have to buy new furniture again."

"I just might, actually. I heard from Wyatt, by the way. They're taking shifts on Peterson, but I guess him and Celena did a number on him. He's in real bad shape. They want to know if they should heal him."

"Is he in pain?" I asked.

"Apparently."

"Is he dying?"

"I don't think so."

"Then no. Don't heal him unless he's about to die. Let him suffer." I took another sip from my coffee.

"That's what I said too," she murmured. Her gaze moved over me for a long moment. "Something happened when you went with that FBI agent, huh?"

"Yep." I continued to stare out the window, watching a bee flutter into a flower. "I'm meeting with a CIA agent for lunch."

"What? Are you serious?"

"While Micah's getting his implants removed," I said. "If Jeremy's not down here soon, I should go wake him. They said we could be back at the hospital at nine, so we have to leave here by eight fifteen."

"Laila, hang on a second." She caught my arm and searched my gaze. "You're meeting with someone from the Central Intelligence Agency. They're involved with this, that's what you're telling me."

"What? What's wrong?"

"Do you have any ideas how much tech the CIA has, man? I'm a hacker, I've seen some crazy shit on the dark web."

"Like Peterson style tech?"

"Not specifically but just, a lot of shit that they could use to prove we did some sketchy shit. Aside from some advanced forensics they could use at any of the compounds you destroyed? Basic tech all around us. Facial recognition, geo tracking us, our phones are an obvious one." She gestured to hers in her hand. "Bugging a phone is nothing, man. If the CIA is meeting with you, they know who you are. They know what we are. And they know what we've done. I guarantee it. And with the CIA, there are no trials. Just missing persons."

I wasn't afraid of the CIA. Not much scared me anymore. Unless they had an incredibly powerful psychic, no one was going to have me turn up missing again. I'd been tied to a table too many times. And I'd be damned before it happened again.

"Well, we seemed to have better luck with them than the FBI so." I shrugged. "Maybe we're already on the same team."

"Maybe," she muttered. "Hey, we haven't really talked about what happened in there the other day."

I frowned. "Not much, actually. Well, I mean, I guess a lot. They injected us with something. Some type of sedative for me. I'm pretty sure he gave Jeremy heroin."

"Yeah, he said that," she murmured.

"I woke up in a cell that was split down the middle. He beat the shit out of Jeremy and put him on the other side." As I told the story I watched employees set up the breakfast bar on the other side of the lobby. Maybe I could've shown a bit more emotion, but it was practically replaying in my mind like a movie. Maybe it was just easier to see it that way. "He passed out for a while. Then when he woke up, Peterson came in. He showed us a live feed of Amy hurting Micah to make us compliant. He... I thought he was going to rape me and make Jeremy watch, but he didn't. He just stabbed me with Jeremy's knife."

"That's what was going on with your heart rate then," she murmured. "We were getting ready to bind Jeremy to Micah when we felt you code but then it started doing weird stuff, beating erratically or something. Then it came back, and we stopped."

I licked my lips. "Jeremy brought me back."

"That's what Hannah said. But who healed you?"

I turned to her with a confused expression. "I think Jeremy did."

Her face screwed up in confusion. "What?"

"With my powers," I muttered. "The light started coming out of my hand, but I grabbed his. And his started doing it."

Leah blinked hard for a second. "Jeremy used your powers."

"It seemed like it," I said. "I think that was the whole point, or at least half of it. Peterson wanted to unlock Jeremy's necromancy abilities for a reason. I think it was always his plan to kill Micah and then have Jeremy bring him back. And I think he wanted to us to realize we can use each other's powers too."

"I didn't know that was a thing," Leah said. "It wasn't in the myths, that's for sure. I didn't know abilities could be shared."

"I guess they can when your souls are connected."

"I wonder if Heylel knows anything about that. Maybe you guys can check with him."

"Once we get Micah home," I said. "I have a lot of people to talk to once things settle down. Moriah, Ray, Heylel, Roland. And that asshole's going to have to wait on my blood this month; I'm not rushing over there. I just got my kid back. He can grab a snack somewhere else."

"What are you guys talking about?" Jeremy said behind me. He wrapped his arms around my neck and kissed my hair.

"Oh, ya know, the usual," Leah said. "Werewolves and murder."

"Sounds about right." Milly extended her arms out to him. He lifted her to his hip. "You guys ready for breakfast? I want to get out of here by eight-fifteen."

I smiled as Leah laughed. "Yeah, let's go eat."

CHAPTER SEVENTEEN

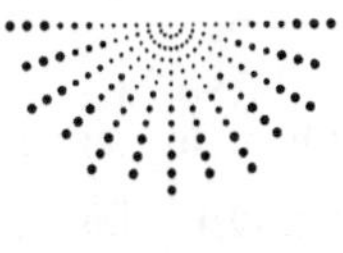

JEREMY

Micah ran from his bed to the doorway. He wrapped his arms around my legs. "Daddy!"

"Well, what am I? Chopped liver?" Laila grinned.

Chris gave an awkward, sad smile when I placed my arms around Micah's shoulders.

Okay, yeah, that had to suck. Prior to yesterday, I'd only met him twice, and suddenly, I was his favorite person in the world. I was so happy that I was, but I understand how that could hurt Chris.

"He's taken to the two of you pretty quick," a woman said, smiling beside Micah's bed.

I had to do a double take at first. I felt like I'd seen her before, but I couldn't put my finger on where. She looked like a teacher or something of the sorts. Her tight brown curls were wisped up into a high ponytail at the top of her head. She wore a pair of thin glasses over her warm mahogany eyes. Her skin was a medium brown. She stood a few inches taller than Laila but not by much. I estimated her to be about twenty-five, possibly a hair younger.

Despite some aspect of familiarity, there was something I didn't like about her. Not in the sense that I thought she was evil. I just... It's hard to explain, but I didn't like her. She was nice. Her smile was friendly.

But she just... I don't know, I looked at her and thought the word 'bitch.'

That wasn't necessarily a bad thing. I also looked at Leah, Celena, and my wife and thought the word bitch. Love them as I may, I didn't always like them. They were, in fact, bitches at times.

"Look, look." Micah pulled away and darted toward the window. When I didn't move fast enough, he turned. "Awen't you coming?"

I laughed and followed him across the room. "Right behind you, kiddo."

"Look," he said again. On the windowsill sat a solar powered sunflower that danced in a brown, plastic pot. "Look, it moves all by itself."

"Wow, that is super cool." I smiled, touching the plastic petals.

"Are you with the hospital?" Laila asked the woman beside the bed.

"No, I'm actually here with Child Protective Services. My name's Naomi. I've been assigned to Micah's case." She smiled and extended her hand to Laila's. "You are Laila Callidy, I'm assuming."

"I am, and that's my husband, Jeremy Skoulda." I gave a wave accompanied by a friendly smile. "And this is my sister in-law, Leah Boucher."

"Great." Naomi smiled and shook their hands. "Great, it's wonderful to meet you all. I'll be here observing the way the two of you interact with Micah today. Just taking some notes, answering questions you might have, just helping to make this process a little easier on everyone. When he goes in for his procedure, there's some paperwork we need to go over. Dotting some Is, crossing some Ts."

"Sure," Laila said. "Sure, do you know if the DNA results came in yet?"

"I don't, not yet. But we're starting the process under the assumption that they'll come back as we expect them to. Pretty hard to deny that those two are related." She looked between Micah and I with a smile.

"Kind of look like triplets with a really weird birth order, don't they?" Leah laughed, plopping on the bed beside Chris.

"It kind of does." She chuckled.

"So do you guys have a roundabout of when they get to leave?" I looked between Micah and Chris.

"Well, Chris can leave once he has his procedure. But Micah's going to be a little more difficult. There's a lot of paperwork that goes into this. We'll have to get him a birth certificate, figure out citizenship, a social security number. Then we'll need to do a home visit and observe the two of you with your daughter. We'll need to see your tax records and review your financial capabilities in raising a child, of course. The two of you will have to provide urine samples, we'll need access to your daughter's medical records, and a few other loose ends. Nothing too exciting."

I licked my lips and glanced at Laila. I wasn't sure when the last time she smoked was; we might need to borrow someone's piss for her too. I knew I'd fail for opioids, maybe benzos too, and definitely THC. Pretty arbitrary to keep me from my kid for taking a few hits off a joint, but at least I had the resources to fake a test.

Honestly, it *all* seemed arbitrary. Had Laila given birth to him in a hospital, they wouldn't have done all of this. Nothing like this needed to happen when we had Milly.

I supposed it made sense though. My kid had been abused and neglected since his birth. They wanted to make sure that wherever he was going, he'd be safe.

"So this is going to take weeks then?" Laila asked.

"At least," she said. "We're working with Child Services in Pennsylvania too, but since this is across states, it means we'll basically have two sets of paperwork for everything."

"So even once he's healthy and ready to leave, you won't release him from the hospital." It came out as a statement, although I'd intended it as a question. "He's been trapped inside a room for three years, and you're going to force him to stay in another?"

"Jeremy." Laila gave me a look.

Naomi smiled. "I know it doesn't seem fair, and I agree that it isn't. But we all have jobs to do. And mine is making sure that this little boy is placed into a healthy home."

"Placed?" My head tilted. "That's a subject of conversation here? Placement?"

Micah leaned into my hip and rested his head on my stomach. "What's wong, Daddy?"

"Everything's fine, buddy." Laila smiled and lowered herself beside him. "It's okay, don't worry."

"Of course we want him to go home with the two of you, Mister Skoulda," Naomi said. "We just have to make sure that the two of you can provide him with a life that he deserves."

Guessed that instinct to call her a bitch wasn't too far off.

I clenched my jaw a bit. "Well, we can. And we will."

She smiled still. "There you have it then. So long as everything checks out, you'll be home with your son by his third birthday."

"They care so much about making sure he has a good life, but they couldn't give a shit less when that bastard was torturing him," I muttered to Laila. "And they're seriously going to keep him from us if one of us comes back positive for drugs? What kind of bullshit is that? This is California. Weed's legal here."

"We have a way around everything that she talked about, baby," she whispered, gazing in at Micah and Chris through the glass window. "But you've got to keep your cool. Don't give them a reason to think we've done anything wrong."

"I have heroin in my system, Laila," I whispered. "We have no idea what Peterson gave you either."

"Then I'll put a bottle of Lydia's pee up my hoo-ha."

"Well, I don't have one of those."

"Then I'll fuck with her head, and you can just hand her a cup of Ray's," she muttered. She turned to meet my gaze. "None of this is ideal, Jeremy. But we're here. Our son is right there. We made it."

I looked over Micah speaking to a doctor who sat beside his bed. "What if they deem us unfit? They could try and take Milly too. And I'll be damned before—"

"Jeremy." She took my face in her hands. Her eyes flicked between mine as her head shook. "No one's taking our babies. No one. We'll play the game; we'll follow their rules. We'll show them our taxes, give them a tour of our house, and let them see how we interact with our daughter. Whatever they want, we'll do it. But if they say we can't have him, we'll take him. Just like we did in the first place."

I said, "Alright. Alright, yeah. As long as we're on the same page."

She swiveled back to the window. "He asked if this would hurt, and I told him just when they prick him with the needle. I hope they call us back in first. He wanted us to be there."

"Laila Callidy," a man's voice said behind us. I turned to catch his gaze. And I instantly realized what Laila meant when she said he seemed familiar. "You must be Jeremy then."

Connor stood a few inches shorter than me, wearing a carefully ironed black suit and white button-up. His brown eyes were only a few shades lighter than his night-colored skin. He wore a pair of thick round glasses that rested against his buzzed cut curls. He appeared around my age, maybe a few years older, but no more than thirty-five.

"I am." I extended my hand. "And who are you?"

"Oh, I'm sorry. Connor, Connor Taylor." He shook my hand and gave a smile. "I saw you in there yesterday, but I didn't want to interrupt."

"This is the agent I was telling you about," Laila said.

"Right," I said. "We're having lunch after he goes in for his procedure, right?"

"That's the plan. I see you've met my colleague." He gestured to Naomi in the room with Micah. "She'll be there too."

I tilted my head. "The CIA works with CPS?"

"When it's necessary." He smiled. "Complicated overlap with agencies on this case."

"Well, I'm looking forward to it."

"Me too." He looked past us into the room. "How is he adjusting? Taking to you two pretty well?"

"Seems to be," Laila said.

"Have you played anything for him?" he asked me.

My head tilted. "Huh?"

"I Googled you." Connor smiled. "You're a pretty talented musician; I figured you would have brought a guitar with you."

"Oh. Yeah, I have one back at the hotel," I muttered. "I wasn't sure if I was allowed to bring it in here."

"Definitely. He'd probably like that." He glanced at Micah then back to me. "Can't just leave it at the hotel after as much as I'm sure you spent to have it checked with your baggage."

"We didn't fly commercial so that's not an issue," I said, quickly realizing the way that these interviews would go. Stating things as facts only to see if we'd correct them.

"Oh, how'd you get here then? You couldn't have driven."

"He comes from a wealthy family." Laila gestured toward me. "His grandparents let us use their plane."

"Wow, that's nice of them," Connor said. "Will they let you use it to fly home too? We'd like at least one of you to be present when we tour your home."

"I'm sure." I forced a smile, realizing he would be coming to our house too. Just a few measly minutes down the road from the torture chamber where Peterson sat tied to a chair.

"Maybe we'll hitch a ride with you then. That way we'd all get there at the same time." He smiled. "If that's okay, of course."

"Absolutely." Laila smiled. "Anything we can do to rush this process along."

"Missus Callidy? Mister Skoulda?" a woman said behind us. We turned to see a nurse carrying a clipboard. "That's you two, right?"

"That's us," Laila said.

"I thought so." She chuckled. "We just got these results in. Everything came back as we expected. Micah is in fact your son."

"Ya don't say." I smiled, glancing at him through the window.

She laughed. "I'll need you guys to sign here stating that you've received this information and this release here so that we can give the results to the according agency."

"Sure." Laila scribbled on the page. I took the pen, signed on the line below, and turned back to the window. Micah sat with his legs hanging off the bed. The doctor tapped his knee with a little metal tool. He giggled when his leg involuntarily jutted forward.

"Great, thank you. And here's your copies." She handed them to Laila and then turned to Connor. "And here is yours."

"Thank you, miss." Connor smiled. "This should help move things along too. Thanks for paying to have these expedited, by the way."

"Just want to bring our son home as soon as we can." I smiled. "Anything we can do to help, we will."

"I want to get your son home too." He placed a hand on my shoulder with a friendly smile.

He was odd. I didn't hate him. I was worried about him finding Peterson, but I didn't hate him. And he... He looked at me the way Asher, the Elvan hand of the queen of the Open Lands, looked at me.

Like he knew me.

"Laila, Jeremy," Naomi said from the door as it pushed open. "The nurse is getting ready to start Micah's IV. He's a little scared about the needle. I think it might help if you guys sat with him."

"Of course." Laila brushed past Naomi into the room.

"I'll wait in the lobby. Once he's out, come on down and we'll walk next door for lunch," Connor said.

"Sure." I started past him. "Thanks."

He smiled. That same, odd, familiar smile.

But I just wheeled Milly's stroller back into the room. I sat on the edge of the bed opposite of Laila.

"What is they going to do?" Micah asked with watery blue eyes. "Is it going to huwt?"

"Just for a second." Laila smiled. "The doctors are going to put some medicine in a little needle that's going to help you sleep through the whole thing."

"But I scwaed."

"There's nothing to be scared of." I smiled and put my hand over his. "The scary stuff's over, buddy."

"It won't be like last time, will it?" he nearly whispered, looking down at the scar on his wrist.

"No." Laila touched his cheek, pushing hair behind his ear. "No, it won't be like last time. It'll hurt some, but not like it did then."

"And you be hewe when I wake up, wight?" He looked between us.

I smiled. "We sure will."

He swallowed hard.

"Hey, maybe me and Mommy can get you something to play with when you wake up," I said. "There was some really cool stuff in the gift shop downstairs. Maybe when you're done, the doctors will let us take you down there and pick something out."

He looked up at the doctor with wide, excited eyes. "Can we?"

He laughed. "As long as Agent Taylor's okay with that, we'll get you guys a wheelchair."

I looked at Connor in the doorway beside Naomi. "That alright with you, agent?"

He smiled. "I don't see why not."

I turned back to Micah with a smile. "What do you think? Does that sound good?"

"Like a pwesent?" A grin spread across his lips. "You'll get me a present, Daddy?"

A laugh left me. "Yeah. Yeah, like a present."

He smiled and turned to the doctor. "Okay, but can Mommy and Daddy stay until I fall aseep?"

"I bet Mommy and Daddy think that's a great idea."

CHAPTER EIGHTEEN

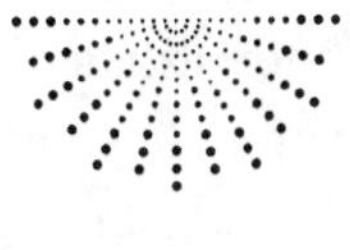

LAILA

Watching Micah's expression as they pushed that needle through his skin felt like a thousand knives stabbing me in the heart. His little body quivered the same way that mine did when I saw a needle. Sweat pearled above his brow, his hands trembled, his teeth chattered.

The doctors had a hard time finding his vein which sent him into a panic. After four consecutive stabs, Micah quaked too hard to sit still for another. I transferred him to my lap and wrapped my arms around his belly. He closed his crying eyes and pushed his head into my chest before they finally got his vein. The doctor told me to move him back to the bed, but I shook my head. I waited until I heard his sobs slow and felt his head roll to the side.

I lay him back on the bed and ran my fingers through his hair. I kissed his forehead and pulled away wiping my eyes. Afterward, they rolled his sleeping little body out of the room.

"It'll be over soon," Jeremy murmured with a hand on my back.

"Just a turkey on wheat," Connor said, passing the waiter his menu. "Thank you."

"That'll be right up." He gave a friendly smile.

"Great, thank you." Connor turned back to me and Jeremy. "Well, it's a pleasure to finally meet the two of you. I've seen your names in my files a lot."

Jeremy forced a smile. I cleared my throat. "Yeah, well. Nice to meet you too."

Naomi smiled back. Connor exhaled a deep breath. "So you're wondering why the CIA is involved in your son's case, I'm assuming."

"For starters," Jeremy said. "But all things considered, it's not much of a shock."

"I am curious why we're just meeting you now that it's over though," I said. "Tina's the only official I knew was working the case."

"A lot of it has been done behind closed doors. You went through a horrible thing, Laila. You needed time to heal." His eyes flittered between mine as he spoke.

I found it odd how genuine he looked as he said it. Rarely did I like a cop. But there was some part of me that instantly thought, *he's a good guy.*

"Well, thanks for that, I guess," I muttered.

"But I think we all know that this isn't over," Connor said. "Robert Peterson's still out there somewhere."

"Well, hopefully not for long. You guys have some leads, don't you?"

"A couple." Naomi's brown eyes washed over me before bouncing to Jeremy. "Everything's pretty circumstantial though."

I sucked my teeth, reading her accusative gaze. It was a strange dynamic. She was the social worker, yet she was playing the bad cop routine.

A quiet chuckle left Connor's lips, shaking his head a bit. "Let me level with you guys here, alright?"

"Sure," Jeremy said.

"I've read the interviews with all seven hundred victims. Which may sound like a lot. But it was only about fifty pages. Because all of the information they've given is incredibly vague."

"Survivors," I said. "We aren't victims. We're survivors."

"Right. All of the survivors gave very little information to explain their capture. But your name is mentioned quite a bit, Laila. Many of them say that you set them free but not very much information is given as to how. Even in your interview with Tina Davis, you don't clearly explain how you got out of that room."

I knew that was coming. I'd worked up a careful lie. It was close enough to the truth to sound as genuine as he looked, but still far enough from it that he couldn't get me on anything.

"You want to know what happened that day?"

"Really, I'd like to know what happened all of those days," Connor said. "I understand how they kidnapped you; they used people you cared about against you. I understand that you don't recall the trip there because you were drugged. But I really need to know what happened when you were inside. It says that you woke up in a cell, but what happened after that?"

My face must've shown my discomfort.

"Does she really have to talk about this right now?" Jeremy asked. "We just got our son back; it's bringing back enough—"

"No, you don't *have* to, Laila. No one can make you do anything you don't want to. But you want us to have a better understanding of all of this, don't you?" Connor said.

I sure the hell did not. But I didn't have much choice. They weren't going to leave me alone until they heard the story. So I supposed it was time to tell it.

My gaze traveled to the wooden table beneath my hands. "I woke up in my cell and started screaming for help. I heard Haley and Chris. Took me a minute, but I realized who Chris was. We talked for a while before two guards came in and shot me up with some anxiety meds. I woke up naked tied to a table. Peterson introduced himself and said a bunch of nonsense. He started cutting into me like a turkey on Thanksgiving."

"What did he say?" Connor asked with a genuinely sympathetic expression.

"A bunch of nonsense," I repeated. "I don't remember it all. It was mostly just him rambling about how happy he was to have the opportunity to be a part of my story. He told me I could scream if it made me feel better, but no one would hear. And he liked it anyway."

Connor grew quiet, moving his head in a gentle nod. "What happened after that?"

"I woke up in my cell. Talked to Chris and Haley for a while. I don't know what day it was, but not long after, they did the first stress test."

"That's when they beat you," he murmured.

I nodded and turned my gaze to my drink on the table. "I think I had twenty of those. I tried to keep track, but it all kind of blurred together after a while. But I don't know, I was tied to that table at one point and... I don't know, one of the locks must not have been tight enough. I can't really tell you how because I don't clearly remember but somehow, I got out. And I tried to run, but one of the guards shot me in the leg, and I went down."

Connor watched my expression. I cleared my throat and went on. "I woke up tied to a table again. A little different than the other time though, it was a maternity table. My legs were bolted to the stirrups, my arms were buckled down at the wrists, and... I don't know, I..."

This part was the one I didn't want to get into. I'd never talked about all of this in such detail in front of Jeremy, and I knew that I probably should have, but I didn't want him to look at me the way I knew he would. Pitifully.

I glanced at Jeremy. He sent me a pained, sympathetic smile.

"He fed me. Chicken tenders, French fries, and a milkshake. I didn't want it, not when everyone else was eating shit. But he swore he'd get everyone pizza if I ate because they were concerned about how much weight I'd lost in there. So I did. I ate and he... He said something. Something about how *our* baby needed to eat. And I just lost it. I barely even remember what I said but he... I pissed him off. Like, really angry. Angrier than I'd ever seen him. And I thought he was going to kill me; I was hoping he would actually. But he..." I cleared my throat, shook my head, and turned my gaze back to the table. "You saw the video, you know what he did."

"I do," Connor murmured. "What happened after that?"

I still gazed down at the grains of the wood in the table. Jeremy moved his hand to mine, gently twining our fingers between one another's. I looked up at him and blinked tears away. I turned back to Connor.

"When I got back to my cell, I started planning. He said he wouldn't do any more stress tests on me until Micah was born, and I knew I had a couple months. That'd buy me enough time for my leg to heal. I figured once I could walk again, that's when we'd make our break. When they came to do bloodwork and stuff, I... Well, I wasn't compliant. I made their lives pretty difficult. But, from the time that I was shot until Micah was born, I didn't leave that cell. I slammed the door every time they tried to come in. I held it with my back, I screamed, I... I made things difficult, put it that way."

"Can you tell me about when Micah was born?" Naomi asked.

I ran my hand through my hair, scratching my scalp. "What do you want to know?"

"How you did it," she murmured. "How you birthed a baby unnoticed when you were being watched every moment."

"We weren't watched every moment. We were caged at every moment, but we weren't watched. Guards did rounds twice an hour. And the cameras were in the hallways, not the cells."

"But how did you handle the mess?" Naomi asked.

My tongue ran along my teeth. "I limped to the toilet to catch as much of the blood as possible. I cleaned it up with toilet paper as much as I could. When I heard the beep of the door opening, I rushed back over to my bed, lay down, crossed my legs, and prayed he didn't start crowning until that door clicked shut."

"That must have been awful," Naomi murmured. "You had contractions at some point or another while the guard made his rounds, right?"

My eyes stayed on the carbonated bubbles rising to the top of my glass of coke now. "I bit down on the inside of my shirt when they did.

I held my breath when they were really bad. Almost fainted a few times."

"I can't even imagine," she said softly.

Behind her eyes, I saw a flash of anger. It wasn't even an expression really. Not a turn of a lip or an arch of a brow. It was something within the irises themselves.

Almost like she hated Peterson too.

I licked my lips and nodded again.

"When he did start crowning, what did you do?" Connor asked.

"I pushed." I gave something between a laugh and a huff. "It's not like you have much choice in that moment. Your body just kind of does it."

"Sure, but when he came. What happened?"

The memory of that little white ball in my hands flashed behind my eyelids. I fought the tears forming in my eyes. "He wasn't crying. So I... I tried rubbing him like I saw in birth videos, but it didn't work. I tried slapping him like they do in old movies but" —I let out a huff of a laugh— "Didn't work. He just... He wouldn't cry. Just complete, deafening silence. So I held him to my chest, and when I looked down, I saw the blood dumping out of me and I... I knew I was about to faint, so I lay him on the crease of my knee, and it all went black."

"Then you woke up tied to a table?" Connor asked.

"I woke up tied to a table. Peterson told me Micah died, and I didn't believe him at first, but it'd been days and the body would have been too..."

"You were in an impossible situation," Naomi said. "No one can blame you for that."

"I blame myself for it every day. But what're you gonna do? Can't change it now. He's alive, and he's healthy, and I know where he is. Now I just have to get him home so I can finally shut the damn door on all of this."

"What happened after that?" Connor asked. "How did you get out of your cell?"

And now, where the lie became more intricate.

"I'd accumulated a good bit of gauze and tape in my room from the wound on my leg. Over time, I gradually worked it into a little stick. Right after a guard did the last check of the night, just as the lights went out, I stuck my little stick through the box they used to feed us. I'm not sure how I did it, but I managed to undo the lock on my door. I cracked it open and waited for the next guard's shift. When he came through, I waited by my door. When he looked in, I opened the door and I... I got my hands around his neck. He was strong, but he was surprised and... Well, he passed out. I took his gun and let Chris and Haley out. They helped me lift him up to use his hand for the keypad.

"Then we moved into the other sectors and started opening doors. Once we got the first two wings covered, we started running. And I honestly can't tell you much of anything after that. I vaguely remember opening more doors, I vaguely remember running barefoot through the grass, I vaguely remember seeing the explosion and hearing the plane. But everything else... I'm sorry, I wish I could give you more, but I just don't remember. And frankly, I don't want to."

They both gave a gentle nod, silence creeping in. As I took a sip of my Coke, Connor broke the silence.

"Did you kill anyone that night, Laila?"

It probably would have been more believable if I coughed on my drink. "Not that I can recall."

Jeremy's fingers tightened around mine.

"I wouldn't blame you if you did," he said. "If I finally had a gun in my hand after what you went through, I'd kill those sons of bitches too."

"Well, I have no recollection of killing anyone."

He paused as he looked between my eyes. "Well, we didn't find any bodies, so I have no reason to believe you did."

"So is that all? Is there anything else we need to go over?"

"That about covers it," Connor muttered. "But let me ask you something, Laila. You don't know where Robert Peterson is, do you?"

"Wish I did. I'd be the first to send him your way."

He smiled. "Would you?"

I forced a smile back. "I sure would, agent."

His smile was still there, but it dwindled a bit. He leaned back in his chair. "Any idea where he might be then?"

"If I had to guess?" I asked. "Probably running. So if that about covers it—"

"Just one more thing," Connor said. "Why is he afraid of you, Laila?"

"Maybe because when you steal a mama bear's cub, you expect to get mauled."

"Maybe," Connor said. "Maybe that's it. Or maybe because you're not just the small-town girl you'd like the world to believe you are."

I leaned over the table a bit. "What else would I be then, Agent Taylor?"

He smiled as he looked between my eyes. He leaned further across the table too. His smile turned to more of a familiar grin than a smug, questioning expression.

That fucking grin. It was so familiar, and I knew it from somewhere. But I couldn't place where.

It was like running into someone I went to preschool with. We both looked different, but that expression brought something back. Not a name, not a memory, but a feeling.

Playful. Fun. Sweet, and...

Familial.

He propped his chin in his palm, smirk still across his lips. "I don't know, Laila Callidy. You tell me."

I didn't have a doubt in my mind that they knew who and what I was. But he wanted me to be the first one to come out and say it. And I wouldn't dare. If they were working with the Chambers or Elders, it could very well be a set up to see if I'd expose our people.

As our elbows touched, I tried to go into his mind. But I hit a wall.

I couldn't touch his thoughts. I turned to Naomi and tried again. But nothing. It was like when I tried to go into Leah's or Adam's head when they were firm on keeping a secret.

Naomi sent me a smile as she watched me struggle to climb inside of her mind.

"This is starting to feel more like an interrogation that an interview," Jeremy said.

"I'm sorry, that wasn't my intent." Connor leaned back in his chair and let his grin fall. "We just want to get to the bottom of what's really going on here."

"Then do it," I said. "Get to the bottom of it, put Peterson behind bars, kill the bastard. I don't really care. But I've told you everything I know, and I'm done talking about my captivity. So are we done here?"

Connor and I stared into one another's eyes for a long moment. I could practically see them screaming, *Just say it. Admit you are who you are.* But mine said the same.

"I'd like to set up a date to visit your home." Naomi broke through our staring contest. "But once that's established, I think we'll have covered all the bases. Right, Connor?"

"I believe so." He glanced at Jeremy.

"When do you want to do that then?" Jeremy asked. "One day this week, one day next week?"

"Tomorrow works for me if you can arrange a flight." Naomi smiled. "Figured the sooner we can get it done, the sooner we can get Micah home, right?"

"Tomorrow it is then. I'll talk to the pilot and let you know about a time," Jeremy said. "You just need one of us there, right? One of us can stay back here with Micah?"

Naomi said, "Just one of you will be fine."

"Great." I stood and forced a smile. "I'm going to go back to the hospital and wait for him to wake up then. I hope the two of you have a wonderful day."

Connor chuckled as he smiled back. "Yeah, you too. But when I say it, I actually mean it."

"So do I."

"No, you don't. You don't trust us." He looked at me and then to Jeremy. "You will though."

CHAPTER NINETEEN

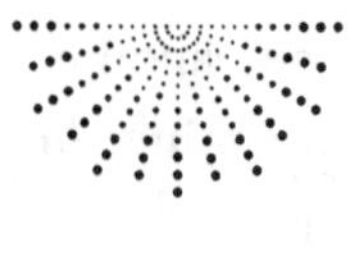

JEREMY

"They aren't human," Laila murmured with a look over her shoulder as we stepped into the revolving hospital door.

"How do you know?" My chest tightened. "I didn't feel anything."

"They blocked me out of their heads," Laila said. "Both of them. I don't know what they are, but they sure as hell know who we are."

"Why wouldn't they just tell us then?" I clicked the up button for the elevator.

"Maybe to get us to tell them first? Get us to tell them something and incriminate ourselves? I don't know," she said. "I don't know, but they're definitely keeping it from us for a reason."

"Maybe they're waiting for us to call them out," I murmured. "I checked their badges, and Tina confirmed. They definitely work for who they claim to."

"Maybe the government's claws have been in this for a while. Maybe they know what we all are, and they knew what Peterson was doing all along. Hell, maybe Peterson worked for them. Maybe that's why they want him back so bad, because he's an agent of theirs."

"I didn't get that vibe." We took a step inside, and the elevator door shut. "I don't think they're an enemy. At least, not the guy. Not sure how I feel about the girl yet."

"I don't think so either. He... He reminds me of Avery." Laila's head shook slightly, and she rubbed her temples. "I don't know. Maybe you'll have a better opinion after tomorrow."

Ironic, because I'd had that exact same thought.

"Yeah, maybe. I'll try and get them to tell me what they are. They'll have to put on a necklace when they come to see our house; their reaction'll tell us something." I thought for a moment. "I don't know that name either. Connor Taylor. I mean, I do know some Taylors in Nebraska but they're low-balling Guardians. They've never met the Chambers, and they definitely don't work for the CIA. And they're white. Connor clearly isn't."

"Must be fake. Common enough. I think it's pretty customary for CIA to use names that aren't actually their names." She rubbed her mouth. "Just try and get what you can. But make sure they don't get to the main house. I'm not losing that fucker until I get to cut his dick off."

I nodded.

We were on the third floor, and Micah's was on the seventh. We still had a minute. And as I looked over her, I walked through that interview in my mind again, taking it all in. The day she was shot, it was because she was trying to escape. I knew she'd fought back, and I wanted to smile and tell her how much of a badass she was. But I also knew that would gross her out. She wasn't proud of those murders, even if I was.

I wanted to ask why she didn't jump at the chance to eat those chicken tenders he'd offered her. Better yet, I wondered why she hadn't tried to persuade him into giving her more than that. He loved her; she could've gotten just about anything out of him, and I wanted to ask why she didn't try to manipulate him.

Laila was good at that; every conversation she had with a cop was proof of that. She knew how to give the right smiles, and stroke egos, and manipulate anyone she met into doing whatever she wanted. Hell, she could've seduced the fucker. That's a horrible thought considering what he did moments later, but it did run through my mind.

She could have manipulated that man into anything, and she hadn't.

But I didn't want her to think I was calling her stupid for not trying more than she had. I didn't want her to think I was upset at how she reacted in there. I wasn't. Whatever she did, I trusted she did because it was the best decision for her in that moment. I just wanted to know more.

I cleared my throat. "A lot's happened in the past few days. You've had to relive a lot of awful things. Are you okay?"

"Yeah. Yeah, I'm alright."

Silence set in as I watched the light flick to the sixth floor. "I never heard it like that."

"What do you mean?"

"The story of what happened to you," I muttered. "I felt it. And I heard bits and pieces from you and Leah and everyone. But I never... You never told me the full story. I know you didn't tell them the full story either but... It's just, it's different to hear it like that."

Her gaze softened, looking between my eyes. "It was hard to tell you. It was hard to tell anyone, I guess, but it was especially hard to tell you."

"But why? You tell me everything."

"I just... I didn't want you to see me like that."

The elevator door slid open, and she began to walk through, but I caught her hand. "Like what?"

She met my gaze and frowned. "Like I was just some helpless victim strapped to a table."

That was the opposite of how I felt. She amazed me. I was in awe of what she'd pulled off. But I didn't know how to say that without her thinking I was like him, obsessed with the feral parts of her she'd prefer didn't exist.

I furrowed my brows. "You know I've never seen you as helpless."

"Not helpless, but you saw me as a victim for a long time. And you blamed yourself for it. It was my fault, but you blamed yourself for not being able to help me. And I knew that telling you those things would hurt you more. And hurting you is the last thing that I wanted."

I frowned. "Well. I don't see you as a victim these days. So if you ever want to talk about what happened in there, I'll listen."

She smiled. "I know."

And yet, she never did.

"Micah did really well. Everything went exactly as planned. He should be waking up within the hour. We brought a wheelchair in so whenever he's ready to stand, you guys can take him down to the gift shop. He's going to be pretty disoriented for a while so try to keep him in the chair."

"Can I hold him?" Laila asked.

"Sure. Yeah, I just mean we don't want him up running around until the sedatives wear off. He's got some ibuprofen and Tylenol in him right now, but if the pain's too bad, we can get a small dose painkiller. He's on some antibiotics at the moment, but that's just precautionary. I'm not sure when you'll get to bring him home, but if it's soon, we'll want you to keep a close eye on the stitches. We'll let you know what stage we're at in the healing process when that time comes, and we'll give you more instructions."

Laila peered at him through the glass window. "He was asleep the whole time, right?"

"Hasn't opened his eyes since you left." The doctor smiled.

I looked at him sleeping on the bed. The slow rise and fall of his chest, the long black hair dangling in his eyes. And it should've brought me some peace, seeing him home and finally healthy, but those chunks of gauze taped to his body made my jaw clench tight. He shouldn't have been here. We all should've been at home playing in the yard, enjoying the spring afternoon.

"So we can go see him now?" I asked.

"Yes, absolutely. Go ahead. And if he needs those pain meds, you tell a nurse, and we'll get them in there."

"Awesome, thank you," I said.

Laila didn't so much as glance at the doctor before she grabbed the door handle and hurried into the room. I pushed Milly's stroller and stayed close at her tail.

Chris's eyes fluttered open. His lips pulled into a smile. "Hey, guys."

"How're you feeling?" I smiled his way.

"I'm high as fu-u-uck." His grinning eyes shut before his head rolled to the side. "I think they gave me morphine or something, man. I'm like, gone."

I laughed. "Guess you don't want to take a trip down to the gift shop then, huh?"

"Nah." He made a shooing motion. "You guys have fun though. Ooh, can you get me a Reese's though? I've been wanting a Reese's for like, ten years."

I laughed again and sat on Micah's bed. "Yeah, we'll grab you a Reese's."

"You're the best." He pointed at me before he rolled over and dramatically yawned. "I'm taking a nap. I expect my Reese's upon my awakening."

I smiled. This was one thing I missed so much about Chris. He'd randomly do stupid shit like talking like he was from the sixteenth century or belting song lyrics at the top of his lungs. I'd almost forgotten, but that instant brought it all back.

Laila laughed, taking a glance at him. "We'll have your peanut butter chocolate when you awake from your nap, good sir."

"Oh, wait before I go to sleep." Chris rolled over and looked at Laila. "Think they'd let us take a trip to McDonald's for dinner? Or maybe lunch tomorrow?"

"Maybe. We could just get Doordash though."

"Door what?" he asked.

"It's a food delivery service," I said. "You pay a few extra bucks, and someone drives your food to you."

"What a time to be alive," he muttered. "Bet they eat your fries on the way though."

"They probably did before the pandemic, but now they seal your bag before the dasher picks it up," I said.

Chris rolled back over, face screwing up in confusion. "Wait, did you just say pandemic?"

I laughed. "You've missed a lot, man."

Micah rustled a bit, letting out a quiet, pained sigh. His brows crinkled over his closed eyes before they slowly peeled open.

"Hey buddy." I smiled, lifting my hand to touch his cheek.

"It huwts." Tears formed in his sleepy big eyes as he looked at me. He turned to Laila with a quivering lip. "You said it wouldn't huwt."

Laila's mouth fell open, searching for something to say. I think tears even welled in her eyes. Her mouth opened and closed a few more times.

"You said no one would huwt me again." His little lips quivered as tears began to course down his cheeks. "You lied."

"Micah." Chris rolled over, giving him a firm expression.

"Hey." I gave him the same parental gaze I gave Milly when she pulled my hair. "Mommy didn't say it wouldn't hurt, she said it wouldn't hurt like it did last time. She didn't lie, buddy. I know you're hurt right now, but it won't hurt for long. The doctors did this because those things that were in you could hurt you a lot more."

"That's why they took mine out too," Chris said. "It hurts, bud, but it'll be better soon. And this is better than last time, isn't it?"

Micah furrowed his brows at Chris. For a second, I thought I was looking in a mirror. It was the exact expression I made when I was pissed. "But she lied—"

"Eh." Chris lifted a finger. "Uh-uh, you don't talk to you mom like that."

"No, it's okay," Laila said.

"No, it's not," Chris said, still looking at Micah. "You don't call your mom a liar again, alright?"

Micah said nothing, only glared.

"I'm sorry," Laila barely whispered. "I'm sorry, baby, I don't want you to hurt. I know I said I wouldn't let anyone hurt you again, but I should have said that a little different. Sometimes, we have to do things that hurt."

"That's what he said too," Micah muttered.

I watched her heart shatter as those words left his lips. Her lip curled inward, her eyes instantly started to water, and her mouth fell open. My heart throbbed in my chest.

And I understood that he was in pain. My heart hurt for that too. But he needed to understand that this wasn't Laila's fault. She wouldn't tell him that, because in her eyes, *all* of this was her fault. But I couldn't let him think that it was okay to talk to his mom like that.

"It's not the same thing, Micah." I lifted his chin to meet my gaze. "Those things that he put inside of you, those little black dots. Those were there so he could find you if you got away. He put them there so that he could control you. So that he could keep you from doing things he didn't like." I looked behind me to make sure no nurses or doctors were around. "Remember when you asked if we were allowed to use our powers at home?" He dipped his head in a nod. "Those little things they took out of you, they kept you from being able to do that. But now that they're gone, you can use all of your powers again. Not here because there's people around but when we get to take you home, you can do it again. You wouldn't have been able to if we let the doctors leave them in there."

He thought for a minute. He looked down at his bandaged arm and back up to me. "Weally?"

"Really." I smiled. "And if they still hurt a lot when the doctors let us bring you home, Mommy can heal them."

He was quiet for a few seconds.

"But you really hurt Mommy's feelings when you said that. That's not how we talk to each other, Micah. Do you think there's something you should tell her?"

He turned to Laila. "I sawwy."

"It's okay," she said. "It's okay—I'm not mad."

"I din't mean to huwt you feewings," he muttered. "I sawwy, Mommy."

"That's okay." Laila smiled. "That's alright. How about we go pick out that present of yours?"

Our first crisis as parents to our son: averted.

CHAPTER TWENTY

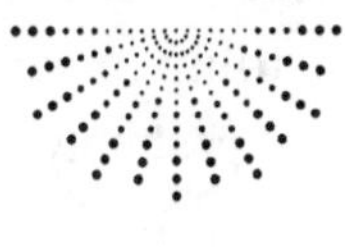

LAILA

"Mommy." Micah ran his fingers along my wrist as we stood in the elevator. "What's this stuff?"

I looked at my hand. "What stuff?"

"This stuff." His finger traced across the vine tattoo that stretched up my arm. He turned his finger and scratched his nail across it. "Why don't it come off?"

"Oh." I laughed. "That's my tattoo."

"But what is it?" he asked. "How'd it get thewe?"

"Well, an artist drew it on for me."

"And it don't wash off?"

"It does not wash off." I laughed. "It's kind of like a scar but with pretty colors."

"I like it." He turned up to me from the wheelchair and pointed to the butterfly on my neck. "I like that one most. It's got pwetty colows."

"I bet you'd love the ones on her back then." Jeremy smirked from behind the wheelchair. "It's *covered* in pretty colors."

"Weally?" Micah asked. "Can I see?"

"Maybe later." I laughed.

"If it's like a scaw, does that mean it huwt?"

"Yeah, tattoos hurt."

"Huh," he muttered. "I don't want them then."

Jeremy and I laughed. "Can't say I blame you, kid."

"I's hungwy," Micah muttered.

This kid never shut up, and I loved it. He just talked, and talked, and talked. I supposed my motor mouth was hereditary.

It was ironic, because when he was born, he didn't make a sound. And now, I wasn't sure if I'd experience silence again. That isn't a complaint though. His little voice really was the sweetest sound.

"Maybe we'll get you something to eat then." I smiled. "There's a cafeteria here, right? They probably have some pudding or something."

"Yeah, I'll grab us all something after Micah picks out a toy," Jeremy said.

The elevator door opened. Jeremy wheeled Micah into the hall, and I followed with Milly. Then Jeremy leaned and whispered something to Micah. Micah laughed and gave a fast nod. Then Jeremy hastily pushed the wheelchair up the slow incline of the hall.

As he did, Micah let out the softest, cutest little laugh. I smiled. Jeremy grinned at me over his shoulder and wheeled Micah into the gift shop.

Damn, I hated hospitals. But that day, I loved it. Even the chemical smell and dull fluorescent lighting didn't bother me.

Because I had everything that mattered to me. Micah was a few feet ahead of me, Milly was in the stroller I was pushing, and Jeremy was with our son. All that was missing was my fur baby.

I trailed close behind, watching Micah's gaze shift around in awe.

"Thewe's so much stuff," he said with wide eyes.

"And you can pick out whatever you want," I said behind him.

"Anything?" he asked.

"Anything."

I attempted to overcompensate for the time I lost with Micah and the horrible life he'd lived so far with gifts. But Micah was never a materialistic kid, even when it was encouraged. He didn't see the need for the abundance of toys like his sister had at home, but rather the emotional value of a gift.

That's why my heart broke when he gasped and pointed to the white stuffed lamb that sat on the bottom shelf.

"Can I has that one?" He looked up at me with big blue eyes.

I froze. Of course, there was nothing wrong with him wanting a stuffed lamb. That was the only gift he'd ever been given. And I could still see it smoldering as I burned that shed to the ground. He loved animals and now had a particular affiliation for lambs thanks to Peterson's cryptic brainwashing.

But Micah just saw it as a lamb. He didn't see the connotation to it that Jeremy and I did. I wanted to tell him no, but how could I? I told him he could have anything in that store. I couldn't refuse him the one thing that he wanted.

"What about this one, kiddo?" Jeremy gestured to a lion beside it. "Don't you like this one?"

"Yeah, but I like that one mowe." Micah's voice was so soft and sweet, practically begging. When his eyes met mine, they did the same. "My lamb's gone, Mommy. Can I has it? Pease?"

That little 'pease' was the cutest thing I ever did hear.

I forced a smile. "If that's what you really want, then sure."

He grinned and nodded fast. "I weally want it."

Jeremy licked his lips and kneeled beside Micah. He handed him the lamb and smiled wide. "Alright, I'll make you a deal." Micah turned his head to the side a bit and waited for him to continue. "You can have the lamb. But only if we get the lion too. That way, they can be friends. And they can help each other, the lion can take care of the lamb because sometimes lambs are too little to help themselves. The lion can keep the lamb safe."

Micah laughed. "It's not a weal lamb, Daddy. It's just pwetend."

"I know." Jeremy smiled. "I know, but just go with me on this one, alright? I'm old, I know what I'm talking about. Hey, and if you do it this way, you get two toys instead of one. That's a good deal, right?"

"I like the lion anyways." Micah grinned, reaching for it. "I can has both?"

"You can have both," Jeremy said. "Can you say that? Can you say *have*?"

"Have," Micah repeated. "I can have both."

"There ya go." Jeremy smiled. "Maybe we'll get some candy too, what do you think? Uncle Chris said he wanted candy."

"What's that?" Micah asked.

I tried to stop letting all of those little things get to me. But every question he asked that he should have already known the answer to formed a knot in my throat that wouldn't go away until Peterson was buried deep in the confines of his memories.

It was easier for Jeremy to talk to him throughout all of this. He knew how to answer questions I was too emotional to explain to Micah. I dreaded him leaving the following day because I wasn't sure I knew how to converse with Micah without a buffer, despite our many conversations in my dreams. I felt completely destroyed after he told me I lied about keeping him safe. It left me second guessing every word before it left my lips. I wasn't tiptoeing on eggshells; I was dancing on broken glass.

"Candy is the best thing ever. Probably Mommy's favorite thing in the world. Next to you and your sister, of course." Jeremy smiled up at me. "What do you think, Lai? What's a good candy for a first timer?"

I smiled and cleared my throat. "Well, there's a lot of great options out there. But for your first candy bar ever?" I grabbed a Hershey bar from the shelf. "This guy is the way to go."

"Okay." Micah looked over it with a smile. "I twy that one."

"Alright." I grinned. "And we'll get one for Milly too."

"But it's so big. We can shawe," Micah said.

"You say that now." Jeremy smiled. "But once you start eating it, you won't want to stop."

"It's sweet of you to share though," I said. "I bet you guys'll be sharing all kind of stuff when we get home."

"But not my sasophone, wight?" He looked between Jeremy and I, eyes radiating concern. "'Cause I just want to shawe my sasophone with you, Daddy."

Jeremy laughed. "No, you don't have to share your saxophone. I didn't want to share my guitar with my little sister either. Babies make too many messes, huh?"

Micah smiled. He looked at stuffed animals in Jeremy's arms. "Can I has my toys now?"

"Have," Jeremy corrected.

"Oh. Can I have my toys now?" Micah asked.

"Right after we pay for them," Jeremy said.

CHAPTER TWENTY-ONE

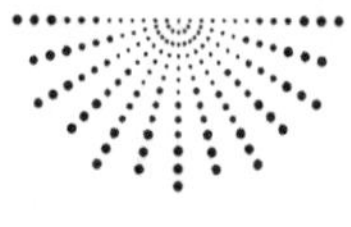

JEREMY

"Holy shit." Chris closed his eyes. His head rolled to the pillow behind him as he chewed on massive bite of a Big Mac. "Fuck, this is good. I thought I imagined it tasting this good, ya know?"

"That's how I felt about cookies." Laila smiled.

I reached across the gap between the two beds to steal a French fry, but Chris smacked my hand. "Get your own."

"Ow," I muttered.

"Can I has one?" Micah asked.

"Have," I corrected.

"Yeah, can I have one?" Micah asked with a look at Chris's fries.

Chris pouted, holding the bag close to his chest. I wondered if it was because he was worried about him choking or if it was because he'd been dreaming about those French fries for a decade. "I don't know, bud."

"But they smell so good." He smiled. "Pease? I shawe with you."

Chris's nose curled at Micah's slobbery spoon. "I don't want your pudding."

"But if you do, you can has some," Micah said.

"Here." Laila grabbed a French fry from the paper bag on her lap.

"But listen, you have to eat it real slow, okay? And you've got to chew like this." She slowly chomped on a fry before she handed him one. "Can you do that?"

"I can twy." Micah took the fry and put it between his lips.

"Now move your mouth real slow," Laila said, chomping on the fry carefully.

"Like this?" Micah said with a mouthful, jaw slowly moving up and down.

"Yeah, you've got it." She smiled and handed him another fry. "What do you think? Do you like it?"

He nodded with wide eyes. "They's so good."

"That should be your catch phrase, kid." I smiled.

"Oh, good, you're eating." Leah came in through the door carrying a few shopping bags and my guitar from the hotel. "I grabbed something while I was out. Here's your card, Lai."

"I'll take that." I stood to grab the card and two of the bags from her hands. "Did you find everything?"

"Yeah, the prices out here are crazy though so, sorry." Leah sat on the bed beside Chris and handed him a few bags. "Got your deodorant, body wash, and shampoo in this bag. And two pairs of sweatpants and a hoody in this one. Oh, and socks and slippers."

"Awesome, thanks." Chris took another bite of his Big Mac.

"And for you, little man." Leah reached into the other bag and pulled out a stack of clothes. "I'm not sure what's going to fit, but you said you liked dogs, right?"

He smiled and gave a fast nod.

"Alright, look at this then." She pulled out a blue T-shirt with a big white dog on the front.

Micah gasped. A big smile came to his lips. "It's like Tink."

"That's what I thought too." Leah grinned. "So you like it?"

He nodded quickly.

"Alright, cool. And you got him a coat, right, Jeremy?" Leah asked.

"I did," I said.

"Okay, awesome. Let me see your foot, kiddo." Micah lifted his leg up on the bed and extended his calloused foot to Leah. She dug in the bag for a minute and lifted out a stack of colorful socks. She slid a pair of green ones over his toes and then grabbed the box from the rolling table between the beds. "Okay, have you ever worn shoes, Micah?"

He shook his head.

"Well, it's your lucky day then." Leah smiled and pulled a pair of sneakers from the box. "Ya know what's super cool about these?" He shook his head. Leah smacked the bottom. Green and blue lights flashed along the soles, and he gasped in awe.

"Those is mine?" he asked.

She smiled. "All yours, bud."

"Thank you." He grinned with wide eyes. "Thank you so much, Aunt Leah."

"Thank your mom and dad, I just went to the store. They paid for it," Leah said.

"Thank you." Micah grinned between me and Laila.

"You're welcome." Laila smiled.

He was so excited over every little thing. The food, his clothes, the pillow of the bed, the blanket Laila had brought with us from home, my guitar. Quite literally, everything he saw blew his mind. And I loved it. I couldn't stop smiling.

But still, these were such basic things. Sure, he made me appreciate them more. But it made me so angry. I wanted better for my children than I'd had; I didn't want them to get a new pair of shoes and think that it was some great gift. They weren't. They were a necessity.

I was glad that he was grateful. I was happy that he was such a sweet child. But *he* shouldn't have been so happy for the bare minimum.

"Can I put them on?" he asked.

"Maybe we'll wait to try them until your foot's all better," I said. "They might hurt if you put them on now."

"Which is why I also got these." Leah pulled a pair of fuzzy bear slippers from the bag. "They might be a little big, but they'll keep your toes nice and warm."

"I love it," Micah said with wide eyes. "I love it, can I weaw it now?"

"Sure." Leah smiled, tore off the tags, and carefully pulled them over his bandaged feet. "How do they feel?"

"Wawm." Micah grinned, wiggling his toes.

Leah looked at Laila and I. "How'd your meeting go?"

"We'll talk about it when we get back to the hotel."

"Great," she muttered. "Oh, I saw Tina in the lobby. Did something happen? I waved, and she completely snubbed me. Looked me dead in the eyes and turned away."

"Not that I know of." Laila's forehead wrinkled. "That's weird though."

"Yeah, it was," Leah said. "Oh, your mom called me, Lai. She's been trying to get ahold of you. And Adam told me to tell you he had to cancel the concerts this weekend because I guess a toilet backed up in the basement or something? I don't know; you'd have to ask him. He said that him and Max cleaned it up and called a plumber, but you're going to have to call the guy to approve the payment."

"Did he already come? Because I'm flying back tomorrow. I might be able to handle it as long as they shut off the valve and cleaned up the water," I said.

"You leaving?" Micah asked.

"Just for a few hours." I smiled. "I've got to take that nice lady to see our house so we can take you home."

"Why?" Micah asked.

"Because they want to make sure you're going to live in a nice house," I said.

"You can't just show them a pitchew?" Micah asked.

I smiled. "No, a picture won't work. They've got to see it in real life."

"Oh." He turned his gaze downward. "But you be back, wight?"

"I will definitely be back," I said.

"Awe you staying, Mommy?" Micah asked.

"Yep." Laila smiled.

"Okay, good." He extended his hand. "Can I has anudder?"

"Have," Laila corrected, passing him another fry.

"Have," he repeated.

"We've been working on that one for a while. Never seems to stick for some reason," Chris said.

"That's alright," Laila said.

"If you leaving, can you play the da-tar first?" Micah asked. "I like the da-tar."

I smiled. "Sure, buddy."

CHAPTER TWENTY-TWO

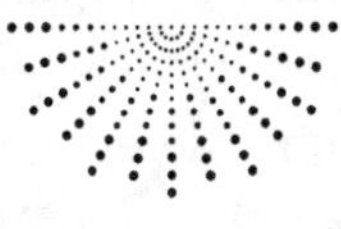

LAILA

I took in a long, exhausted yawn as I rubbed lotion up my arms. My gaze shifted to Milly sleeping in the basinet. Jeremy plopped face first onto the bed beside me. "I'm exhausted."

"Me too." I lifted my legs under the blanket and lay onto the pillows. "I can't wait until I get to sleep in my bed again, holy shit."

He rolled onto his side to meet my gaze. "Do you want me to grab you anything while I'm home?"

"Not unless you can bring the actual bed. I wish we could bring Tink. I miss her. She's probably so lonely; I feel like I haven't seen her in a week."

"She's probably chasing Wyatt and Celena through the woods having the time of her life right now," he said. "Well, maybe not right now. It's midnight there. But you know what I mean."

"Yeah, I know. I just want this to be over already. I want to lay in my big bed with you and my babies and watch TV and just finally call it a damn day."

"Won't be long." He smiled, reaching up to touch my cheek. "Almost there now."

"The home stretch. Yeah, yeah, I know."

He laid his head on the pillow beside me. "So what do you think those CIA agents are?"

"Well, not wolves or vamps; they wouldn't be able to keep me out if they were. Maybe Guardians like you? Or Fae? Maybe even Angels or Demons, who the hell knows."

He chewed his lip. "Should I take Milly with me? Or do you think she should stay here?"

"She can stay here. If something goes awry, I don't want you to have to worry about her. No, she'll stay with me. But you're going to get her medical records while you're there, right?"

"And our taxes from this and last year," he said. "I've got a list going of all this stuff I need. Oh, should I grab some extra clothes for Mills? She's going through them quick."

"Yeah, probably a good idea," I said. "Ya know what you could grab me? A variety box from Beverly's. See if she'll give you the softer stuff. No toffee or pretzel bark or anything."

"Will do."

Clunking further into the pillows, I tugged them to my face. "We should get some sleep though. You're leaving early, right?"

"Yeah, our flight's leaving at seven, so I've got to get out of here by six. I'll try and be quiet though."

"Nah, it's alright. The mornings are pretty out here. Me and Milly will go for a walk again. I saw a Waffle House down the road too, maybe we'll go there for breakfast."

"You and your damn Waffle House." He pulled the blankets over his legs. "I'm exhausted though. Can you grab the light in the bathroom after you brush your teeth?"

"Sure." I kissed him and started to my feet.

Once I hit that pillow, I was out like a light. I slept dreamlessly all night long for the first time in a long time. Things weren't exactly as I wanted them to be. But they were getting better. Perhaps the best they'd ever been.

Our lives started to make sense again after we found Micah. We believed that we finally reached our happy ending. But of course, it was far from the end. The dominoes started tipping over three years prior when I walked into that van. Or at least, so I thought. Really, they'd been falling over long before that. But we could enjoy the bliss while we had it.

Jeremy kissed me and Milly goodbye before he started out of the hotel room to his Uber. I got myself dressed, then Milly, made the bed, dusted on some makeup, and then called myself an Uber. Milly and I had breakfast at the Waffle House down the road, went back to the hotel, and grabbed Leah. Then the three of us went back to the hospital.

When we arrived, Micah was in an appointment with some specialist that watched him eat to help him learn to chew properly. Before they brought him back in, the doctor asked to speak to me in private. My heart hammered against its cage as we sat in the small exam room a few doors down from Micah.

The doctor explained that they'd gotten all of Micah's bloodwork back and had some concerns. Unsurprisingly, his vitamin D levels were incredibly low, and his electrolytes were way out of whack. He showed me x-rays of his legs that apparently appeared slightly bowed. He went on to explain that Micah had something called rickets disease.

He said that rickets is essentially a direct cause of lifestyle. Since Micah had been held captive his entire life, he got very little sunlight. We still had no idea what was in that mush they fed us but clearly it didn't have much vitamin D either.

I found myself on the verge of a panic attack when he said it could cause developmental delays. But he said that Micah tested high for his age range in most intellectual regards so he didn't think that would be a concern. He continued explaining that rickets is essentially curable if treated with high dose vitamin supplements, proper diet, and plenty of sun exposure.

He told me that I should take him outside to soak in some of that much needed vitamin D. Micah was ecstatic, and Chris was excited too. I pushed Micah's wheelchair, Leah pushed Chris's, and Chris held

Milly. When we started to walk out of the lobby, Tina approached me with a forced smile and said she'd be accompanying us outside just in case anything was to happen.

When we made it to the small courtyard in the back, we video called Jeremy. Micah thought it was the coolest thing in the world, which really surprised me since he could essentially do the same thing inside of his mind. He was on his flight with Naomi and Connor so he couldn't talk for long, but it made Micah's day.

Then Micah and I sat in the soil and watched ants crawl through the green patches. He gave them names before excitedly helping me look for four leaf clovers. I tried to show him how to make a whistle from a blade of grass but failed on every attempt. Chris couldn't do it either, but Leah could. Micah gaped in amazement and spent the next hour trying to do it himself.

Tina didn't say a word to me for the first hour or so. At first, I thought it may be because she wanted to give me as much time as I could have with Micah. But she kept looking at me with the oddest expression. It wasn't sad necessarily, but sympathetic. Maybe even a little fearful. Not fearful *of* me, more like she was afraid *for* me.

Eventually, I met her gaze and stood. Leah and Chris took over with Milly and Micah when I asked if we could speak for a minute. She still forced a smile. Then we walked around the edge of the garden and sat at a bench.

"Is everything okay?" I asked.

"Yeah, everything's fine." She smiled, looking over Micah a few yards away. "He seems to be doing really good."

"Yeah. Yeah, he is." I studied her expression for a moment. "Tina, what's going on? You've barely said a word to me, and Leah said you walked away when she waved at you yesterday."

"Everything's fine." She tried to make her smile appear more genuine, but it looked faker than Dolly Parton's chest.

I frowned. "No, something's wrong. What is it?"

She turned her gaze down for a moment. "It's confidential, Laila."

"Is it about Micah? Is something happening?"

"No, Micah's fine. From what Agent Taylor told me, they'll probably release him into your custody by this time next week. You don't need to worry."

"Well, what is it then?" I cocked my head to the side. "Something's wrong, and it has to do with me. I can see it; you keep giving me a really weird look."

She let out a slow breath. "You don't need to worry about it, Laila."

I thought for a moment. Realizing she wasn't going to tell me what was up, I reached for her mind. But I hit a wall.

"How did you do that? Why can't I read your mind?"

Tina sighed but stayed silent.

"Well, you're human. Someone must have done it for you. It was them, wasn't it? Connor and Naomi?"

"Sure," she muttered.

I knitted my brows. "C'mon, Tina. Talk to me. We're friends, aren't we?"

"We are," she murmured. She grew quiet again. She ran her tongue along her lips. "But we can't be any more."

"What? Why?"

"I know why Peterson sent me that video now." Tina met my gaze. "He told me that I had a part to play in this story, and now I know what that is. I'm here because I can work your case without exposing you. That's why Ward got kicked off. It had to be me."

I paused for a moment, thinking hard. "Did you talk to the other person you guys found? Is that where this is coming from? Do you know something about why he did this that I don't?"

"I know a lot of things now, Laila." She held my gaze. "And you will too. But I'm not the one to explain it to you. I'm not the one who makes it make sense. You'll see it soon. But for now... For now, ignorance is bliss, alright? Just... Just spend some time with your babies. Enjoy being a wife and a mom."

"What... What do you mean, Tina?" I said. "What do you know?"

She turned away. "Look, it's not bad, alright? You and your family are okay, and you're gonna stay that way. It's not... I can't get into all of it. I just can't, Laila. I wish I could, but that's why we can't be friends right now. I'm not a good liar, not with you. I'd have to lie to keep this stuff from you. And I won't lie to you. So instead, I'm just going to be silent."

If it weren't bad, I didn't understand why she wouldn't tell me. But clearly, she wouldn't. And I couldn't make her. Maybe I could torture it out of her, but finding out why she couldn't be my friend anymore didn't exactly justify something like that.

She confirmed that it was them though. Connor and Naomi, they told her something. Which meant they knew something. Maybe Jeremy would get it out of them on his trip home.

I looked around for a minute, searching for what to say next. "Can you at least tell me about that other person you captured that was working for him?"

"She's a doctor. OB, actually. She won't give us her name, but she said you'd probably remember her. Other than that, she doesn't have much to say. Doesn't matter anyway though, they're going to kill her. She doesn't have anything they want. She was just a blind sheep following Peterson. She doesn't know anything of value. Peterson's who they want."

"Why?" My face screwed up in confusion. "He doesn't work for them or anything, does he?"

"Does Peterson work for the CIA?" She arched a brow. "No. No, he's an international terrorist, Laila. A raping, kidnapping, torturing terrorist."

"What do they want then?"

"The same thing that you want. Answers."

CHAPTER TWENTY-THREE

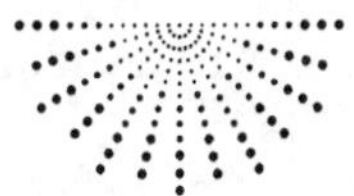

JEREMY

"Look, Daddy," Micah said from the screen on my phone. He held a ladybug up to the camera on the tip of his finger. "Look how pwetty."

"That is a really pretty ladybug." I smiled. He turned the camera back to his face. Or at least, he tried to. But it only showed the top of his head and the blue sky above. "You like hanging out outside, huh?"

He smiled wider, nodding fast. "It smells diffewent."

"Fresh air usually does," I said.

"Mommy said we can play outside all the time when we get home." He grinned. "But she says it wains a lot thewe."

"It does rain a lot, but you can still play in the rain."

"But we'll get all diwty."

"Dirt washes off." I smiled. "Hey, can you put your mom back on the phone for a minute, buddy? I'm getting off the plane soon, so I've got to get off the phone."

"Can you call again when you done?"

"Yeah, I'll call you again later, okay? I have some errands to run so it might be a little while though."

"Okay." He smiled and handed the phone to Laila. "Hewe, Mommy."

"Thanks, buddy." The camera shifted. Laila looked into the screen with a smile. "Hey, you."

"Hey, baby. What's going on? They let you take him outside?"

"Yeah." She flapped her lips together in a trill. "Yeah, they want him to spend a lot of time in the sun. I'll tell you the details when you get back."

"Is something wrong?" I asked. "Is he okay?"

"Yeah, it's not that big of a thing. But apparently his vitamin D levels were super low, and I guess that's really bad for babies."

My heart dropped. "How bad?"

"They said that it didn't affect his mental development, so it'll reverse with diet, supplements, and sun. So that's good. They mentioned braces and surgery on his knees if it doesn't improve, but they think everything's going to be fine."

My heart picked up in my chest. My stomach flipped. I wasn't sure if from the turbulence or the fact that my son might—again—have to be put to sleep and cut into because of fucking Peterson.

"Braces and surgery," I muttered. "That doesn't sound like not a big thing, Lai."

"That's just a worst-case scenario. They don't think it'll come to that."

I clicked the home button and opened Google. "What's it called?"

"Don't dive down the Web MD rabbit hole, babe. It's not a very severe case and he's really young, everything's going to be fine."

"Alright, but what's it called?"

She sighed. "Rickets disease. It doesn't even really exist here anymore unless it's the genetic type, and Micah's isn't. It's a direct cause of not having proper medical care, malnutrition, and lifestyle. Everything says it's not only treatable but basically curable."

That slowed my racing heart a bit.

I smiled as I clicked back to the video call. "So you've already gone down the Web MD rabbit hole."

She chuckled. "A little bit. But the doctors said it's pretty mild. His legs are almost normal so after a couple months on the vitamins and a proper diet, he should be fine. If not, we'll have him fitted for braces. But I think it's going to be fine."

"Alright. Alright, if you say so. I'm still going to Google though." I smiled. She smiled back. "I could be back before the hospital closes so I might get to see Micah before he goes to bed. Don't tell him that though. I don't want him to get excited in case I don't make it in time."

"Sounds good. You have your room key, right?"

"Yeah, I've got it. We're getting ready to land now so I should probably get off of here. But I love you, tell Micah I said I love him too. And hug Mills for me."

"Alright, I love you too. Drive safe."

"Always. And Lai?"

"Yeah?"

I smiled. "You're beautiful."

Her cheeks got red, and she grinned. "Shut up. I'll see you later."

I smiled. She ended the call. As I pulled my headphones from my ears, Naomi met my gaze with a smile. "What?"

She cleared her throat. "You two are just a lovely couple."

"She's my world. Her and the kids, I mean."

"Yeah, I can see that." She smiled, still looking me over. "You know that I'm not doing these things to make your life difficult, right? I'm just doing my job, Jeremy. These provisions have to be made. And believe it or not, I'm the best person available to help."

"I get it," I said. "Yeah, I'm sorry if I was kind of a dick yesterday. But I've been waiting three years to bring my son home, almost four if you count Laila's pregnancy. I'm just tired of waiting."

"Well, I'm hoping we can expedite this process. It's just a very complicated case."

I nodded again, body veering to the side as the plane shifted.

"Was everything alright?" Connor asked. I made a face, and he gestured to my phone. "You said something about surgery. Is everything alright?"

"Oh. Yeah. Yeah, I guess. She said Micah's got something called rickets disease? I guess it's a result of lack of sunlight and poor nutrition. The doctors said everything should be fine with supplements though."

"Oh, good. Good," Connor said.

Naomi looked my way. "When we land, should we get an Uber? Or do you have a ride arranged?"

"Yeah, my brother's picking me up. You're welcome to tag along if you don't want to wait. We kind of live in the boonies, takes a while for a taxi around here."

"Sure, thank you," Connor said.

"Yeah, of course." The plane jutted to the side a bit as I continued, "Look, maybe I should have told you this sooner. But we're Wiccan."

"Oh?" Naomi raised a brow over her smile. "*You're* Wiccan?"

"Not something we typically announce," I said. "People can be judgey. But to enter our home, you've got to wear a necklace. If you don't, you can't come onto our property."

Connor stifled a laugh as Naomi struggled to hold down her smile.

"Kinda weird, I know. Sorry. But this is America. Freedom of religion and all that," I said. "It'd be greatly appreciated if you could respect our beliefs and wear the necklace."

"What's it for?" Connor lifted a brow, still smiling. "What's your spiritual purpose behind this necklace?"

"It's for protection."

"Does it work?" Naomi asked.

"Seems to." I smiled. "Haven't had any issues so far."

"Sure," Connor said. "We'll wear the necklace."

Their reactions left me believing that Laila may have been wrong. They practically laughed at me. No one in our world would laugh at the mention of a protection spell.

Little did I realize that they were laughing at the irony. Because they knew I hated Witches.

"So this is it." I stepped from the Forrester and looked up at the house.

"Whoa," Connor murmured with a look around. "Jesus Christ, how much does that diner bring in?"

"We used an inheritance Laila got for materials. Me and my siblings built it. Laila was pregnant with Milly, she couldn't do much. But she helped where she could." That was a lie, it would've taken twice as long if not for her telekinesis.

"Impressive," he muttered. "How long did it take?"

"Little over five months, almost six. We ran into a couple issues along the way," I said. "Wasn't too bad though."

He huffed, walking along the flagstone path behind me. "Wish I'd get a damn inheritance."

"Well, care to show us around?" Naomi asked. "Shouldn't take long really. Just a general inspection."

"Yeah, of course. Follow me."

Brody hopped from the car. "I'm going up to the house. Stop by before you leave." I sent him a wave and continued up the walkway.

When we got to the porch, Naomi ran her fingertips along the wicker furniture. "This is beautiful."

"Oh, thanks. They're Laila's babies. She found them at some flea market years ago. They sat in storage at her mom's forever."

Naomi smiled, looking over it a moment longer.

I turned the doorknob and held it open. "After you."

Connor took a step inside. Naomi followed. "Damn. Just... Damn, this place is beautiful," he said.

"Thanks. Kind of my pride and joy." I smiled, looking around. "Aside from my car, this place is the only materialistic object that matters to me."

"That Charger parked over there?" Connor asked. "She's beautiful. What kind of engine does she have?"

"Six point four liter V8."

He laughed. "With these gas prices?"

"She doesn't get out much these days. We're usually in the Forrester. Laila thinks it's safer with the baby."

"Psh, that thing's a tank. That Subaru would crunch like a soda can in an accident."

"That's what I tell her."

"Women."

"So the tour?" Naomi asked.

"Oh, right. Sorry," I muttered. "The kid's bedrooms are upstairs, the master's around the corner there, the kitchen's back there. You're welcome to look around, open cabinets, look in drawers, what have you. Literally everything is baby proofed. Every cabinet, the refrigerator, and the toilets all have locks on them. Every doorknob has a baby proof handle on it. Laila's neurotic about organization, and she follows the same code here as she does at work. Cleaning products are never stored in the same place as food, meats are always in the bottom drawer of the fridge so they don't leak and ruin the produce."

And I meant that. There was nothing in this house I was afraid of them finding. I'd even stopped by last night, taken my miniscule amount of weed to Adam, and had him stow it away at his apartment.

Our entire home was safe. It was beautiful. And honestly, the only object that meant a great deal to me. I was proud of it. And I liked showing it off.

"What do you do about the fireplace?" Naomi asked.

"We've got a wraparound gate we put up when we light it. I know it's kind of a safety hazard, but it's sentimental. My dad lived here when it was a cabin, and when we added on, that was about the only thing that stuck."

"Gate works." She scribbled onto a notebook in her hands. "What about the backyard? I saw it was fenced in, are there any hazards back there?"

"No more than any other yard in America," I said. "We have a dog; she's back there with Laila in the garden a lot. Oh, wait, actually, we do have a little pond. Maybe two feet at its deepest. I don't know if that's a hazard, but we can get a fence around it if we have to."

"No, that's okay." Naomi walked toward the back door and smiled out the window. "Beautiful garden though."

I smiled. "I'll tell Laila you said so."

"Do you have a gate for those steps?" she asked with a nod toward them.

"We do. The handrail's actually custom made. There's two more pieces that clip onto what's there to form a gate, but Milly's not walking yet so we haven't put it on. We can though."

Naomi looked around the living room one more time. "Where's the master?"

"Back here." I started past the powder room and opened the door to our bedroom. "The bed and dressers are bolted to the walls 'cause that's what the parenting books said to do. Our closet isn't baby proofed, but I doubt the kids'll be playing in there so unless we have to, I'd like to keep it as is."

Naomi walked through the door, looking around. "And the bathroom's that door back there?"

"Yup. We bathe Milly in there sometimes. We'll probably bathe Micah in there at some point too, the tub's bigger. Go ahead and take a look."

She opened the bathroom door as Connor gestured to the French doors. "Where do they go?"

"To the garden out back. Laila loves it out there. Sometimes she's out there with Milly all day."

"Huh." He thought for a moment, still gazing out the doors. "You built this place after she got back, huh?"

"Yeah, just moved in last May. Why do you ask?"

"An exit everywhere you go." He smiled. "Almost poetic."

I smiled back. "There's a door in Micah's room to the balcony upstairs too."

He huffed, still smiling.

"Everything looks good down here," Naomi said. "Want to show me around upstairs?"

"Sure, follow me."

It'd seemed like a normal tour so far. She looked at everything, she checked to make sure it was a stable environment for my child. It all seemed fine. Maybe this really was just a routine thing. Maybe it really was just crossing Ts and dotting Is.

As we walked, Naomi cleared her throat. "So what's you and Laila's work schedule like, Jeremy?"

"It varies. Some days I'm there for an hour, others I'm there for twelve. But Laila hasn't been working much since Milly was born. She's come down and helped a few times, but she's mostly home with the baby and running errands. Plus, our general manager was out on bereavement for a while so I was working more than I would have liked. But he's back now, and he's taking on just about everything until Micah adjusts."

Naomi gazed around the living room and kitchen from the staircase. "That's good to know."

"Well, right here is Laila's home office. Not too exciting really." I pushed the door open and walked to the next one. "Kind of like my music room. A lot more exciting than the office." Connor chuckled as I walked to the next door. "Guest bathroom, guest bedroom. Here's Milly's room. As you can see, everything is tediously organized. Even the toys. Not like it matters, she just throws them everywhere anyway." I frowned as I opened Micah's door. "And the bedroom I built for the son I just met two days ago."

"Wow." Naomi's eyes widened slightly as they settled on the door. "He's got his own balcony?"

"There's another door at the end of the hall; it kind of wraps around the back end of the house. But yeah, I wanted him to have a lot of light."

"And a door to the outside world." Connor gave a gentle smile.

I smiled back, nodding. "That too."

"You keep this locked, I'm assuming?"

"We do," I said.

She walked further into the room and looked around. "Well, this looks like a wonderful room for a little boy. I assume you'll customize it as you learn his preferences?"

"That's the plan."

She ran her finger along his saxophone in its stand by the window. "And your brother. He'll be staying here too?"

"Unless he decides to stay at my sister's, then yeah. We've got enough room, and it seems like the best option for Micah." I leaned against the desk.

"Yeah, I agree." Naomi placed her hands at her hips and glanced up. "Is there an attic?"

"Not one that's easily accessible, but yeah. I'd have to stand at the bottom of the ladder for you to get up there though."

She looked around for a moment. "That's alright."

"What about the basement?" Connor asked.

I raised a brow. "You want to see the basement?"

They knew who we were. They knew we had our own torture chamber, everyone in our world who knew my family did. Almost every clan had a similar setup. But they didn't realize that our torture chamber was located half a mile up the gravel road.

"If you don't mind." Naomi smiled.

CHAPTER TWENTY-FOUR

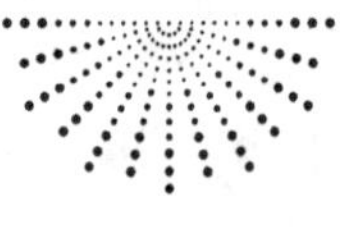

LAILA

The rest of the day was pretty peaceful. We got food delivered via Doordash again. Micah's was feeling better since the surgery yesterday, Milly was her usual happy self. It'd been a good day. I couldn't wait for it all to be over, but it was fine enough.

Micah dreamed against my chest and Milly slept in the crevice of my other arm. It was only seven thirty, but that time in the courtyard seemed to have drained the kiddos. I hoped it wouldn't mess up Milly's sleep schedule, but the jetlag had probably done that already.

"Laila," Chris muttered from his bed.

"Yeah?" I said.

He forced a smile against the pillow. "We should probably talk."

I rolled over to meet his gaze. "What about?"

He laughed. "The last three years?"

"Oh," I murmured. I summoned a playful grin. "You Skoulda men always want to talk about things."

"Probably because we were raised by a woman." He smiled.

I didn't want to have this conversation. I didn't want to tell him I'd fallen into a pit of depression and substance abuse after losing Micah. I wasn't proud of what I'd done when I'd thought he died. I wasn't proud of what I'd done once I learned he was alive. I didn't want to talk about how Jeremy and I had separated for almost a year of our marriage.

There was so much I was ashamed of. I hated that we weren't picture perfect. But he was going to find all of that out eventually regardless.

I looked down at Micah's eyes fluttering beneath their lids. "Who wants to go first?"

Chris chuckled. "Most of the past three years for me has been sitting in a room with him. Pretty boring for the most part. The parts I remember, anyway."

"So it wasn't…" I trailed off. "It wasn't like last time?"

He looked down and fell quiet. "It wasn't routine. It wasn't as calculated. But I… I never knew when it was coming so that kind of made it worse. But on average, it was less often, I guess."

I turned my gaze away, allowing a slow breath to leave my lips.

"But more than anything, it was boring. He's chatty though." He smiled at Micah. "So once he started talking, things lightened up a bit."

"When was that?" I asked. "When he started talking. How old was he?"

"I don't know exactly. A few months when he said his first word. Maybe a year ago, he started talking in full sentences. The year before, he knew a few phrases." His eyes shifted over him with a smile against his lips. Then it slowly fell. "That's when we were still at the second compound. Things were pretty light there. Almost felt normal. Still fucked up, but I had a cot instead of a table so that was good."

My heart swelled. "What was it?"

"Huh?"

"His first word," I barely whispered. I cleared my throat and summoned a smile. "Was it Chris?"

He chuckled and looked down. Again, he grew quiet. "He called her mama."

That bitch. She'd coached him into calling her his mother? She held him down for that bastard to put the fucking implants in.

Fuck, I hated her. I was so relieved that she was dead.

I swallowed the lump in my throat and looked down at Micah. "Was she even around? Was she the one taking care of him?"

"When he was that little," he said. "I couldn't really... I mean, have you ever tried to change a diaper blindfolded?"

I ignored the chill that rose to my skin. "Can't say that I have."

"Yeah, well. He was little at first, and I couldn't be trusted to handle him on my own. When he got bigger, it was pretty much just me. Once he started holding his head up and moving around on his own and everything."

It made my chest so tight. She'd stolen all of those beautiful moments with him. I'd never even know what he looked like as a baby because Chris's only memories of him would be the other senses.

I clenched my jaw and looked away, giving a nod.

"You have to take that from him if you haven't already," Chris murmured. "Killing her. He shouldn't have seen that."

I knew that I had to, but I'd been so overjoyed that he was home, I almost forgot. But I looked over Chris's pained gaze and gave a nod.

I closed my eyes and focused on Micah's mind. Thoughts are more complex to manipulate in children because of how quickly they're learning. As we age, most of our thoughts fade. We remember important things, but most minute details get cast away. But kids are building their thought processes on those minute details. Though complex, still relatively simple for me.

I didn't take the part where Jeremy entered his mind. That short conversation was a building block of their relationship. Daddy swooping in to save the day. He needed that memory.

Instead, I cleared the memories of the bodies on the ground. I took the smell of burned flesh from his nostrils. I erased the evidence of what happened, the things that would haunt a child. I made sure he didn't realize that his hands killed Amy. I made him believe his eyes stayed closed and that he hurt no one. Technically, he didn't anyway. Jeremy did.

"It's done." I looked back to Chris. "I didn't want it to go like that, Chris. You don't remember it because she was in your body, but we tried to grab you guys and get out. She was in you, and you were..." I glanced at Micah and back up at him. "You were holding a knife to his throat. We had to go with them. And then we had to come up with a new plan to get rid of Amy. We had to get the immediate threat off of Micah."

"But they killed us anyway, Laila," Chris said.

"And if Amy would have done it, you would have been brain dead before Jeremy brought you back and your body wouldn't have been worth coming back to." I gave the same tone. "It wasn't ideal, but it worked."

"But what did it do?" Chris said. "What happened when they killed us, Laila? What box did we just open?"

I looked at the ground. Technically, we did it. We saved Micah and Chris. But not until after the sacrifice was completed. They died. They all died, and then came back. I wasn't sure what that meant. Was that what the zombie in the basement was talking about when he referred to the 'resurrection?'

"I don't know."

We both got quiet for a moment. I looked out the window as a bird flew by. For a half second, I wondered what it was like to be that bird and not have to give a shit about a time travelling lunatic kidnapping and sacrificing my baby to bring on the apocalypse.

"Well, maybe you should fill me in on everything that's happened here then. I've been in the dark for a while," Chris said, pulling a gentle smile to his lips. "Pun intended."

I laughed. "Where should I start?"

"How about with what happened after you got shot the day that you escaped?"

"Right. So." I paused and squinted a bit. "Wait, I'll get to that. But what happened to you that day? How did you get back there?"

"I didn't get to leave," he muttered. "The crowd started shifting, and Haley let go of my hand. I heard Jeremy, and I tried to follow his voice. I know you said to jump but... But my little brother literally ran into a bomb site where I had been held captive for seven years. So I started following his voice, and I fell down a flight of stairs. Next thing I know, a guard's got a gun to my head."

I frowned as I looked him over.

He forced a smile. "But go ahead, tell me what's happened here. And what's up with that book Jeremy was talking about in that dream?"

I huffed. "Well. You aren't going to believe this shit."

CHAPTER TWENTY-FIVE

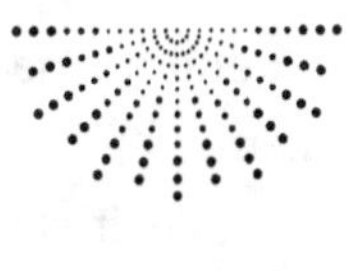

JEREMY

"Sorry, I know it's a little creepy down here." I flicked on the light as I started down the rickety basement steps. "Eventually I'll get around to finishing the remodel on this part of the house too. We put in a French drain system to reroute the water away. Sealed off any cracks where it was coming in and haven't had any issues since. I just didn't have the time to insulate and hang drywall before the baby came. She did. And I *really* didn't have the time. So we just put on a quick coat of paint and threw some carpeting down."

Naomi brushed past me, then the pool table, to the small closet in the corner. The only area where we could have been hiding a person. I fought the smile that tried to climb my cheeks. They should have known the main house was farther back. But maybe they didn't know as much about us as we thought they did.

"We made sure to get all the mold out first. Poured bleach everywhere, let it sit for a day, came by a few days later and cleaned it up. We had fans blowing for days just so we could breathe. Then we poured the cement, let it dry, and everything's been dry as a bone since. If you want to run some tests though, you totally can. Wouldn't hurt to check for mold spores anyway." I crossed my arms against my chest.

She opened the door and moved the coats from side to side. She tapped the block wall and turned her head to the side to listen for an echo.

I smiled. "Like I said. Cement."

"It's small down here." Connor looked around. "The house is huge though."

"Like I said, this was a hunting cabin," I said. "Digging out a bigger basement was a waste of money. Why would we need a big basement? Our house is big enough."

"I don't know, Jeremy." Naomi turned and narrowed her gaze. "Why *would* you need a big basement?"

She said it so casually. Jeremy. As if she'd said it a thousand times, as if she knew me.

I gave a huff of a laugh. My hand ran along my scruff as I lowered myself to the steps. I narrowed my gaze and looked between them. "Alright, ya know what, let's cut the shit. We all know what we know, who's going to say it first?"

Naomi clenched her jaw. Connor laughed, shaking his head slightly.

"Not you?" I looked between them. "Alright, fine. We don't have to talk. But let's not play pretend like children either. We all know what we know. But if you know who I am, you have a lot more reason to trust me than I have to trust you. So either spit it out or quit expecting me to say it first."

Naomi fell silent.

Connor sighed. "You're Jeremy Skoulda. Par animo to Laila Callidy."

"There we go." I joined my hands together in a clap.

"We know *who* you are, and we know *what* you are." Connor leaned against the pool table. "That's why we know that you have Peterson."

"I don't have Peterson." I gestured around. "You just toured my home. He's not here."

"But you have him." Connor smiled. "We know that you do. Word's been out since a few hours after you got home. Everyone's ecstatic over Micah's return."

"Including you?" I asked.

His smile heightened. "Including me. But we need Peterson."

"Then find him," I said.

"We can come back with a warrant," Naomi said. "Even if you move him. Think you can move the mass burial you have around this place?"

Smiling, I arched a brow. "Thought the CIA didn't need warrants."

Connor said, "We both know why you have to let us take him."

"Mhmm." I gestured toward the necklace at his chest. "I'm guessing you're not teleporters, or you would have gone to the house and grabbed him the moment that I gave you that. So what are you?" I looked between them, waiting for an answer. "One of you is a psychic, I know that. But both of you have your powers seriously hidden. I can't feel them at all. How'd you pull that off?"

"Good Witch." Connor smiled. "You should look into it. Might want to go incognito once in a while."

I smiled back. "That's what you call it?"

He shrugged, holding his grin.

"Well, if you're disguising it, that means you're powerful. You wouldn't work for the CIA if you were nobodies, right?" I looked between them. "I'm going to go with Demon for you, Connor. But older, maybe? First generation?"

"Eh." He made a buzzer sound, pulling off his jacket.

"Completely wrong? Or you're just not first generation?" I asked.

Connor grinned. He glanced at the table behind him. "You any good?"

I looked it over. I was a boss at pool. Aunt Annie taught me when I was a kid, and I taught all of my siblings. Leah was the only one who ever stood a chance against me. "I'm alright."

"Beat me, and I'll answer as many questions as you want in five minutes."

Sounded too good to be true. "What's the catch?"

"No catch." He smiled. "But one rule."

"What's that?"

His smile widened. "You can't ask me where the information I give you came from. You've got to respect that it's from someone who's on your side and that's it."

I huffed. "So there is a catch."

"A spy can't give away his sources." Connor laid his jacket on the back of a chair in the corner of the room. He sent me an ironic smile. And his voice changed. "'Specially not to a massacrist like the lot of yous."

I smiled. I stood. My tongue ran along my lips as I shook off my hoody. "Not from this realm, are we?"

Connor smiled and shrugged again. "Rack 'em up, Nix."

My brows dipped, and his smile widened.

Nix. That's what Kai said the name of one of the gods in the Fae Realm had been. The god that *I* had been.

CHAPTER TWENTY-SIX

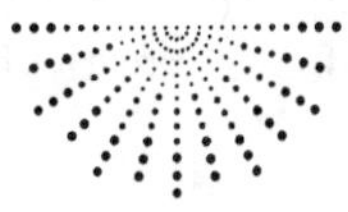

LAILA

Micah and Milly slept on either side of me as I told Chris what happened on our side since I gave birth to my son. I went into vast detail, going on tangents with side stories about the other siblings and what they'd lived at that time. I tried to avoid Jeremy's addiction before he said that Leah told him. I went into a bit more detail there, but still not much. It wasn't my place to talk about with the brother Jeremy hadn't seen in ten years, but it was a part of what happened. Jeremy and I weren't even together when we learned that Micah was still alive. We probably would have gotten back together either way, but learning Micah was alive started the healing process that brought us to where we were.

I explained how we saved the second compound because of his message. That brought a joyous smile to his lips. I told him how we learned who Nastya was. I explained the book we found at the first compound and told him he could read it if he wanted as long as he promised to skip the sex scenes.

Chris didn't believe me when I told him about our meeting with Heylel. He literally laughed at me, very condescendingly, might I add. When I told him that Jeremy planned to invite him to the welcome home party, I watched him fight back the urge to yell. I quickly started to see what Jeremy meant when he said that Chris was the golden boy.

I didn't realize how different Chris was from the rest of his siblings when we were in captivity. It seemed that their grandparent's ways of following the Elders and the Council ran deeper through Chris's blood than the others, at least at that point.

He was quirky at times, but incredibly structured. Had he been around when I first met Jeremy, I would have hated him. Even then, his obedience to the rules of our world kind of irritated me. But we meshed well.

We built a type of friendship that can't be broken. We had a mutual love of Micah and the same understanding of what it's like to have your world ripped away from you. Granted, Chris was gone longer, and his torment was far worse than mine in many ways. But we agreed on one thing. We'd both rather have our eyes cut from our skulls and backs lashed than lose Micah again.

At nine, a nurse came in to tell me that visiting hours were over. She saw the kids curled against my chest, held her forefinger over her smiling lips, and shut the door. I texted Jeremy to let him know I was still at the hospital and to try to sneak in if he could. He texted back about an hour later and said he'd try but his plane got held up. But if he didn't make it back in time, I needed to get back to the hotel because we had to talk. I asked if something was wrong, and he said no, but we had to speak in person. I brushed it off and continued talking to Chris.

Around eleven thirty, another nurse came in and told me I *had* to leave. Micah stayed asleep as I rolled him back to the bed. Milly woke up so I changed her diaper after I ordered an Uber. She fell back to sleep on the ride back to the hotel. I strolled her to our room, shocked that she stayed asleep when I placed her in the basinet.

I tried to call Jeremy when I lay down, but it went to voicemail because it was on airplane mode. He messaged me on Facebook to tell me that he'd be landing around four. He wouldn't make it back to the hotel until five and he said I should get some sleep. So I did.

Then, I had my first in-depth memory from my first life. But Jeremy wasn't in it.

———

It was so realistic that I felt like a whore when I woke up. So much so, in fact, that I ran to the bathroom and dumped everything I'd eaten into the toilet.

I wasn't surprised at first. In almost all polytheistic tellings of the gods, sexuality was a huge part of their religions and gender had little to do with that. But I expected to see my husband when I opened my eyes, despite the fact that my knees were outstretched around another woman's face.

Still, I can't imagine kissing Jeremy as he thrusted in and out of another woman. But I wasn't a stranger to threesomes, even in my current life. Before Jeremy, anyway. Neither of us were the 'let's share' type. But the man who held my face in his hand wasn't my husband. Or at least, not the husband I'd give my life for. And I didn't seem to mind that he was balls deep in the woman who had her head between my thighs.

I don't want to go into too much detail of the sex itself, because it wasn't relevant. Pleasurable and exciting, absolutely. But not intimate. And it wasn't going the way that group sex is supposed to.

I barely even paid attention to the man. I noted his brown eyes, strong attractive jaw, and the waves of blond that hung to his defined, nearly sculpted shoulders. But I was more into her. I felt connected her. Not the way that I connected to Jeremy, we weren't in love. But there was attraction. And friendship. Companionship, perhaps. Almost sisterhood.

Just as I paid little mind to him, the blond-haired man in front of me paid little attention to her. Even when he was inside of her, he looked at me. When I gave her too much attention, he physically pulled me back to him.

Which I suppose is fine in random threesomes once in a while. But at the end, we curled into the bed together. She and I rested our heads on his chest and smiled at each other. He kissed each of our foreheads. And he cupped his hand over mine and let the other hand hang limp.

The connection I had to her led me to believe that the three of us didn't randomly decide to hook up. I didn't want to face what that meant because it contradicted my previous notion.

I'd believed that Jeremy was my other half. I thought that we were always together; two parts to one whole. But what I didn't realize was my age in that memory.

In my first life, I was a little older before we got together. And the life I lived before we bonded was just as important as my life once our souls paired.

CHAPTER TWENTY-SEVEN

JEREMY

"So you're Fae." I pointed at Connor with my pole. I turned to Naomi. "But you're not. You're too mean. Kind, in a way, but you don't have that softness to you that the Fae do."

Naomi arched a brow. "Laila's soft?"

"Unless you piss her off." I smiled. She ignored me, focusing on Connor leaning over the table in attempt to line up a shot. The eight-ball sat directly beside the cue an inch or two from the corner pocket. "Your name's biblical. Naomi, she lost her husband and her two sons. Guess there's a connection to be made there. I'm seeing them every-where these days."

She ignored me still.

"Angel, maybe? I know Mary was named after an important biblical figure."

"Maybe." Naomi crossed her legs in the chair at the corner of the room.

I ran my hand over my mouth and looked over her for a moment. "You wouldn't happen to be working for them, would you?"

She narrowed her gaze and curled her lip. "Fuck the Angels."

"So we're on the same side." I smiled.

The balls clanged together in the pocket. "Damn it," Connor muttered.

"Eight ball's in, start a timer." I sat my stick down.

Naomi pulled her phone from her pocket, tapped for a moment, set it on the table, and pressed start.

"What are you?" I asked with a look between them.

"Fae wolf hybrid," Connor answered.

"Hence why you didn't go to the main house." Not because they couldn't teleport there, but because Wyatt and Celena would smell them.

I looked at Naomi.

"Demon Angel hybrid."

"Called it." She rolled her eyes, and I smiled. "Why do you want Peterson so bad? Yeah, he's a terrorist, but what do you know?"

"Enough," Naomi said.

"We know what happened when they killed your son and you brought him back from the dead," Connor said.

My stomach sunk. "How do you know that?"

He smiled. "We had a deal. You don't ask me where my information comes from."

"Fine." I looked over him for a moment. "Why do I feel like I remember you from somewhere?"

He raised his hand outward. Reddish light that nearly resembled smoke erupted from his skin, sparkled with specks of twinkling silver and dots of gold. It was like a parallel of my gray and blue energy. The same substance that floated in that dark dimension I'd traveled through to bring my son back to life.

"You are not just Fae."

He smiled. "Did you notice that Naomi didn't introduce herself with her last name, Jeremy?"

I glanced down at her hand, noting a golden engagement ring and wedding band. My gaze shifted to Connor's hand where another gold ring wrapped around his third finger.

"You're..." I looked between them as a whitish light with hints of blue spun from Naomi's palm.

"Par animarum," Connor said. "Not the mother and father gods. But the fact remains."

"That's why your powers are concealed. But... But why? Who don't you want to find you?"

"The twenty-four-year curse didn't just hit the two of you." Naomi's gaze could cut glass. "You're the only one who had the apocalyptic baby part. But this was the first life where we made it past twenty-four, too."

"How did you know about it?" I asked. "Did you remember on your own?"

Connor said, "No. But we had a deal. You don't ask for my sources."

"Well, can you ask them why the fuck they didn't tell us to keep our mouths shut too?"

Naomi chuckled.

I thought about saying something snarky, but I was running out of time.

"So the par animos are connected to Peterson because of the apocalypse." I leaned on the pole stick, eyes shifting between them. "What do you know about it?"

"That it's coming. Probably unavoidable now for most of us." She strummed her fingers against her notebook in her lap. "But you know. Still trying to beat it before it gets here."

"When you opened the door and brought Laila back, you broke a seal. When they killed Micah, they broke a seal. When you brought him back, you broke another," Connor said.

Naomi licked her teeth. "There were four broken already. You and your wife can be blamed for them too."

"You're saying Laila and I are responsible for the end of the world."

"Technically, the bastard who made the deal is responsible. He set you up for failure. But also for your failure to be your one chance at happiness. Quite a paradox, if you think about it," Connor said.

"No shit," I blurted. "So that means God is connected to Peterson? Is that what you're saying?"

"We don't call him that. He is no more god than the three of us. But yes. They had a common interest," Naomi said. "Putting you and Laila through horrible shit. But Peterson's kind of the better of the two evils once you know the whole story. At least Peterson only fucked you over in the life you're living."

My face screwed up in confusion. "This is all because we were going to lock him up. But he's had us in these cycles for at least twice as long as we were going to jail him. Why does he hate us so bad?"

"Don't know," Naomi said. But the way her tongue flicked against her teeth and her brows twitched said otherwise.

My gaze narrowed. "You're lying."

"Well, since you're a shit telepath, I guess you'll never know."

"Fuck off."

Naomi smiled. "Thousands of years later, and our banter still never gets old."

Connor rubbed his mouth. "That's something I don't know enough about to discuss."

"But you do. You know something," I said. "What is it?"

"You, him, and Laila were the first of us all. And you two had something he never will," Naomi said. "Let's just say he's got a little green monster and call it a day."

"So did the other twenty-two," I said.

"Like Connor said. We don't know enough to discuss it."

They definitely did, but the clock was ticking.

"Fine." I watched the time hit three minutes and forty-three seconds. "How many others are there? I mean, twenty-four total, I know that. But how many have found each other?"

"Most of them, let's put it that way," Naomi said.

I scoffed. "And me and Laila were exclusively left out of the conversation?"

"Well. Not exclusively," she said. "Celena and Wyatt didn't know either."

I paused to think for a moment, not wasting time with her pointless argumentative rhetoric. "Who is Wormwood? And how do we stop them?"

"We don't know everything, Jeremy," Connor said. "We know that they're ruthless. They're coming here with a purpose; they want their land back."

"And when they take it, they'll take whatever souls are still living on it that don't make it to the first heaven."

"They're taking the souls of the people of earth?"

"That was the deal we all agreed to a few thousand years ago," Connor said. "Whatever souls didn't ascend are theirs. Slaughter the bodies and take the souls for themselves. Basically, it's going to be hell on earth unless we can stop it."

"That's why you want Peterson," I said. "You want to know what's coming. He's from the future, he can tell you."

"That's the plan."

My gaze narrowed. "You'll do anything to get that information, won't you?"

"Just about," Connor said.

"Like, setting him free?" I asked. "Immunity for information that could save the planet?"

Naomi laughed. "That man will never get immunity."

"Either way. You can't have him," I said. "Laila decides what we do with him."

"We don't have to take him," Connor said. "We can come here. As long as you don't mind us cutting into him a little bit."

"We?" I asked. "We who?"

"Colleagues." Naomi smiled. "All that need be said, Jeremy."

I thought for a short moment. I wasn't crazy about the idea, but I also didn't want the CIA breathing down our necks, even if we did have supposed old friends within it. "Well, Laila and I would have to meet them and agree on boundaries before it could even be a discussion. And like I said, it's her call."

"That's not going to happen," Connor said.

"How do you think you're going to torture him if I don't get to meet these people? What—you think we're going to leave you home alone with him?"

"Not alone." Naomi stood. "Someone in your family can stay. Teleporter, if you prefer as a safety measure."

"Great, then me or Laila."

"No," Naomi said. "It can't be a telepath that can send you a live stream of what we're doing."

"We'll have to clear their memories before we leave, too," Connor said.

"And what does that do for us?" I asked.

Naomi crossed her arms against her chest. "I'll get Micah released within twenty-four hours from the time that you agree to this."

"Before you get to interrogate Peterson?"

Naomi said, "I'll get him home to you first. But if you go back on your word, I'll go back on mine. We'll come back, and we won't just take Micah. We'll take Milly too. Wouldn't be hard to pin you and Laila as unfit parents. You're a drug addict. Laila's a survivor of captivity, not to mention on a million watch lists for murder cases."

I laughed. "Nobody's taking my kids."

"We won't do that," Connor said.

"But we can." Naomi's eyes rapidly shifted between mine. "We both have leverage here, Jeremy. You have him, and we have the fate of your family."

My heart hammered as my gaze shifted over her. "So if we don't let you interrogate Peterson, you're going to build a case against us to take our children?"

"If we make a deal and you go back on your word, I'll take your children," Naomi said. "It's a business transaction."

I laughed. "I mean, you can try. You'll probably end up a pile of ash if you do. But what if we don't make a deal?"

"I can make this process drag out for months, maybe even years. I can have him temporarily placed in state custody. I can make it so you and Laila get court ordered, supervised visitation. Or no visitation at all. If I tried hard enough, I could probably even get him deported. You'll get him back one way or another eventually." Her eyes were steadier than stone. "But we'll bury you in lawyer fees. We'll take more time from you and your son. We'll do whatever we have to until you give us what we want."

I didn't like it. But I didn't see much choice either.

I narrowed my gaze. "I can't give you shit until I talk to my wife. If you knew us in a past life, then I'm sure you understand."

"Course." Connor smiled. "Talk to her when we land."

I gestured to their necklaces. "In the meantime, I'm going to need those back. I'll get you an Uber into town. Try out our diner. It's on the outskirts but best cup of coffee on the east coast." Connor pulled the necklace from his chest and held it in his hand. Naomi clenched her jaw as she did the same. I extended my palm and sent them a smile. "I'll give you a call about when to meet up for our flight."

Then they dropped the necklaces to my palm and disappeared.

CHAPTER TWENTY-EIGHT

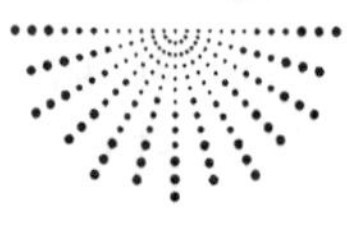

LAILA

"Hey, beautiful." Jeremy kissed my cheek, the smell of his citrusy cologne wafting to my nose.

My eyes lifted open in the dark hotel room. I rolled to meet his gaze. And the moment our eyes met, my stomach spun. I knew it was a dream. A few hours prior, I was not having a threesome with two strangers.

But I really felt like I had.

I tasted that man's lips on my tongue. I smelled that woman's perfume in my nose, like flowers and fruits. And I felt that man's dick inside of me.

But it was a dream. It was a dream; I hadn't actually done that. I'd never cheat on Jeremy.

I forced a smile and cleared my throat. "How was your flight?"

"Boring." He situated Milly on his hip. "Flying sucks."

"When the alternative is teleporting." I stifled a yawn, sat forward, and pushed hair behind my ear. "What time is it?"

"A little after five. Sorry I didn't get back to you much yesterday, there was a lot going on."

"It's alright." I rubbed my eyes and flicked on the lamp. "What happened? Did you find out who they are?"

"Not really who. But what," he said. "Connor's Fae and Wolf. Naomi's half Angel half Demon."

Outside of my family, I'd hardly met any hybrids at all. In fact, come to think of it, Wyatt, Liam, and his siblings were the only others I'd met. There was Gwen, but she was a hybrid by bite, not by blood.

"That's incredibly uncommon."

"Nothing they said was common. Do you want to get up and talk about this over breakfast? Or do you want to get some more sleep?"

"I'm up now. Let me get dressed, and we'll get going. We won't have much time to talk once we get to the hospital so we should do that now."

He gave a smile. I looked between his sweet gaze, and I felt so gross.

Whoever those people were in that dream, I didn't want them. All I ever wanted was the man that sat before me with my daughter in his lap. Jeremy was exactly the person I'd wanted for as long as I could remember.

And I hated the fact that I felt my vagina contract around another man's dick a few hours prior. Even if it weren't real, even if it were just a deep buried memory. I hated it.

I leaned forward, put my arms around his neck, and rested my head against his chest. "I missed you."

Rationally, I knew that I shouldn't have felt guilty. Whatever happened in that memory was from a time when the two of us weren't a couple. But it left me feeling so gross.

And I had to tell him. I didn't want to, and I doubted that he wanted the details. But my mind brought that memory front and center for a reason. Yet, I didn't know how to bring it up. Bullshitting for a while was a little easier than springing it on him.

He laughed as his hands twisted around my back. "I missed you too."

I pulled back and kissed Milly's forehead. "What took you so long, anyway?"

"They had to do some shit with the plane, I don't know," he said. "They told me I had to wait until the evening to fly so I just stayed back at the house for a while. I stopped by the diner and took a look at that toilet in the basement. I could fix it, but I didn't have the time to get to the store, so I just turned off the water down there and put an out of order sign on the door. We can still have the shows, there's just less toilets at the moment."

"Yeah, we should keep them going," I said. "With us being off, we need the money to pay Max and keep us from having to dip into the savings. Especially because we're going to have to pay Helena seventy grand for this."

He released a slow sigh. "Ya know, we should find out where Peterson kept his money. He had to have had a lot of it to pull off all the shit he has."

"Maybe, but he had Nastya. Good Witches are good alchemists. She could have made him money." I stood and dug through my suitcase for an outfit. "I doubt there's any trace of him anywhere. We searched for more than three years and only just found him. And I'm not in the mood for a treasure hunt."

Jeremy laughed and set Milly beside him on the bed. He teleported a diaper and wipes to his hand. "Yeah, me neither."

"Did you talk to him while you were there?" I asked.

"I tried. He's in pretty bad shape, wasn't even faking when he couldn't keep his eyes open. I guess everybody's kind of been using him like a punching bag so," Jeremy said, "didn't get anything out of him."

I pulled off my shirt and lifted a blouse over my shoulders. As it brushed past my face, an image of that woman lifting my dress over my head flashed behind my eyes. I didn't really know how to go about it, but I couldn't keep seeing that memory in my head and not tell him. It'd only been a couple minutes, but I already had to get it off my chest.

"Okay, listen. I need to tell you something."

"I have stuff to tell you too. I thought that's why we were getting breakfast."

"Yeah, but this is a different kind of thing. Not something I really want to talk about in a restaurant," I murmured. He lifted Milly back to his chest. "Like... Kind of like your dreams before we left."

"Oh." A wide smile pulled at his lips.

Aw, damn it. He thought I was about to tell him about some wet dream I had of him from a past life. This was gonna hurt his ego.

I looked down at my jeans, lifting them over each ankle, unable to meet that soft, boyish grin. "But not exactly like yours."

"What do you mean? Not just a sex dream?" he asked.

"No. No, it was definitely a sex dream. But... you weren't there."

He turned his head to the side. "Who was it then?"

"I don't know, but it wasn't an it. It, uh..." I awkwardly scratched my head. "It was a them."

He blinked hard for a second. "As in, like a nonbinary person? Or more than one person?"

I loved that as a straight white man, he was considerate enough to the LGBTQ+ community to ask that question. And it just made me feel so much more guilty.

My lips pressed together. "More than one person."

I couldn't tell if he looked confused or sad. "And none of these people were me."

"They were not you."

He frowned. "Damn."

I laughed and rubbed a hand down my face. "I was pretty surprised too. Kind of a weird memory to get after the last one was you holding my dying body, right?"

"Little bit." He paused to think for a second. "What did they look like?"

"Him or her?"

"Him."

"I don't know, I was paying more attention to the girl to be honest. She was hot. But he was blond. I can show you if you—"

"No. No, thanks. I'll pass on that." He pulled Milly's jacket on and turned to meet my gaze. "Did he kind of look like Heylel but just, like, a little less soft? More masculine features?"

Huh. I hadn't thought of that. But yeah, he kind of did.

"Maybe. I don't know. Like I said, I was more into the redhead," I said. "But maybe. I don't know. He looked young. Maybe even younger than me. Couldn't have been more than twenty-five. Strong though. Muscly."

He rolled his eyes and lifted Milly to the car seat. "Well, I ask because I had a memory too. When you died, right before I brought you back. It was that day in the Elder's Hall. You died in my arms, and I went to that place. The one that we go to when we die, but I couldn't find you. And I looked up, and this guy was standing there. He was blond, tall, brown eyes. And he said something, and he... He was almost crying too. He looked down at you and he... He definitely felt guilty. But it was almost like he was the one who kept me from bringing you back? I don't know. Either way, I yelled at him, and he looked terrified. And I woke up."

I lifted my palm out for his. "Show me what he looked like."

He extended his hand to mine, and I closed my eyes. Then flashed an image of the same man I'd seen in the dream. He looked older, not significantly, but more manly and less boy-like. His jaw looked more defined, his shoulders appeared broader, his forehead seemed a bit more prominent. But they were definitely the same man.

I pulled my hand back and gave a slow nod. "Yeah. Yeah, that's him. Older though."

He thought for a moment. "Heylel said that his dad was responsible for our murders when we were the Elders. So it stands to reason that that man was God."

My stomach gurgled. "And Heylel said God was your brother in that life."

"And you were fucking him before we got together."

Ew.

Ew, ew, *ew*.

I was fucking his brother. I was in a *relationship* with his brother.

It didn't seem possible. Then again, most of my life didn't. But there was no way the world was going to end because I fell in love with some dude's brother.

"This can't come down to a love triangle."

"No, it's bigger than that. Otherwise, the other par animarum wouldn't have been cursed." He rubbed his mouth. "But it might explain why he hates the two of us so bad."

I raked a hand through my hair. "I wish these little flashes would give me the whole damn picture."

"Might help if we knew the language," he muttered. He thought for a moment. "But ya know, even if you would have chosen Brody over me, I wouldn't have cursed you for thousands of years. I definitely wouldn't have killed your children."

"Well, maybe that's why I picked you." I put my hands on my hips. "We're talking about a guy who asked a man to kill his son to prove his loyalty to him. Someone who tells women to submit to their husbands and not to speak in church."

"Yeah. I know, pretty gross," Jeremy muttered. "Ya know... The Bible also says to stone adulterers."

I met his gaze. "I guess your wife fucking your brother might light a big enough fire under your ass to make a rule like that."

"Maybe. But Heylel said we had children. And he doesn't remember anything like that. So whatever happened between the two of you must have happened well before Heylel was born. He would have been over it by that time if the twenty-five of us were ruling together."

"So that's not what this is actually about," I said. "But yeah. Might explain why he hates us."

"That is a pretty shitty thing to do though."

"Yeah. Yeah, it is." I scratched my head. "But if that's true, how are we soulmates? I thought that we were one soul split in half."

"The myths got twisted on the way down. I'm banking on these memories to tell us the truth. I trust myself more than I trust old stories, ya know?"

"Can't disagree with you there."

"Speaking of the par animos, we need to talk about Connor and Naomi."

CHAPTER TWENTY-NINE

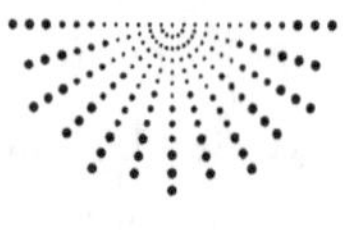

JEREMY

"Well, that's not happening," Laila said over her coffee. "We can't just let a bunch of CIA people into our house alone with him."

"I agree, but do you want to get caught up in a legal battle to get our son back?" I cut through my waffle and passed Milly a chunk of banana from my fruit bowl. "Because we won't look good in court, Lai. And if they dig deeper, they're going to find more. A lot more. Things that could have us both sent away for life. Yeah, we could escape to the Fae Realm with the kids, but do we *want* to do that? I like the life we've built; I don't want to lose it."

"Neither do I, but if we lose Peterson, we'll spend every day for the rest of our lives looking over our shoulder." She leaned over the table and glanced at the Waffle House waitress as she walked past. Once she rounded the corner, she turned back to me. "I busted my ass for three fucking years to give him what he deserves. I'm not letting him go that easily."

"They aren't going to take him. They just want to torture him." I lowered my voice. "Which, frankly, I'm completely cool with."

"Well, yeah, so am I. But if we're not present, there's nothing stopping them from taking him. Then we're back to square one," she said. "No, I don't like it."

"They said someone can be there, but they can't be a telepath that can live stream what they're doing." I took a gulp of my coffee and raised a shoulder. "Adam would be a good option. He can stay on Peterson, and if they try to take him, he could teleport right out."

"But what are they hiding from us then? They don't want us to see something, what is it?"

"My guess? The colleagues they wouldn't mention by name."

Her head shook. "See, I don't like that. What if their colleague is him? God or whatever, I mean."

Nah, Naomi meant it when she said, 'fuck the Angels.' Plus, all of us were cursed by that bastard, not just me and Laila. They probably hated him as much as we did.

I rubbed my mouth. "What if we make a deal? Adam gets to meet them first, gives us the okay, but he doesn't disclose their identity. Then they wipe whoever it is from his thoughts once they're done. If it's someone we can't trust, it's off. But we trust Adam's word. And he's strong enough to keep them from manipulating him into saying they're okay if they're not."

She stared down at her coffee for a minute. She looked back up. "They'll give us Micah back first, you said. So we'll know that no one's taking him from us."

"That's what they said," I said.

"And did you ask Adam about this? If he'd be willing to be there when they do this?"

"He said sure. I'll have to tell him about this part of the deal if Naomi and Connor agree to it, but yeah."

She rubbed her temple. "Well, if all they want to do is torture him, I'm in no position to stop them. The more the merrier. But we need some type of leverage. Like some temporary barrier around the basement that no one can leave for a specific span of time once it's up. When the spell goes down, Adam takes them where they need to go, and they clear his memory of whatever it is that he saw."

Helena had cast a spell that could contain Laila. Surely, she could cast something similar for these people. "I think that Helena could work up a teleportation barrier linked to Adam. No one else can go in or out of it but him. Won't last long if they're powerful, but we can give them a time limit."

"That'd work," she said. "Well, let's meet up with the bitches and get our kid home. I need to get Milly back on a normal sleep schedule, or we're going to be in hell when we get back."

"Well, they said they'd be by around lunch time. There's a bunch of papers we need to sign about Micah."

"Lunch it is then. In the meantime, let's go see our son."

———

Warm California sun shined against my arms. The smell of fresh cut grass and the hum of a mower sounded from the hilltop behind us. I was so happy to sit in that small courtyard with my wife and kids, but every time I looked at Laila, I pictured that guy in the memory fucking her.

I knew that wasn't fair. It's not like I thought she was having an affair with the guy in this life. But shit, was it weird.

The myths had led me to believe that it had always been her and I as one. But the myths also led me to believe soulmates were fairytales. The past few years had proved how far that was from the truth.

Still, I had to wonder. What had happened between them? How could I have justified ending up with my brother's girl? I wouldn't have done it in this life, why had I done it in that one? And why had she? She made it abundantly clear when Brody had shown his feelings for her all those years ago that she wouldn't do that because it'd hurt me.

So how badly did he hurt her?

He had to have. In any life, I knew her moral compass. She wouldn't have hurt anyone she loved that way unless they'd hurt her first, and she felt justified in doing it.

Then again, that answer seemed obvious. He fucking killed her in the end. I didn't care what any of my exes had done, I would never do something like that. I'd never kill someone I once loved.

But it brought me back to that same question. Why would I have done something like that to my brother? What had he done? Who was he?

"So what would you think about having a little party when we get home, buddy?" Laila asked Micah.

Oh, yeah. The welcome home party. I was glad she'd brought it up. I needed to get my mind off of this shit anyway. But I was so excited for it. We had big plans for Micah's homecoming. Leah mentioned renting a bounce-house, I couldn't wait for Micah to try some of Beverly's famous chocolate cake, and it'd be so cool to introduce him to all of my brothers and sisters.

And it also seemed like a good time for Heylel to meet the kids.

He'd mentioned it that first day we met, and it wasn't until recently that I felt comfortable enough with him to actually go through with that idea.

"What's a pawty?" Micah looked up from the dandelion in his palm to meet her gaze.

"It's where all the people you care about and all the people that care about you come to see you." I smiled. "We eat all kinds of food, and we listen to music, and we play all kinds of games and stuff."

"That sounds fun," Micah said.

"I need to meet everybody too," Chris said. "There's all of these new people around these days. Who all's going to be there though?"

"Just family. Maybe a couple friends." I roughed up Micah's hair. "A lot of people helped us get to where we are. They want to meet the kid all this fuss has been about."

Chris licked his teeth. "Like the devil?"

"Chris." Laila gave him a disapproving gaze. "Not right now."

I didn't care for that phrasing. But that's what I'd called him until recently too. "Maybe," I said. "Why?"

"You think it's a good idea to have the King of Hell at our welcome home party?" Chris asked.

I laughed. "It's a long story, Chris. But if you don't want him to be there, that's alright. We can have dinner with him or something."

"With Micah?" Chris raised a brow.

"Possibly." I cocked my head to the side. "Is that a problem?"

"Well, he's your kid. Do what you think is best." He looked away.

I turned back to Micah. In Chris's shoes, I'd probably feel the same way. But he didn't know Heylel like I did. We weren't close, but we were connected. He felt like family to me too. I understood Chris's perspective, but Micah wasn't his kid. He didn't get a choice in which of my friends he got to meet.

Plus, with the new information I'd gathered in the last few hours, I definitely needed to talk to him. He hadn't mentioned anything about Laila fucking his dad. I needed to know if he knew that. And if he did, why in the fuck he hadn't told us.

"Will I get to meet Lydia?" Micah looked up at Laila. "I don't see hew when I close my eyes no mowe."

I laughed. Killing Nastya had broken the bond between them. And I was grateful for that. I imagined Lydia would be too.

"Yeah, Lydia will be there. So will all of your aunts, and your uncles, and my mom. Your little cousin, Luka. And one of my friends from high school is really looking forward to meeting you. I think you'll like him."

"What's his name?" Micah asked.

"Max." I smiled. "But you can call him Uncle Max."

"Uncle Max," Micah murmured with a nod. "What about Tink? Will she be thewe?"

"She will." Laila grinned.

He nodded with a big smile. "Yeah, that sounds fun."

"Any word on how long it'll be 'til they let you guys take him?" Chris asked.

"Could be really soon," I said.

It'd better be, anyway.

"We'll know more after we meet with the social worker for lunch. It could be tomorrow," Laila said.

"Really?" Chris's eyes widened, smile pulling at his lips. "That soon?"

"Maybe," I said.

"Is you leaving fow lunch then, Mommy?" Micah asked.

"Just for a little bit," Laila said.

"But we won't be long, kiddo. Maybe we'll even stop and get you some ice cream on the way back, what do you think?"

His smile stretched across his cheeks. He gave a fast nod. "The same kind from the other day, wight?"

I laughed. "Chocolate it is."

CHAPTER THIRTY

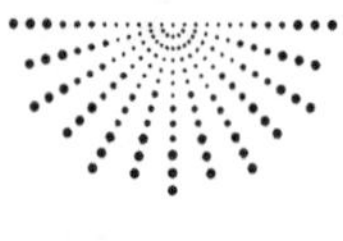

LAILA

It shocked me how quick Naomi and Connor agreed. Our terms were reasonable but from how Jeremy made their conversation sound, I expected an argument at the least. But they agreed to every bit of it. Then they started the process of getting Micah home. I was still wary, but the fact that they agreed so effortlessly gave me hope.

By dinner, they told us to prepare a flight for the morning. Then we got Micah in his new shoes. We tried on a few different outfits Jeremy grabbed from the house. We made sure his coat fit. And we packed our bags.

Although I wanted to, I couldn't fall asleep that night. My heart raced with excitement to finally bring Micah home and move the fuck on. But the more I thought about it, the more I realized how deep we were in shit.

The glimpses we'd seen of our past lives were simply that. Glimpses. We knew a droplet in the pond of our history. We'd thought our lives were always centered around each other, but my last dream proved that to be false.

I started to think about what that meant. If I was God's wife at one point, that explained why my soul was so powerful. But to my knowledge, God had no wife. I was no expert, but I always thought that it was the father, son, and holy spirit. In fact, that's why I shied away from Christianity. Its lack of a female deity and its suppression of women.

So I took to Google as Jeremy dreamed beside me.

Simple question. Did God have a wife?

And I got thousands of results. Until that moment, despite my studies of the Christian religion after learning of my Angelic heritage, I never once heard the name Asherah.

Turns out, scholars believed that God did in fact have a wife.

She was a deity known as the mother goddess, goddess of fertility, goddess of the sea, and the queen of heaven. Interestingly enough though, she's scarcely mentioned in the English translations of the Bible. In the Hebrew version, she was mentioned only forty times—just about as often as it tells women to submit to their husbands.

In some stories, Asherah's even associated with a tree of life depicted on her stomach. That fact backed the myths Heylel informed us of a few months prior.

Even more interesting is how much God grew to hate the bitch. In 1st Kings 14:23, God says "You shall not plant any tree as an Asherah beside the altar of the Lord your God..." Again, in Exodus, verse 34:13 "Break down their altars, smash their sacred poles, and cut down their Asherah poles."

More strange than that even was the fact that she was mentioned multiple times in the book of Jeremiah. Couldn't really see that being a coincidence. In which, Ezekiel, Hosea, and Jeremiah attribute Asherah as "making Yahweh jealous." After the dream I'd had the night before, couldn't say I blamed the guy in that regard.

"What fault did your ancestors find in me they strayed so far from me? They followed worthless idols and became worthless themselves."

Little harsh, but okay, dude.

He went on a rant about the Jews worshipping other deities, AKA yours truly, for a few verses. Verse nine stuck out to me too, but in fairness, I think he was talking about the Jews. Either way, it said "I will bring charges against your children's children."

Considering the Jews were his holy people, and the Guardians were also told they were his holy people, I couldn't help but wonder if that was a little foreshadowing from our man God.

He rambled some more about the Jews worshipping other gods. Like, a shit ton. Just kept going and going about it.

But another verse that really stuck out was Jeremiah 2:20. "For long ago I broke your yoke and tore off your bonds." That line really stuck out to me, but so did the next. "But you said, 'I will not serve!"

Although in fairness, I think he was referring to the Jews there too. What sent a chill to my skin, though, was how deeply a lack of obedience infuriated him. Why would someone supposedly all powerful and all-knowing expect such ideation from people so small and tiny? Why did he need that reassurance so badly? Unless he had a serious complex about people that told him to fuck off.

Either way, with a confused, annoyed huff, I tossed my phone to the bed and stared at the ceiling.

It seemed like Asherah kind of ruined women in his eyes. He *really* hated that bitch. And if she was symbolized as a tree, and I literally gave people immortality through the tree of life...

If I didn't feel the weight of the world on my shoulders before, I definitely did after exploring the idea that my soul was responsible for the oppression of women since the Abrahamic religions took over the world.

A feminist for as long as I could remember. Just to be the bitch that ruined women for God and caused millions of women to be ordered into submission for centuries.

Yeah. Didn't get a lot of sleep that night.

I lay awake and pondered if that could even be true. I never cheated before, I prided myself in that fact. Would I really cheat on a man with his brother in *any* lifetime?

Then again. He was fucking another woman in front of me. Another wife maybe? Maybe I rationalized it. Maybe that was the falling out. Maybe I didn't like that he got to fuck more than one woman and I had to settle for him.

But I kept coming back to the soulmate thing.

If Jeremy and I were soulmates, why would I be with his brother? Did I meet him after already marrying his brother? Or did we just not realize what we were yet? If we were the first, we wouldn't have known what a soulmate was. Even now, we hardly knew what it meant.

Another thought occurred to me. Could divine love really be traced back to infidelity? Loyalty was more important to me than anything, I doubted that would have been any different in any life I lived.

So it bared another question. What had he done that made cheating justifiable in my eyes? But that answer seemed pretty obvious. He clearly didn't respect women.

'Wives, submit to your husbands. Submit, submit, *submit.*' Do as you're told. Listen to your husband, he knows best. And don't ask questions. Women are the lesser sex, they dare not question a man. Be modest, cover your body.

The thought of being married to a man who viewed women that way made my stomach churn.

Actually, it all but made my stomach spill. Especially when I remembered that sound I heard when Peterson's hand grazed my underwear. Was preventing him from raping me again to save me the agony? Or Jeremy? Or was it simply over territory?

I wanted to sleep. But those thoughts chased each other like a bad acid trip. Part of me worried what I would see if I closed my eyes. Because I didn't want another group sex dream from a distant life I lived a few thousand years ago. I wanted to understand.

The only way to do that was to interrogate Peterson. But I refused to be the parent that searched for their child for years just to spend the time he deserved chasing folklore and fairytales.

Yes, something big was going on, and I was the center of it. But so was Micah. And being a good parent to him, and to my daughter, was just as important. Later, I'd realize that raising them to be good people was even *more* important.

"It looks like you're all ready." I smiled, looking over Micah in his khaki pants and cute blue button up.

"Mommy, it's itchy." He scratched beneath the collar at his neck.

Jeremy smiled. "See, that's why I don't let your mom dress me."

I waved Jeremy off. "We have some sweatpants in your bag. If you're that uncomfortable, you can change on the plane."

"Okay." Micah grinned. "Is we still going to the beach? Or is we going home?"

"Where do you want to go?" Jeremy asked.

"I want to go home." He smiled. "I want to have that pawty."

I laughed. "We're having your party tomorrow so that'll be perfect."

"Okay." Micah clenched his lamb closer to his chest. "I weddy."

I laughed again, stood, and walked around the wheelchair. Chris laughed as he started the wheels on his. Jeremy grinned, grabbing ahold of Milly's stroller. "Home we go."

"Finally." Chris grinned.

I smiled before we each started from the room.

That moment felt like it did when I pulled down the doors three years before. Or maybe when I blew the roof off and watched the survivors jump from the precipice.

Liberation. Freedom. Triumph.

We finally fucking made it.

CHAPTER THIRTY-ONE

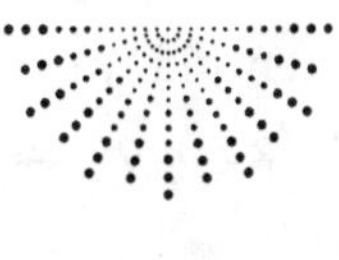

JEREMY

Micah looked out the window for an hour or so before he closed his eyes and fell asleep watching the clouds drift below us. Laila transferred him to her lap beside me and rested her head on my shoulder. Milly dreamed quietly in my arms as Chris excitedly binge watched Breaking Bad for the entirety of our trip, mumbling some rhetoric but mostly watching in awe.

In all honesty, I blocked out the instinct in me that knew we were buried in some deep shit. I just wanted to be happy for a damn minute. Or a month, or a year, or however long we had.

I hated Peterson, and I wanted him dead, but I didn't care to torture the guy. He deserved it, and I wanted him to suffer too. And sure, I wanted to know what he knew. But what would he really give us? He knew we were going to capture him; he knew we were going to torture him. He already mapped out what he would and wouldn't tell us. I wished we could just kill the bastard.

But we had to do what we had to do. Getting Micah home was more important than a quick vengeance. And helping the CIA try to prevent the end of the world seemed like a good idea too.

As arbitrary as I found it at the time, I'd eventually realize taking Peterson alive was one of the best decisions we ever made.

"I can't believe they stayed asleep." Laila smiled, looking in the back seat. "Still out like lights."

"Maybe this transitioning to two kids thing won't be so hard after all." I glanced at her, grinned, and turned back to the road. "Hasn't been too bad yet."

"Well, Micah's older. I think it's hard when you bring in a little one who needs your undivided attention, ya know?" She situated the seatbelt around her shoulder. "We got a buffer. Not that we wanted it, but we got it."

"Yeah. Yeah, that's true," I muttered. "Hey, do you think Micah can eat marshmallows? I know graham crackers are probably too hard, but we could roast marshmallows, right?"

"The specialist said that he can have harder foods. We just have to be careful and monitor him closely. Remind him to chew, be ready to do the Heimlich and all that. I'm a healer and you can resurrect the dead; we can't keep this kid from eating because he hasn't learned. We just have to teach him."

I smiled. "S'mores it is then."

"Hey, what do you know about that anyway? We haven't really talked about it since it happened. Did you talk to Hannah?" She turned down the music and met my gaze.

The whole necromancy thing wasn't something I'd given much thought. I'd grown up in a world that made it out to be evil, dark magic. I didn't understand why, and I didn't particularly want to.

Although, now, knowing that was the only ability capable of taking immortality from someone who's eaten from the tree of life, I realized that was why. Not because it was dark magic. No, it was so that he, God, was the only one capable of doing it. So that he was more powerful than anyone else.

There was enough on my plate at the moment. I didn't care about this. Yeah, it was great that I had the power to save people from death. But I just wanted to be a dad. I had to learn how to do that before I took on some massive set of abilities that were looked at as evil and got nearly every bloodline with said ability wiped from the planet.

"Not yet. I didn't have much time when I was here yesterday, and she was at school. But yeah, I don't know. It's pretty weird."

"What's it like? I never really remember it once I'm back. I swear I heard my dad's voice the first time, but that part might have just been a hallucination. Otherwise, I just remember darkness."

"It is dark," I said. "But not... Not like pitch-black dark, ya know? I guess that's why my name was Nix in the Fae world, that means night in Latin, I think. But it's like looking up at the stars and traveling through them at the same time. But I've never been to space, so I guess I'm not the best judge."

"Do you think that's what it is? Somewhere in space?" she asked.

"Maybe," I said. "Maybe, I don't know. It kind of sounds like the Greek interpretation of Tartarus. But the myth says that isn't where souls go where they die, that's Hades. Tartarus is like a place of imprisonment. It's where Zeus locked up the Titans."

"Huh. Almost like an interpretation of purgatory, if you think about it. Hannah's always called it the abyss, but it is essentially purgatory. Where your soul goes before it moves onto the next life."

"Yeah, I guess. It could be," I said.

Laila tilted her head to the side. "How many Titans were there again?"

I thought for a moment. Then my breath caught. "Twelve."

That number really was everywhere.

Twelve, and twenty-four. Twenty-four hours in a day, twelve months in a year, twelve stars on the whore of Babylon's crown in Revelation, the twelve apostles. It was a popular number in other religions too. Odin had twelve sons in Norse mythology. In the legend of King Arthur, he allegedly won twelve battles. His roundtable had twelve knights. He took out twelve princes. Bodyguards in ancient Rome carried weapons bound by twelve rods.

Even in science, it was a relevant number. The Beaufort scale that measures wind maxes out at twelve. Everyone has twelve sets of cranial nerves that affect bodily senses. The first part of the small intestine is called the duodenum which comes from the Latin translation of the word twelve. There are twelve pairs of ribs in a human body.

In art, there are twelve basic colors.

Twelve basic zodiac signs.

I wasn't exactly sure how that all connected. But the fact remained.

Twelve was a number used repeatedly throughout human history.

Maybe that had something to do with the twelve sets of gods that brought life to this planet.

"That's what I thought," Laila muttered. The car fell silent for a moment. "We know the myths got a lot of things mixed up. We need to look at keywords and repeating patterns."

"Like the number twelve." I blew out a slow, calming breath.

"And the overlap in associations like the lion and the lamb in multiple cultures. The recurring number three with the binding spells and whatever the hell Nastya did that day. We also need to look into the myths about brothers, right?"

"Yeah. Yeah, I think so. Loki and Thor might be a good place to start. And we should look into Ragnarök a little more, that's another major end of world myth."

"Yeah. But speaking of mythology, I did a little bit of research last night and let me ask you something. In all the times that you've read the Bible, have you heard the name Asherah?"

Vague memories floated back to me. "When I read the Hebrew version with my grandpa as a kid, yeah. She's also mentioned in ancient Sumerian texts. She was a Canaanite deity. Earth goddess, right?"

"Earth goddess, mother goddess, fertility goddess, goddess of the sea. She's also represented by a tree of life."

I pause, thinking hard for a moment. That title, Asherah, she brought back another memory.

In my adolescence when I started shying away from religion, I'd been doing some research on other mythologies. Specifically, I'd been doing research on the Canaanite deities. That's how I learned what the Elohim were.

But I remembered reading once about another god.

Ba'al.

He was hated by Abrahamic religions, interpreted as a demon. After all, the Bible said he requested child sacrifice in exchange for a good crop. Although, in my opinion, it was Yhwh that really enjoyed killing children. Including his own. In fact, in one telling in that book, people sacrificed an animal side by side to Yhwh and to Ba'al. Ba'al's sacrifice was not taken, but Yhwh's was. That had always made me wonder who the one actually requesting a sacrifice had been.

Despite how the biblical texts framed the photo, the Canaanites knew him as Ba'al Zebul, Lord Prince, King of the Gods. In the bible though, he became known as Ba'al Zebub, later turned into Beelzebub.

I remembered reading about that clearly. It made me laugh and shake my head.

Ba'al's classification from a god to a demon changed because of a pun. Ba'al Zebul translated to "Lord Prince." But Ba'al Zebub meant "Lord of Flies." Quite literally, one letter was changed to make a joke. And from there, a deity so strong he was depicted holding lightning was turned into a demon with the head of a fly.

Lightning. I supposed he and I had that in common too.

Based on a story from the Ras Shamra tablets, Ba'al was also associated with death and resurrection.

Overall though, he was a god of fertility. And either the consort, or the son, of Asherah.

But see, that's where the myth got confusing. Because in some tellings, Yhwh was the consort of Asherah. In others, it was Ba'al. In some, she was listed as their mother. That made me wonder though. What would one call the woman who granted them eternal life? Perhaps great mother.

I supposed it was all confusing. Myths are. They're stories passed down around campfires for generations, turned into songs, words changed so they rhyme, and meanings nearly erased to make for an entertaining tale.

There were consistencies though.

Like the way people worshipped Ba'al and Asherah.

Fucking.

I mean that literally. To worship Ba'al and Asherah, people fucked. I guessed I could see why that would be a logical way to honor fertility deities who manifested new abilities when they had sex.

According to Heylel, and the myths on the Fae Realm, I also was allegedly a god of fertility. I also held lightning in my hand. And now, apparently, I was also associated with death and resurrection.

Laila blew out a deep breath. "In the Bible, God says to destroy any temples or poles that honor her. Even goes so far as to say not to plant a tree near an altar for him."

"And you think that's you?" I asked.

"Heylel said I was known as the great mother once. And that I was the living personification of the tree of life. My research last night seems to point to Asherah having been God's wife, who was also personified as a tree and goddess of fertility, and then him having some pretty strong feelings about her. So it'd make sense, right?"

I could definitely see the parallels. It'd explain why our lives had been so shitty, and it did back up a lot of Heylel's story. "Yeah, I guess. But I can't think of any specific myths about a set of brothers with a love triangle over a woman."

"We'll have to dig. But Asherah was practically washed from the Abrahamic tellings. When her name wasn't being dragged through the dirt, anyway."

"Ba'al's was too," I murmured.

"Huh?" she asked.

"I don't know. It doesn't matter. They were just stories anyway, you know? I'm sure they got just as misconstrued as the stories of the par animarum did." I took my hand in hers, twined our fingers together, and raised her knuckles to my lips. "We can worry about all this later. I do want to talk to Heylel though."

"Yeah, you're right. Let's just get home. We'll have dinner and make some s'mores. Get our kids to bed. Then call Heylel and set up a time to meet. We'll deal with all this shit then. But I don't really care what Chris says either, I like Heylel. I trust him. And if we're right about all of this, which I think we are, he deserves the opportunity to meet his nephew."

Relief loosened my shoulders at the subject change. "Yeah. Yeah, I get why Chris feels the way he does. But it's really not up to him. I know he loves Micah and everything, but he's our kid. And it's not our fault we haven't gotten to spend the last three years with him."

"Well." She paused. "It's not *your* fault."

I glanced from the road and met her gaze. "It's not yours either."

"It is." She turned out the window. "Wish that it weren't. But it is. And I've come to accept it. I've got to own up to it. This happened because of what I did. But so did saving the seven-hundred survivors. If there was a way to rewrite it, I would. There isn't though, so I've just got to accept my fate. On the bright side, he's young enough that he might not remember all of this. He might not remember Peterson at all in five years. I mean, I don't remember anything from before I turned three, do you?"

"No. I don't." I glanced her way. "But I still don't think this was your fault."

She shrugged. "Regardless."

CHAPTER THIRTY-TWO

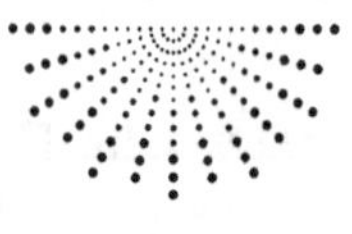

LAILA

"Hey, buddy." I shook Micah's shoulder in the car seat. "Look, we're home."

His eyes fluttered open, balled fists rubbing against them. A yawn escaped his mouth as he looked around. A smile pulled at his lips. "Can you cawwy me, Mommy?"

I smiled and unstrapped the buckle at his chest. "Can you get Milly, babe?"

Jeremy smiled back and stepped around the car. "Yeah, I got her."

I grinned and turned down to Micah. He outstretched his arms and placed them around my neck, legs wrapping around my hips.

Walking up that flagstone path with my son in my arms and my husband carrying our daughter behind me felt like shackles falling from my feet.

In that moment, nothing else mattered.

Just the warm little body wrapped against my chest, the cooing little girl behind me, and the man who helped me create them.

I let the theories, and the drama, and the nonsense wash away for a moment. I just focused on absorbing the instant I was in. The soft crisp wind's smell as it brushed hair into my face, the hue of the sky turning pink in the distance, and the overwhelming sense of peace.

The beauty of freedom.

Later that night, we did exactly as we'd planned to months before. We lit the fire. We blasted the A/C. And we roasted marshmallows.

Chris went back to the main house with Leah and the others. I think the rest of the family recognized how badly we needed that time together. Just the four of us and Tink, getting to really know one another and enjoying each other's company. We sat around the living room for a while, then we meandered outside. Micah loved the pond, but he loved the trees just as much. I passed Milly to Jeremy at one point and levitated the two of us above their early blooming tops.

He looked around in fear for a moment, but he stared at the views around him in awe. I brought the small green blossoms to large leaves and watched his eyes widen in amazement. I found it beautiful how enthralled he looked at what I could do, but it also sent me into a quiet fury.

Milly had been using her abilities since birth in some form or another. She learned from watching, from picking up on what we did and how we felt as we did it. But Micah was filled with wonder from it. Because his potential had been suppressed since his birth yet used for it in the same instant.

But I pushed that thought aside.

This night was about my family.

I sniffed Micah and Milly's hair. "They smell like smoke."

"Usually what happens when you sit around a fire all night." Jeremy grinned, plopping onto the bed beside me. "Plus, you smell like smoke all the time."

"Not *all* the time."

"A large amount of the time."

"But I don't want them to smell like smoke." I glanced over their sweet, sleeping faces. "I want them to smell clean."

"Then give them a bath." He laughed as he pulled himself up the bed. "But you're going to give them baths in the morning anyway. And it's late, they just fell asleep. If you wake them up now, we're really going to fuck up their sleep schedule."

"Fine. But we have to wash the sheets in the morning."

"Sounds reasonable." He rolled against the pillow to meet my gaze. "Ya know what's crazy?"

"What's that?"

His smile stretched wide. "It's not the home stretch any more. We made it. We're home." His hand raised and coasted it along my cheek. He looked down at the kids. "I know I shouldn't have, but I kind of lost faith once in a while. I didn't think we'd ever get to this moment. But we did."

I smiled, gazing down at their two sleeping faces against my chest. "Yeah. I had my moments of doubt too. But we pulled it off."

"We did." He grinned and raised his palm. I laughed and tapped my hand to his, trying to be quiet enough to keep the kids asleep. He twined his fingers through mine and brought them to his lips. "Now we get to enjoy it for a little while."

"Probably just a little while, huh?"

"Knowing our luck. But ya never know, maybe everything's going to be fine. Maybe the CIA's doing its job taking care of it."

"I guess time will tell."

I kept pushing the theories I mustered up to the back of my mind. But they kept creeping back up. It just made so much sense. A lot of it didn't, but my memories weren't a lie. Neither were Jeremy's.

As Heylel had said, how would one hurt the goddess of motherhood? Take away her ability to be a mother. And that's exactly what had happened. In each and every life, I never got to the moment I was at now.

I loved each and every second of it. My heart skipped with joy as Micah's sleeping hand tugged my shirt. A sweet burst of love jumped from my brain through my body as Milly rolled her head against my chest.

But it was laced with fear and guilt.

I remembered Heylel saying the war was over the tree of life, then that we wanted to imprison that man. But what had he done to deserve it?

Had a decision I made caused mine, my husband, and my children centuries of suffering? Could I really have been to blame for all of this? Was my failed marriage with a man I hadn't even met truly the reason the world would end?

What the hell would the point of saving Micah have been if the world were going to end and we'd all die anyway?

"Usually does." Jeremy frowned. "Can we just... Can we not think about everything we may or may not have learned in the past few days? A lot of it's just theories anyway. We aren't those people anymore. Whatever happened then isn't who we are now. That's what Helena said when she showed us our past lives, remember?"

"So you want to hop onto the ignorance is bliss train?"

"Maybe for a little while." He smiled and gazed down at Micah. "This is his first day home. I just want him to get the attention he deserves right now."

He was right. I had to push it back. For years, I'd been dreaming of the moment I'd hold my son in my arms. And I was finally living that moment. I needed to embrace it.

"Yeah. Yeah, I agree." I ran my fingers along the dark black curl beside his ear. "Let's enjoy the time we have. We don't know how long it'll last."

"So let's dance in the rain."

CHAPTER THIRTY-THREE

JEREMY

Quiet, stifled sobs pulled me from my dreams early the next morning. I wrinkled my brows, blinking through the morning light in my eyes. Micah stood beside the bed, pushing a small throw blanket into the corner of the mattress where he fell asleep beside Laila.

"What're you doing, bud?" I rubbed my eyes, trying to meet his gaze. But he just froze. His jaw fell open and shut a few times. Tears glistened his big blue eyes. "What's the matter, Micah?"

He ran.

Just bolted to the master bathroom and shut the door behind him. Laila barely flinched as I stood from the bed and examined where he stood with the blanket. I picked it up and felt a warm, wet substance beneath my hand. I did what just about every parent does in that situation. I smelled it. And it smelled like piss.

Not a big deal. He wasn't even three yet. And even if he were, even if were ten or fifteen or eighteen, it wouldn't have been a big deal.

"Hey, it's alright, buddy," I said at the bathroom door. "Accidents happen, we'll just clean it up."

He didn't say anything, but I heard muffled, heaving sobs beneath his palm.

I spun the doorknob and pushed the door open. Micah sat on the ground in front of the counter with an arm wrapped around his knees and the other at his face. I lowered myself to the ground beside him and put my hand on his trembling shoulder.

Still in too much of a slumbered haze to really take it in, I softened my voice and summoned a smile. "It's okay, kid. Nobody's mad about a little pee. Your sister pees on us all the time."

"I sawwy." He kept his head tucked against his knees. The sound of his teeth clattering together cut through his sobs. "I-I-I didn't mean to. I twied, I twied weal hawd."

I stifled a yawn and rubbed his shoulder. "It's alright, dude, I promise. Your mom wanted to clean those sheets anyway. Nobody's mad at you, alright?"

"Mommy won't be mad?" He looked up and met my gaze.

As those big, watery blue eyes shifted between mine, my stomach sunk. Why was he crying and trying to clean it up himself? Why had he run from me?

What happened that made him think he head to run away from me because he peed?

My heart started to drum against my ribs. That fucking bastard. Had he hurt my kid? He must've. Micah wouldn't have had that terrified, heartbroken gaze if he'd been treated the way any child in the potty-training stages should have been treated.

But angry as I may have been, it wasn't at him. I had to make sure he knew I wasn't upset with him. Because clearly, he was afraid. And I didn't want my kid to fear me.

"I don't think Mom will ever be mad at you, buddy." I managed a smile as I thumbed a tear from his cheek. "How about we—"

"Hey, what's going on?" Laila said in the doorway. She raised her hand to her mouth to cover a yawn. Her eyes shifted to Micah. "What's wrong, baby?"

"He wet the bed," I said.

Laila kneeled beside us. "Oh, that's all?"

"I twied to get to the bafwoom but I-I—"

"It's okay. You aren't even three yet, it's okay to have accidents once in a while." She coasted her hand over his hair and brought a smile to her lips. "It's no big deal, I promise."

"You'we not mad?" he asked.

"No. No, I'm not mad," Laila said. "Why would I be mad?" Micah swallowed hard. "Were they mean to you when you had an accident?"

Micah turned his gaze to the ground.

That fucking piece of shit. He had; he'd hurt my kid.

My brows fell. I tried to pull them back up, but I almost couldn't believe what I'd just heard.

He was two. They didn't even have a working fucking toilet in that cell. I was fairly certain Peterson pissed himself when I cut that crystal into his back, and he was a grown ass man.

"Well, you don't have to worry about that here." Laila smiled. "We'll get you a bath while Daddy starts the laundry. Then we'll have some breakfast and sit outside on the patio. How's that sound?"

He gave a slow nod as he wiped his fists against his eyes. His eyes fell on the gauze wrapped around his wrist. "Can you make dese bettew, Mommy?"

She frowned. "I can. But it'll hurt."

"But then they'll be all gone, wight?"

"Yeah. Yeah, then they'll be all gone."

He looked over them and thought. After a moment, he said, "I weddy."

I smiled. "Let me get your sister in the play pen, and I'll help."

"Can you get undressed while I talk to Daddy for a minute?" Laila asked.

He nodded. Laila helped him to his feet and gestured toward the doorway. I headed that way. We glanced between Milly sleeping in the bed and Micah undressing in the bathroom. "What happened?"

"I woke up, and he was dabbing up the pee with Tink's blanket. I asked him what he was doing, and he just ran away."

Her brows were deep in her eyes. "You didn't yell at him, did you?"

I returned her expression. "Did you hear me yell, Laila?"

Her gaze softened. "No. No, I'm sorry. He just... He looked so upset."

"Yeah, his teeth were chattering and everything," I said. "There's a story there, something happened. I'm going to ask Chris."

"But if he was abused, we would have known, right?" Laila asked. "Lydia didn't tell us about every scraped knee and bumped elbow, but if he was being hurt, we would have known."

"I would think. But I don't know. I don't understand why they treated him the way they did. He was their lamb. Their god, their sacrifice. They should have worshipped the ground he walked on."

"I think they did until they moved from the second compound. I think that's when resources got scarce." She paused, looking over him in the bathroom for a moment. "Plus the whole, 'he that overcometh' bullshit."

I took in a slow, calming breath. "Well, I'll go start the laundry and get breakfast going while you get his bath. I can take over with him if you want to get Milly's bath done."

"Chris stumbled in around midnight. I think I heard him yelling at a nightmare an hour or two ago. He's probably up. Try and talk to him before Micah comes out there if you can."

"Never thought I'd see the day." Chris smiled, wiping sweat from his forehead as he pulled off his tennis shoes. "Jeremy Skoulda up before seven with a baby on his hip."

I laughed. As I flipped the sausage, I met his gaze. "I'm not sixteen anymore, ya know."

"Yeah, I'm picking up on that." Chris pulled off his hoody. He sat at the bar on the other side of the island. "It's a really nice morning out there. The sunrise was beautiful."

"Couldn't sleep?" I asked.

"And a little hungover." He smiled. "It's been a while, what can I say. I'm actually legal to drink now, so that's cool. Where're Micah and Laila?"

I set Milly in her highchair. "He's getting a bath. We had our first little meltdown this morning."

"Uh-oh, what about?" he asked.

"They fell asleep in our bed last night. And I woke up to him crying as he tried to clean his piss off the bed with the dog blanket." I looked up and met his gaze. "I'm sorry if this is painful for you, but can you give me some background here?"

He pressed his lips together and gave a slow nod. "Yeah. Yeah, um... So when Micah got scared, he'd pee himself. I did sometimes too, I think we all did. And this one time..." He paused again. He cleared his throat, hand rubbing against his jaw. "Nastya needed our blood for something. Couldn't tell you what, but Micah... Well, he hates needles. He was scared, and he pissed. This was right after we transitioned from pull-ups, maybe six months ago? Anyway, he pissed, and Peterson started yelling at him. Telling him to quit being a cry baby or something, I don't remember. I got mad and copped an attitude with him. And he... Well, he started hitting me around a bit. He told Micah it was his fault. I told him it wasn't but... Yeah."

I clenched my jaw. "The bond that you two had through Nastya. Did that make it so he felt it?"

Chris cleared his throat. "Yeah. Yeah, he did. He felt the bruises too. I think that's when Peterson realized he could hurt Micah without Lydia knowing. Hit me, he'd feel it, but Lydia wouldn't so you guys wouldn't know."

My hands tightened to fists. "He beat you regularly?"

"I wouldn't say regularly. But it wasn't infrequent either."

"And Micah felt it."

He nodded again.

My heart pounded, and my palms grew sweaty. I felt my jaw clench. To keep my angry hands from shaking, I had to tighten them to fists.

That man had been beating my two-year-old. Not a slap on the hand or a pat on the bum, although I didn't agree with that either. But *beating* him.

We didn't know.

We had no idea what our kid had been living through. And in some way, I was grateful, because I wasn't sure we'd have made it through the last few years if we knew that he'd been beating our baby.

That's what he was. He wasn't even a kid, not really. Two years old is a baby.

And he didn't just watch them beat his uncle. He felt it.

"Look, Dad," Micah called, running down the hallway. "Look at my new shiwt." He spun in a circle. He wore a pair of light gray pants that almost resembled slacks and a white cardigan with brown buttons.

"He picked it out; don't you dare say I dressed him like a prep school kid." Laila grinned with her hands at her hips.

"Do you like it?" Micah asked.

I smiled. "Very serious. Like a little college professor."

"It's not itchy. That's why I like it."

"That is the number one thing to look for in clothes." I held my smile. "Go ahead and sit down. I'll bring you and Uncle Chris a plate. Can I talk to you for a minute, Lai?"

CHAPTER THIRTY-FOUR

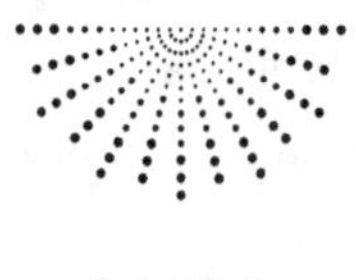

LAILA

As Jeremy explained why Micah was so afraid, my brows fell heavy over my pulsating green eyes. He placed a hand on my shoulder and told me to breathe, but I gritted my teeth to a line and shook my head.

I asked him if he could feed the kids breakfast and give Milly her bath. He started to say that it could wait until after the party, but I said, "I'll get him now. You can get him later."

I forced my glowing eyes to dull. I kissed Milly good morning and gave Micah a quick hug. I lied and told him I was going to the store. He seemed pretty content to stay with his dad and little sister.

I teleported to the kitchen of the main house and felt my blood come back to a boil. I hadn't had the drive to beat the shit out of that fucker since we'd captured him yet. But the fear in Micah's gaze as I walked into that bathroom infuriated me more than almost anything. He was only two and a half when that fucker beat him for peeing himself in a moment of terror. At least he wasn't consciously unaware when they sacrificed him. But to brutalize him for a bodily reaction?

No, that hit differently. There was no reason behind it; it was cruel just for the sake of being cruel.

As I stepped to the cement of the cellar, Brody stood from his chair in the corner. "Oh, cool. Are you my relief?"

"For now. You can leave." I pulled off my sweater as Peterson's swollen eyes struggled to open. His head rolled to the side in a strain to meet my gaze. He smiled.

"I wouldn't be smiling if I was you."

He released a huff of a laugh.

"I think I'll stay," Brody murmured, bringing himself back to the chair. "Let me know if you need a hand."

I started to the armoire. "Might need you to hold his in place."

"I should have let you wear jeans in there," Peterson said. "The scrubs didn't do that ass justice."

I teleported in front of him and grabbed ahold of his hair. My fingers twisted in the short, bloodied locks. I yanked downward. The chair toppled forward, his knees absorbing the shock of his weight when he hit the ground. He groaned. I raised my knee in a swift motion into his face. He gasped. I yanked the chair back into place and grabbed ahold of his hair again. "Say a word about my ass again."

He smiled as blood oozed from his lips. "What about your pussy? Can I talk about—"

I raised my burning hand to his throat and gripped as tight as I could. He tried to scream, but I squeezed tighter, watching smoke escape from the cracks of my fingers as his eyes widened in agony.

When I watched his blood vessels begin to pop through the whites, I smiled and released my grip. "You know what comes next, Peterson? Now... Now I heal you. Nice fresh and clean canvas. Then, I'm going to get my favorite ice pick over there. And I'm going to pry off each of your fingernails one by one."

He looked between my eyes with a straight face, panting hard.

"Oh, now you're scared, huh?" I grasped ahold of his hair and wrenched his head to the side. He grimaced at the pain from the charred flesh at his neck. I twisted his hair tighter around my fingers. "You can pretend that you're not, but we both know that you are. I'm going to make you wish you were dead, but I won't kill you. Not here. Not now. Not for a long time. Because a lot of people want to see you die. We're going to run a poll on how it should go, did you know that? We're also going to give every living survivor the opportunity to torture you. We'll heal you in between, of course. Can't have you dying on us, can we?"

He tightened his teeth together.

I smiled. "How does it fucking feel? How do you feel to finally be the one that's scared? I've lived the past three fucking years in constant agony because of you so answer the damn question, Peterson. How does it fucking feel to be the one tied down?"

His eyes bounced between mine. Still serious as ever, he said, "Like I'm getting what I deserve."

For some reason, that statement just made me angrier. I wanted him to beg me to stop the way that I'd begged him. I wanted him to plead for his life.

I clenched my jaw and slammed my fist into his cheek.

Peterson wept quietly from the chair. I looked over him with fast moving breaths. As I watched the blood drip from his hand at the arm of the chair to the puddle of crimson beneath him, I expected to feel something. Some sort of accomplishment or triumph. But I felt nothing.

No remorse. No sparking joy of vengeance. Even the anger had faded. The feeling of relief had just settled and left me more vacant that I'd ever felt.

I felt *nothing*.

I heard the basement door click open, unwavering gaze still locked on Peterson. His body shook with fear and anguish, but I stood steady as a tree on a windless day. I heard Jeremy murmuring with Brody but the sound of blood dripping from the piece of metal in my palm to the concrete floor was louder than the beat of a drum.

"It's almost eleven, Lai." Jeremy's hand brushed my elbow. "Everyone's coming around one."

I continued staring at Peterson, wanting so badly to feel better. Like the pain of what he'd done could be washed away by the misery my hands caused moments before. But it didn't.

Because trauma doesn't work that way. Nothing could take away the pain he'd caused. Nothing could erase the fact that my baby was only two years old and knew how it felt to have his head bashed off of concrete.

Yeah, Peterson deserved what we'd inflict on him in the coming months. But it wasn't a cure for what he'd done. I'd sewn up the scars he'd given me, but if I bent too hard, they'd rip back open. Wounds like that never completely heal.

"You should probably get cleaned up." Jeremy gently placed his hand at my shoulder.

I didn't respond, I just kept staring at him.

"I did a good job," Peterson managed out.

"What was that?" I took a step forward. He shook his head, sniffing up bloodied mucus. I grabbed him by his hair and turned him up to meet my gaze. "What did you just say?"

"With you." He looked at me with his one good eye, struggling to see me through the swelling in the other. His bloodied lips pulled into a smile. "I didn't think I could, but I did. I pulled it off."

"You pulled what off?"

"I took away your humanity." He smiled. "You couldn't have done this when we first met. You didn't have the drive in you. You didn't have the fuel for your fire. You needed to hate someone enough to become this. You had to hate like you've never hated anyone before.

"When your best friend killed you, you felt sympathy for her. After what Mary did, you were hurt but your hatred faded over time. Even your first husband in the old lives, you didn't hate him. You should have, but you understood. You always understand other people's wrongdoings, Laila. Maybe not at first, not in the heat of the moment, but after a while, you sympathized. And you needed someone that you could hate with no sympathy. That's why it had to happen, don't you see? You had to become like this. You had to hate me to become *this*." He looked between my eyes for a moment. He smiled as tears glided from his eyes. "I had to become your villain because you had to learn to fight. You've taken on the qualities of a fearless, ruthless leader because of me. Don't you see? I did it, I created you."

My breaths got shorter, vision growing black around the edges.

I was right.

I'd assumed that I was, but to hear him admit it...

All that pain of suffering, what he put almost a thousand people through. He did all of it just for me to become this. Someone who could pry off someone's fingernails, someone that could cut through another person's body with a straight face, someone that had just smiled to hear a man scream out in misery.

This was supposed to make me feel better. But now I felt so much worse.

Jeremy grabbed the pick from my palm and thrust it into his hand. He let out a long, ear piercing cry, fingers flexing and releasing. Jeremy turned the metal about forty-five degrees. Peterson screamed again. Jeremy grabbed his face and turned it up to him.

"What do you know about him?" Jeremy said. "How are you connected to him? Is he the one that had you do all this?"

"Ask him yourself. Don't think he's available at the moment though."

He turned the knife again, and Peterson gasped in pain. "What the fuck does that mean? Are you connected to him?"

He breathed heavily through sobs for a moment. I gritted my teeth to a line, watching him tremble in utter agony. After a few slow breaths, he turned his eyes toward me. "You needed me, Laila. You needed to hate me so that you could learn to do what needs to be done. It won't be easy. There will be sacrifice, but you've already given the biggest sacrifice imaginable. You'll be ready when that time comes."

I grabbed the knife, ripped it from his fist, and thrusted it into his other hand. He screamed out, turning to a desperate, sobbing cry as I spun the knife. "I didn't sacrifice my son, you stole him from me!"

He continued to sob as I lifted the metal pick and stabbed it into his arm again, that time between the forearm and hand.

Then again.

And again.

Peterson kept screaming, and I kept stabbing. I wanted to stab it through his chest or his face but at least I had enough self-control not to do that. Instead, I just continued raising the metal pick into the air and thrusting it down into his skin.

I must have stabbed him fifteen times before Jeremy put his arms around my shoulders and yanked me away. With flailing hands and glowing eyes, I commanded he get off of me. But he held my shoulders and yelled for Brody to get Kai.

Jeremy grasped the metal pick in my palm and tossed it to the ground. He took my face and turned it to his. His serious eyes shifted quickly between mine. "Do you want to kill him right now? Because we can. But is that what you want? Or will you hate yourself for it in two hours?"

I tightened my jaw to a line, shaking breaths panting from my body. The basement door slammed open. Kai and Brody ran down in a full sprint. My hands trembled, and Jeremy wrapped his around them.

I did, I wanted to kill him. I wanted to kill him more than I wanted anything. But he'd just confirmed my theories that yes, I was in fact married to God, and that he somehow played a part in everything the past few years had entailed.

We needed more intel.

Jeremy's hands coasted over my tense upper arms. "Let's go get cleaned up."

Peterson erupted in screams.

A chill rose up my spine, and I nodded.

CHAPTER THIRTY-FIVE

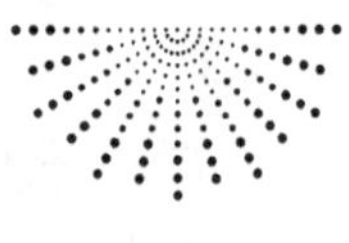

JEREMY

"Daddy," Micah said.

I lifted Milly's jacket around her arms and looked up at him. "Micah."

"Whewe's Mommy?" He looked around the living room. "I haven't seen hew since bweakfast."

"She had to handle some stuff at work." I smiled and sat Milly on the floor. "But she's doing her makeup now. She'll be out soon. Then we're going to go pick up your cake from the bakery, how's that sound?"

"What's a cake?" he asked.

I sighed. "Just... just assume that when I get excited about something, it's probably a cool thing you should be happy about."

"But you always escited." Micah grinned.

I laughed. "It's a big world out there. There's a lot to be excited about."

He smiled back and sat on the couch beside me. He pointed to the picture of him and Chris on the mantel. "Whewe'd you get that?"

"We found it when we were looking for you." I looked over him, holding my smile despite how hard it tried to pull down. "First picture we got to see of you."

He thought for a moment. He looked back up to me. "I seen youw haiw befowe. But the fiwst time I seen you face was when I came to Lydia that day."

I smiled at the way he said Lydia more like Wid-di-uh. But to keep the conversation going, I said, "Uncle Chris didn't show you me?"

"Yeah, but you looked diffewent." He reached up and poked my beard. "You didn't have this."

I laughed. "Well, I was pretty young the last time me and Uncle Chris saw each other. Just a little bit older than Lydia, actually."

He smiled. He leisurely leaned back on the couch. "I like it hewe."

"Oh, yeah?"

He nodded, looking around. "It's so bwight."

"We do have a lot of windows."

"I like it."

I laughed as the door to the master bedroom clicked open. "What are you boys talking about out here?" Laila asked, fixing her sweater over her shoulders. She smiled as her gaze met Micah's. "The big party everyone's putting together at Aunt Leah's maybe?"

He grinned as he stood. "We can go get the cake now?"

"We can go get the cake now." Laila grinned, putting her hands at her hips. "And you can meet the sweetest old lady in the world."

She looked better now. Not the makeup, though the winged eyeliner and red lips were pretty. More so that she was no longer covered in blood. And that she wasn't hyperventilating anymore.

I understood why she had to do it. She probably wouldn't have been able to get through the day with the thought in her mind of that man beating our son if she hadn't. But I wasn't sure it made her feel that much better either.

Torturing someone never made me feel better either. Killing them —eliminating the threat—that would. But not torture.

Micah smiled, and Laila looked at me. Her smile seemed to carry heavy weights she struggled to keep lifted. "Why don't you start out to the car, buddy? We're right behind you."

"Can I do it without walking?" His wide eyes looked between mine.

"Just make sure you go to the car right outside, okay? Right out there." I gestured out the window. He smiled, gave a quick nod, and disappeared.

I turned to Laila. "You alright?"

"Yeah. Yeah, I'm okay." She cleared her throat. "My cheeks aren't blotchy, are they?"

"You look beautiful." I smiled. "But you're sure? You're okay?"

"Yeah, I'm fine. I expected to feel a little better than I do but... But ya know. Got the worst of the anger out."

I'd learned the lesson years ago that torture doesn't take away the pain someone else has caused you. The only thing that even slightly helps is once they're in the ground and you know they can't hurt anyone again.

"We always think that hurting them's going to make us hurt less. Never really works though."

She chewed her lip for a moment or two, gaze shifting over the ground. Her shoulders fell with a deep breath. "Yeah, I guess it takes a certain type of person to enjoy something like that. It felt good for a second, and then it just..."

"I know." I kissed her forehead and glanced at Micah waving from inside the car. "But let's go get our son's cake. Then introduce him to his family."

The sweet smell of pastries filled my lungs. Bright spring sun shined onto the linoleum through the large windowpanes behind me. Gentle fifties music played over the speakers above us. The warmth of Milly's skin radiated into mine against my hip.

This place had a similar feel to it as Moe's. Classic, homey, nostalgic. I'd been in and out of Beverly's Bakery since I was a kid too; it was one of the few places in town that my dad absolutely adored.

He always said that her bread was the closest to French bread that he'd found stateside. And he wasn't wrong, it was the closest I'd found too. The flavor wasn't sweet, the crumbs were light and airy, but the loaves themselves always had a thick, hard crust.

"Just a minute!" Beverly called from the hallway behind the glass case of baked goods.

"Take your time," Laila said. Micah clenched the bottom of her jacket. She smiled down at him, running her hand over his head and looking into the pastry case. "Does any of this look good to you, buddy?"

He shifted his shoulders in a low shrug. I pointed to the coconut cream cupcake and smiled. "That's the type of cake me and Mommy had at our wedding. They're really good. You should try one."

"Oh, and these are really good too." Laila pointed to the cookies and cream cupcake.

"What kind is the cake?" he asked.

"Chocolate and chocolate and more chocolate." She grinned. "You'll like it, I promise."

"Sorry about all that. I was in a war with the bag of flour." Beverly dusted powder from her torso, laughing as a cloud of white floated from the apron. "Guess you can say it won the battle. What're you kids in for today?"

Laila straightened up to meet her gaze. "We have a welcome home cake to pick up."

Beverly's gaze shifted to Micah hiding behind the bottom of Laila's coat. Her eyes widened and a near gasp left her old, cracking lips. "This is the little boy you've been talking about? The one you were pregnant with when you bought all of my chocolate covered Oreos for weeks?" Laila laughed and gave a nod. Beverly looked at me, then at him, and laughed. "Well, of course he is. Looks just like you, Jeremy."

"He does, huh?" I smiled and ran my fingers over the top of his head. "Micah, this is Beverly. Beverly, this is Micah."

"Well, it's honor to meet you, sweetheart." Beverly's grin stretched up her wrinkly cheeks as she reached over the counter. "You're just a little angel, huh?"

He awkwardly reached forward, touched her palm, and quickly retreated back to Laila's hip.

"He's a little shy." Laila laughed. "This is his first trip out and about actually."

"Well, I am honored." Smiling, she placed her hands at her hips. "I'll tell you what. How old are you, dear?" Micah held up two fingers, and she smiled. "Then you can have any two things you want. What's it going to be, mister?"

"Anything?" he asked.

"As long as Mom and Dad say it's okay." Beverly glanced at us. I smiled in answer, and she looked back to the box. "But I've got to say. I highly recommend these chocolate covered graham crackers over here. And these little truffles are really good too."

Micah pointed to the coconut cream cupcake. "Can I has that?"

"You sure can. And maybe that graham cracker?"

Smiling, he nodded and pushed his head into Laila's hip.

"What do you say, kiddo?" I asked.

"Thank you," Micah murmured.

"You're very welcome." Beverly smiled as she handed him the cupcake. She turned to Laila. "He's beautiful, dear."

"Thank you." Laila tightened her arm around his shoulder, beaming with pride.

"Something in his mouth reminds me of your dad. Yours too, Jeremy." Beverly smiled, gaze shifting over him. "Can't see an ounce of your moms, but I see your dads in there, alright."

"Yeah, a little bit, huh?" Laila looked at him and then back up at Beverly. "But he's perfect either way."

"That he is." She smiled down at him. "Well, it looks like you all have a party to get to so I won't keep you. Let me go grab that cake."

CHAPTER THIRTY-SIX

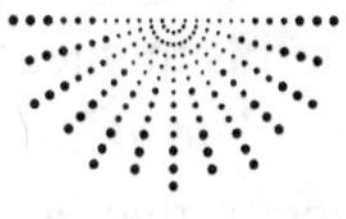

LAILA

"Where is he?" Jenna looked around the bathroom. "Isn't he supposed to be with you?"

"Well, yeah, when I'm not pissing." I stood from the toilet and pulled my jeans up over my legs. "He's out there with Jeremy, you must have walked right past him."

"Nah, I think they're out back." Jenna lifted herself to the counter as I washed my hands in the sink. "You need to introduce me; this is a really weird situation."

"You aren't meeting the president." I laughed. "He's your nephew. Just talk to him like you talk to Milly."

"Yeah, but he's old enough to understand me when I call them all little shits."

"Well, don't call him a little shit."

"That's easier said than done."

My big sister. My obnoxious, bitchy, annoying big sister. She used to do this when we were kids too. She was so blunt and to the point with me, but when she had to meet anyone else, she'd become meek and awkward. I always had to be the one to break the barriers down with new people.

Not that I really minded though. I wasn't exactly a social butterfly, but I knew how to talk to people.

I dried my hands on the hand towel and laughed. "I don't know what to tell you, Jen. Just be nice. He's shy, but once he starts talking, he doesn't stop."

"Must take after his momma." Jenna followed me from the bathroom. "But what went down in there? Are you alright? We haven't even talked since the day before you guys left."

I really wanted to focus on this moment. I had time to dwell on the bullshit once my baby adjusted to our lives together. "A lot. A lot happened, but we'll talk about that another time. Today's about Micah."

"Fair enough. But that's him down there? In the basement?"

I turned to meet her gaze. "Yeah, that's him. And if you want to go meet him, or beat the shit out of him, you're welcome to. I don't care. But for now, I don't want to think about that man. I don't want to see his face or hear his voice or even the mention of his name."

"Does that invitation extend to Mom? Because she's... Well, she wants to get a hit in."

"Knock yourselves out. But not a word about the past three years today. Today is about Micah. And relay the message to Mom when she gets here. Don't ask me about Peterson, don't ask me what happened in there, and don't expect me to explain anything. Today is—"

"About Micah." She smiled, giving a nod. "I got it, Lai."

I summoned a smile to my lips. "Let's go introduce you to him then."

"Alright," she said. "Let's do it."

As we walked through the kitchen, I continued. "Couple things though. Don't look at his scars, alright? I don't want him to be self-conscious about them. They're not that bad, and they'll probably fade as he ages. But ya know, just be cautious."

"Yeah, of course."

"And he really likes chocolate. But don't offer him anything you wouldn't give to someone with dentures. He's still learning to chew so just soft stuff."

"He can't have anything hard?"

"No, he can. But like, pretzels and stuff might be too much of a choking risk for him right now. He's doing okay with crackers, but they dissolve pretty quick. We can probably start on lollipops, but no hard candy."

"Sounds good," Jenna said. "Anything else I should know?"

As we walked through the living room toward the back door, I continued speaking. It came out casual, because I'd already come to terms with it all. "He has something called rickets disease. It's from a lack of sunlight and vitamin D. His forehead seems a little bigger than most kids his age because of it but his hair kind of covers it so you can't really tell. His legs look a little odd if you pay real close attention. He might need braces or surgery if it doesn't improve but the doctors are sure he's going to be fine. It should all go away with supplements, diet, and lots of sunlight."

Her eyes shined with sympathy. "Oh, Lai—"

"No, it's fine. Really, it's okay. He's already getting a lot more energy. And in a few months, any of the skeletal deformities should go away. They're not that prominent anyway, but it's okay. You're not going to be able to tell at all. He's going to be fine." She forced a smile, and I opened the patio door. "It's fine, really. I promise."

At least, that's what I had to keep telling myself. But he was perfect either way.

Jen forced a smile. "I believe you."

Then, we stepped outside. It looked familiar. The welcome home banner, the white tent, the buffet of hamburgers and hotdogs.

But this time, Jeremy sat beside Chris with a guitar in each of their laps. Micah looked like a doll in the camping chair twice his size next to Leah. Hannah held Milly at her hip by the desert table. Celena and Wyatt sipped wine and beer next to the gifts. Kai, Adam, and Brody shared a joint at the foot of the steps.

This time was different. Everyone was here. Everyone was happy. The last three years hadn't been for nothing. Every single person Peterson held captive that still had a beating heart was home. Safe. Where they were always meant to be.

A long, gentle breath left my lungs. My shoulders fell in relief. A soft smile pulled at my lips.

For the first time in a very long time, everything really was okay.

I engulfed myself in it for a moment. That fucker was going to get what he deserved, but not now. Because now, all that mattered was enjoying our family.

And I was already doing just that.

"Mommy!" Micah exclaimed from his seat beside Jeremy. He hurried to his feet and started toward me.

I smiled, trudging down the steps. "Hey, kiddo, did you meet your Aunt Jenna yet?"

He smiled up at her. "I'm Micah."

"Well, nice to meet you, Micah." Jenna lowered herself beside him with a grin. She extended her palm to him. "I'm your mom's sister."

He smiled, gave a nod, and leaned against my hip. His gaze tilted up to me. "Me and Tink was playing."

Jenna's hand fell back to her side, and I stifled a laugh.

Well, that was easier than I'd anticipated. Maybe it was just strangers that he was shy around. Because near our family, the people Jeremy and I trusted, he seemed just as happy as he'd been when it was the four of us.

"Oh yeah?" I asked.

He nodded, lifting his hand toward me. "It huwts a little but she didn't mean to." I thumbed the scratch on his palm. "She jumped a little too hawd."

"You're tough though, huh?" I smiled. "You can handle it."

Micah nodded again with a big smile. He turned to the small crowd and pointed toward the food. "Can we have cake soon?"

"Yeah, but let's say hi to everyone first. You met your Aunt Jenna, did you meet anyone else?"

"That's Uncle Adam." He pointed down the steps at Kai. "But who's that guy? I like him, but he talked funny."

I laughed, hoisted him to my hip, and smiled at Jenna. "We'll be over in a minute so you can introduce him to Luka."

"Alright." She grinned. She ran her hand over Micah's upper back and walked away. I started down the steps with Micah at my hip. When they saw us descending the stairs, Brody put the joint out and smiled up at us.

"What's that?" Micah gestured toward the smoke wafting away. "Is thewe a fiwe?"

"Something like that," I muttered.

Kai laughed as his gaze fell on Micah. "Bloody hell, he really don't look a lick like ye, do he?"

"See?" Micah rested his head on my shoulder.

I huffed, smiling. "He has my lips; the lady at the bakery just said so an hour ago."

"Well, I've got those lips too, and I don't see 'em on your lad." Kai smiled and looked at Micah. "Ye look just like your dad, ye ken."

He grinned, shyly pushing his head further against my shoulder.

"Micah, this is my brother, Kai. Can you say hi?"

"Hi." He waved, still smiling. This kid was always smiling.

Kai grinned, looking between his eyes. "Happy to meet ye, lad."

"And I'm your Uncle Brody." Brody smiled. "I'm your dad's little brother."

"You already know me, huh, kid?" Adam leaned forward and playfully tickled his side. Micah giggled, and Adam laughed.

"Making all the introductions without me?" Jeremy's hand slid over my back, lips pressing into my cheek.

"Why don't you take Micah for a second?" Brody smiled his way, glancing at me. "I need a word with your wife."

"Come here, bud." Jeremy reached for Micah.

I passed him over and smiled. "I'll be over in a minute. Daddy can introduce you to your other aunts and uncle."

"And then we can have cake?" he asked.

"Definitely your kid." Adam laughed.

I stuck my tongue out.

Brody and I took a few steps away. My arms crossed against my chest, head tilting. "What's up?"

"You good?" His eyes flicked between mine with concern.

Ah yes, my torture session this morning.

Well, I was done with that. I didn't want to think about it, I didn't want to talk about it; it didn't matter. All that mattered was looking on the bright side of things.

"I'm fine." I smiled. "Cried in the shower for an hour, I think. But yeah. Yeah, I'm good. Where's Gwen?"

"I think she went to change Luka's diaper. I don't know. She's around here somewhere." He glanced around. "Well, I noted a few things that I think you were too... ya know. In the groove to notice."

Well shit. There went my vibe.

"What is it?"

"None of us can get in his head. Peterson, I mean. I tried, Adam tried, Leah, Celena. We all tried, and we can't get in there. He said something about God, right? He probably wasn't talking out of his ass. He's probably the one keeping us out. Also, I... I don't think any of us are going to get anything out of him. He didn't say a word when I hit him or when Celena and Wyatt were beating the living shit out of him. But the second you came down, he started talking about your ass." I cleared my throat and gave a slow nod. "Sorry, I know this is a sen—"

"No, it's fine. Go ahead."

"I just... I think you're the only one he's going to respond to. Just like the guard did. And maybe... Okay, I know this is a really uncomfortable idea. But he's obsessed with you, ya know? Maybe you should... I don't know, be a little nicer."

"Be nice." My forehead crunched into my eyes. "Be nice to the terrorist that tortured me, kidnapped my son, and ruined my life."

"I didn't mean it like that," he said. "Shit, man. I don't know. I just mean, like try being a little more gentle in your approach. He knows you're going to kill him, but maybe if you do the opposite of what he expects, you know? Make him think you see his perspective."

I tightened my arms against my chest. "Peterson doesn't like me when I'm me. Really me. Bubbly and smiling and happy. That's not what he wants to see. He enjoys watching me run circles around him, screaming at the sky."

"Then don't give it to him. Do the opposite of what he expects. Then cut his dick off."

I didn't agree on the idea of a seductive approach. But I kinda saw his point. Doing the opposite of what Peterson expected was how I got my son back.

"Maybe. Maybe," I said. "I don't know. That was kind of... that was hard. I can kill, but I'm not cut out for torture."

"Only sickos are." Brody glanced at Wyatt and Celena. "And animals."

I laughed and turned my gaze to the ground. "Hey, thanks by the way. For everything. Helping us bring them home, staying up all night to watch our prisoner."

"Don't thank me. They're my family. I'd die for either of them. I know I just met Micah, but family's kind of a big deal around here."

Forcing a smile, I said, "But listen, can we not talk about all that today? We will. We'll figure out how to go about questioning him, and deciding what questions we need answered, and... We'll get to all of that. But I've spent so long being stressed about everything with that bastard. I just need to..."

"Breathe?" Brody smiled. "Yeah. Sure, I won't mention it again."

I smiled back. "Thanks—"

"Laila, am I allowed to shift for Micah?" Celena called. "He wants to see it."

"You can shift in the woods and show him when you're in wolf form," I yelled.

"Told you," Jeremy said.

"Peeaase, Mommy?" Micah begged, grin so wide it reached either ear.

"You'll get scared," I said. "Maybe when you're a little older."

"I won't," Micah said. "I won't be scawed."

"C'mon, Lai. Bonding!" Celena grinned with a gesture between them.

"Peeeeaase," Micah insisted.

"It's really not scary as fast as we can do it," Wyatt yelled.

I rubbed my temple. "Ask your dad."

God damn, I had no clue how nice it would feel to say that.

CHAPTER THIRTY-SEVEN

JEREMY

A smile edged up my cheeks, breathing in the scent of barbecue from the grill before me. Warm air blew hair into my face. I looked out over the yard, squinting through the bright sun. Milly sat in the grass with Adam, Jenna, and Luka. She had the biggest, sweetest smile.

I knew she hadn't known her brother. But she was so happy to see him too. It was almost like she missed him.

"Jeremy," Rachel yelled from the edge of the house. I peeked around the corner. She carried an array of brightly colored bags, tissue paper spilling from their tops, and a large box. "Sweetie, where's Laila? I called her to help me bring stuff in—" I teleported in front of her and took the bags from her hands. She chuckled as I lifted the box. "But I should have just called you, huh?"

I smiled and gestured toward the house. "She's inside. Micah got mud all over him when he was running through the yard with Wyatt and Celena. She's getting him cleaned up."

"Oh, okay." She brushed ashy blond hair from her mint green eyes. "I should wait out here then, right? I don't want to walk in on her changing him with... Well, you know. The scars and everything."

"His aren't that bad. Just the tw—" I paused for a moment, only then putting it together.

I'd traced my fingers along every scar on Laila's body a thousand times. I'd tried to count them all once, but when I tried on her back, it was like counting the stars in the night sky.

But in that moment, I realized that she had twelve scars from the implants. So did Micah, and all the others.

"Just the what?" Rachel asked.

"Just from the implants. He doesn't have the ones on his back," I muttered. "But Laila caught you up on everything, right? The chewing, the Rickets disease?"

"Yeah, she told me. I'm not worried about it though, I Googled," she said. "He's young enough that the damage will reverse."

I set the bags on the table. "But otherwise, he's really good. Happiest kid in the world. He's a little shy, but you're family so he'll warm up to you pretty quick. He seems to understand that concept."

"I can't wait to meet him." She smiled, shoulders raising in glee. "I got him some toys. I don't know what he likes, but Laila said he liked music, so I got him one of those little xylophones. And a few stuffed animals that sing. But I grabbed a couple cars too because every little boy I've ever met likes toy cars. One's remote controlled. Maybe you can show him how it works."

"That'll probably end up being more my toy than his." I laughed.

"Well, then it'll go to good use." She placed her hands at her hips and looked around. "But where's this long-lost brother of yours?"

I looked past her to the fire pit where he stood with Brody assembling wood into a teepee. "Chris," I yelled.

"What?"

"Get over here."

He turned, and Rachel gasped. "Jesus, you two aren't twins?"

I laughed. "Nope, just strong genes. Two years apart."

"What do you want?" Chris asked as he drew closer.

It was funny how that sibling banter hadn't changed. This was the same way we interacted as teenagers. I'd wondered if it would be different, but really, the only difference was the fact that I was a parent now. Even so, our relationship stayed as it'd always been.

I laughed. "This is Laila's mom, Rachel. Rachel, this is my brother, Chris."

"Oh, it's nice to meet you." Chris extended his hand. But Rachel leaned forward and wrapped her arms around his chest. "Oh, okay. You're a hugger."

"She's Laila's mom." I smiled.

"Thank you." I heard her murmur. "Thank you so much."

"Yeah, sure." Chris awkwardly patted her back and sent me a 'help me' gaze over her shoulder. I stifled a laugh as she squeezed him tighter.

"Hey, Mom!" Laila yelled from the porch, hoisting Micah to her hip. "You want to meet your grandson?"

Chris released an awkward breath of relief as Rachel pulled away. She raised her hand to her mouth. Her mascara lined eyes overflowed with tears.

"Oh, c'mon now." Laila walked down the stairs with a smile. "No crying today. This is a good day."

Rachel wiped at the tears that engulfed her eyes. She continued to nod and fought the urge to sob. Laila laughed. "Mom, it's okay. Don't cry."

"What's wong?" Micah asked Rachel. "Is you okay?"

She laughed and gave another fast nod. "I'm just so happy to finally meet you."

"Mommy cwies when she's happy too sometimes." Micah smiled and looked up at Laila. He quietly murmured, "Who's she?"

"This is *my* mommy." Laila smiled. "That means that she's your grandma."

"Gamda?" Micah asked.

Laila laughed, turning to Rachel. "Milly and Luka haven't really come up with a name for you yet, huh?"

Rachel was still trying to collect herself as she said, "Not yet."

"How about Gam then?" she asked. "Can you say Gam, Micah?"

I couldn't help the smile that came to my lips. Me and my grandparents didn't have what any would call a good relationship. But I knew Rachel and Micah would. Rachel was one of the kindest, easiest going people I knew. I guess she had to be to be Laila's mom.

It just made me so happy. He hadn't yet, but I was going to make sure from here on out that he'd had better than I did. And Milly too. They had two parents that were crazy about them. Their grandma was going to be a huge part of their lives.

They were going to have the life that they deserved.

"Gam." He smiled. "I like youw haiw. It kinda looks like Daddy's."

Laila bit back a laugh.

Rachel looked at me, and her eyes widened. "My lord, you got gray quick."

"Yeah, well. Two kids'll do that to you." I roughed up Micah's hair.

He giggled.

"It's just a little bit of gray." Laila looked at the top of my head with a grin. "But I like it."

I smirked, leaned down, and touched my lips to hers. "Well, I'm not dying it, so you better."

She laughed as Rachel turned back to Micah. "I really like your hair too. And your eyes, my goodness those eyes are beautiful."

His cheeks turned red, leaning his head into Laila's chest. Rachel smiled, and Micah turned his head to the side a bit. He looked at Laila. "Is youw dad coming, Mommy?"

Her smile fell. "No. No, my dad's not coming. He passed away a few years before you were born."

"Oh," he murmured. He turned to me. "What about youw mom and dad, Daddy?"

I gave a sad smile and shook my head. "No, buddy. My mom and dad died a long time ago."

He thought hard for a minute. "I'm weally lucky then, wight? Because I have a mommy and a daddy."

I held my smile. "Yeah. Yeah, you are."

He laid his head back to Laila's chest and smiled. I looked her way. "We're just waiting on Ray, Lydia, and Helena now, right?"

"You didn't go to grab her?"

"I was supposed to?"

Her gaze narrowed. "Yes, Jeremy. You were supposed to."

"Then I'll be back." I leaned forward, touched my lips to hers, then kissed Micah's forehead.

CHAPTER THIRTY-EIGHT

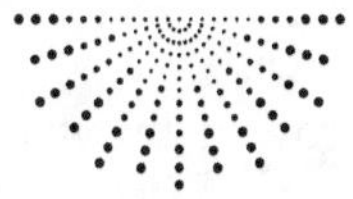

LAILA

Jeremy sat in a camping chair with Milly in his lap. Micah stood on the ground beneath him, tugging on a stick with Tink. The harder she pulled, even when it sent him toppling to the ground, the louder he laughed.

My smile just wouldn't go down.

This was it.

This was the dream. My husband, my kids, our dog, all in our backyard enjoying a spring day with our big family.

It brought my mind back to the Christmas before last. As I walked in the patio door and gazed at our family all together, breathing in the smell of fresh food, and listening to the music, and thinking, 'Micah deserves to see this. He deserves to be a part of this.'

And now, he was.

"Wow." Helena gazed over Micah. "I feel like I'm about to meet a celebrity."

I laughed, taking a gulp of water from my cup. "Well, he's a very Keanu Reeves kind of celebrity, you know? Sweet, happy, funny."

She chuckled, still looking over him with a gentle smile. "He was worth all that risk."

I smiled. "Yeah. Yeah, he was."

"And that fucker. You got him, right?" Helena asked.

"We got him," I said.

Her shoulders fell with relief. "And the other two are dead." I nodded. "And your baby's home."

My smile widened. "He is."

"So where's my seventy grand?" she asked.

Supposed I knew that was coming. And not like I had any intention of failing to pay her, but damn, bitch. She was just jumping straight in there.

I turned to her with furrowed brows. "Really? You need it right now?"

"Well, soon would be nice. I've only been waiting two damn years."

I huffed. "A year and a half. And you've got plenty of money from us in that time. You weren't struggling."

Helena scoffed, glancing at her polished stiletto fingernails. "Bitch, I haven't had a professional manicure in two months. Ya girl is struggling."

Her nails looked fine. Granted, I was no expert. I'd had my nails done in a salon maybe five times in my life. But still, they were pretty.

"When this is over, I'll go down to the safe and get your damn money," I said. "But I thought we were friends you know. You could have asked nicely."

"We are friends. You think I would've put my life on the line like this for someone who wasn't?"

"Well, you came out peachy-keen. So chill," I muttered.

"Yeah, yeah." As the back door swung open, she glanced at Ray and Lydia making their way down the steps. "Ya know, I've always wondered what that beauty looks like naked."

"Phenomenal." I glanced over him. "Perfect abs, big shoulders, tight butt. But his dick's pretty small. Still gets the job done though."

She cocked her head to the side. "You slept together?"

"Once," I said. "It was a good time. You should give it a try. He does this thing with his thumb, and my lord."

"I don't know that I'm really his type." Helena laughed. "I know your generation's pretty open to people like me. But ours isn't."

The way she said that implied that they were elderly. Neither of them were. Helena was in her early mid-life and Ray was still in his thirties. Still, I saw her point. Not that Ray was a homophobe to my knowledge, but he was also an asshole. He might be the type to say, 'I can't be with someone that used to have a penis.' But I could've just been making assumptions. I wasn't sure, we'd never exactly talked about the trans community.

"Hey, you won't know until you try." I dusted my hands on my pants. "But tonight probably isn't the best time. I'm about to tell him that we killed his wife."

"Oh, shit," she murmured. "Good luck with that one."

Ray caught my gaze. I struggled a smile, heading his direction. The smile in his slowly fell from his warm brown eyes. He knew.

He knew how this was going to end when Lydia made it back to him. He knew we'd kill her. But knowing something is *going* to happen and recognizing it once it's occurred are two very different things. Kind of like how I would feel when the world started to end.

Lydia's expression was different. She knew too, but her pale blue eyes looked relieved. Her shoulders that always seemed so harsh and stiff softened.

Maybe it sounds cruel to find relief at the death of your parent, but I understood. Amy tried to kill her. She helped that excuse for a man torture the toddler she was magically linked to. Amy prevented her from going to school, having friends, and simply living. I think if she'd have had the opportunity, she would have killed her mother herself.

"Where is he?" Lydia grinned with a look around. "He's here, right?"

"Over there with Jeremy." I smiled. "He's really excited to meet you."

She grinned and rushed past me. Ray waited until she was out of hearing distance. He opened his mouth but struggled to form words.

"It's over, Ray." I gave a sympathetic frown. He closed his mouth and slowly expelled a deep breath. "She's gone."

He drooped his head slightly. "Was it... It didn't hurt, did it?"

Truthfully, I didn't know. I'd hardly gotten a look at her before I burned the body. But I assumed it was fast, at least. It was certainly quicker than I'd have made it.

"Not for long," I murmured.

Ray was quiet for a moment. "Did she... Did she have anything to say? To me or Lydia, I mean."

"Her last words were, 'the shift has begun,'" I muttered. "Whatever the hell that means."

"Guess her prediction was wrong then, huh?" he murmured. "You didn't bring the three of us together after all."

Well, I'd brought the two of them together. Maybe he misunderstood what she said that day. Peterson knew I was going to kill him; Amy probably knew the same. Perhaps he'd misinterpreted what she meant before she went missing.

"I guess so."

"But I have her." He smiled toward Lydia with her arms around Micah. "This must have been what she meant."

"Yeah. Yeah, I guess."

"Still. Thank you," Ray said. "I wish things were different, but I have my baby back. And I'm glad you have yours."

I glanced at Micah, then to Milly. A soft smile came to my lips. "Micah's been dying to cut into that cake. Are you hungry?"

Ray gave a smile as if in answer.

We started toward Micah and Lydia, still tightly embracing one another. Jeremy gave me a sweet, almost sad smile. Micah's eyes stayed closed against Lydia's long dark curls. Her arms around him were tighter than a lock.

It must've been so strange for them. But at least I knew that they would have a friend in one another. Eleven years apart in age or otherwise, they knew what the other had been through. They could always relate on what it was like to spend so many of those young years in that awful place.

"I bet it's nice to finally see each other face to face." I smiled down at them.

Lydia leaned back. Micah opened his eyes, and Lydia raised her hand to cup his cheek. Tears surged from her eyes, smile coming to her lips.

"I was so worried about you," Lydia murmured. "I felt you get hurt, and then you were just gone and I... I wasn't sure if you were okay. But you are, huh? You're alright."

"I okay." Micah smiled. "Is you okay? You's cwying."

Lydia smiled. She gave a fast nod. "Yeah. Yeah, I'm okay. I'm just so happy to see you."

Micah looked up at Jeremy. "Why do giwls cwy when they'we happy?"

He laughed. "Boys cry when they're happy sometimes too."

"Do you?" Micah asked.

"Sometimes." Jeremy smiled.

"I don't think we've met." Chris extended his hand to Ray. "Who are you again?"

"Ray Ramirez," he said. "We've met actually. But you wouldn't remember that, I guess."

"Ah." Chris pressed his lips together. "Well, I'm sorry for whatever whoever was in my body did to you. But it's nice to meet you."

"Yeah. Yeah, you too."

"Chris, this is the guy that got us looking for you. He's the one that made us question whether or not you and the other survivors were still out there somewhere," Leah said. "He started it all."

"That I did," Ray muttered.

Grateful for it or not, that still must've been one hell of a cross to bear. I'd been angry at him over the years for leading us to what caused me to lose my son. But had it not been for that day at the back of Moe's, had he not caught me on film using my powers, we wouldn't have known that Chris was alive. We wouldn't have saved the hundreds of others Peterson had been holding.

I'd never be happy that I missed out on those years with my baby. Nothing could take away the regret I'd always feel from it. But I had my baby back now.

And nothing would ever take him from me again.

Chris smiled. "I guess I owe you one then."

"I've got everything that I need," Ray said. "Thank you though."

"Hey, everybody," Max's voice called from the side of the house. He toted a few intricately wrapped boxes in his arms, struggling against Tink jumping at his legs. "Can I get a little help back here?"

I teleported to him, pulled Tink from his legs, and grabbed the boxes on top. "Down, Tink."

She huffed and scampered off. Max's eyes met mine. His lips heightened into the biggest smile. "How ya doing?"

"I'm great." I smiled. "Amazing, actually."

He smiled, glancing at Micah over my shoulder. "That him?"

"Come on. Come meet him."

CHAPTER THIRTY-NINE

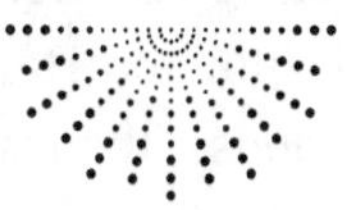

JEREMY

As the night went on, we laughed and sang. When Chris and I played our guitars, Micah put his finger over Chris's lips and told him 'shhh.' Then we laughed. We danced. We talked. We ate. It was like Christmas without the eggnog. But we had hot chocolate and music and a cloudless night sky.

Most importantly though, we had each other.

It felt surreal. Joyous and peace filled, but almost as if it wasn't my life. I'd grown so used to fighting a battle. I spent so long thinking I couldn't win. I didn't think I'd get it all. But somehow, I did.

I got the girl. We brought our son home. We had our daughter. We found my brother. We made it.

Or so I thought.

The past three years had essentially been a prologue for the next twenty-six.

***

"So mission finally accomplished. Want to celebrate?" Adam extended a joint to me.

I took a sip from my water and looked at Micah running after Wyatt in the field. "Nah, I'm good. I don't want to be foggy today, ya know?"

"Yeah, of course." Adam raised his hand back to his lips and took another hit. "When do I need to be here tomorrow? That is still going down, right?"

"As far as I know," I said. "Haven't heard otherwise so I'm assuming. I'm meeting them at the gates to give them the necklaces at eleven. Everyone else is coming back to the house, but you're going to be waiting in the basement with him and Helena. She'll put up the spell, you teleport her back to our house, then we give them the clear to go through."

"Got it," Adam murmured. "Do you guys want me to, like, try and record these guys or something? So we can try and piece together who they are?"

"No, they're telepaths. As strong of telepaths as us. I know you'd be strong enough to keep them from making you believe they're decent if they're not, but they'd know if we tried to go against our deal," I said. "It's not worth it. Honestly, I don't give a shit who they are. We're letting everybody and their mother torture the guy, why not let one more."

"That's true. But aren't you curious?"

"I'm more concerned about the lunatic linked to a god who hates us so badly he set up the entire apocalypse around my wife and kids," I said. "If they want to interrogate him, that means they're looking for information too."

"Yeah, but that's why I think we should set them up. Maybe we're just not asking the right questions."

"Or maybe, the wrong person asked the right questions." I glanced at Laila playing with Milly and Luka. "She's the only one he's going to talk to, and she's not ready for that. And I know she hates him but..."

"Torturing someone isn't easy," Adam murmured. "It's been a while for me too. Kind of makes me nauseous these days. I prefer the less invasive options. Starvation, dehydration, psychological torture. I don't like the blood and gore."

"Yeah, me neither." That look on Micah's face when he'd wet the bed that morning flashed behind my eyes. I clenched my hand to a fist. "But the bastard deserves it."

Adam took a sip from his beer. He blew out a quiet breath before he turned to meet my gaze. "What happened in there anyway?"

"He punched me around a little bit. He stabbed Lai. And I had this memory from our past life. The first one, when we were gods or whatever. After she died, I tried to bring her back then too. But I couldn't find her there. She was just... I don't know, she wasn't there. And I think he did it. He moved her soul somewhere so that I couldn't bring her back. We started arguing, but I don't know what we were saying. Whatever language that was doesn't exist anymore. If it does, I've never heard it, and I'm fluent in at least fifty."

"Well, yeah. Some alien language that existed thousands of years ago probably doesn't exist anymore. Shit, Latin's not even close to as old as this planet. And it's dead."

"Really wish I had a Rosetta Stone for it though. It wasn't the language we spoke in the dreams where we were fucking either. It was harsher. Kind of like Enochian, but a little different? But the other one was closer to Gaelic, even, but softer. More dainty, you know?" I paused. "And alien isn't a fair word."

"Well, that's what you were."

"Technically, that's what we all are."

"Yeah, but you remember being an alien."

"Not really. I just remember fucking my wife and then watching her die."

"Still."

"Hey guys," a quiet voice said behind us. I turned, and there Mary stood. She wore her hair tied back in a neat bun at the back of her head. Her flowing gray blouse rested neatly above her finely pressed black slacks. A soft, nearly sad smile pulled up her creamy white cheeks. "I'm sorry I'm late. I didn't miss all the fun, did I?"

But I smiled back.

I didn't care about the last few years that much anymore. None of that mattered now. I had my kids. I had my wife. My life was good, and

I didn't see the use in holding a grudge. Dealing with a shitty in-law was just a part of the territory.

Plus, I knew how much this moment would mean to my brother. With Annie gone, Mary was the only one he had left to view as a parent. I had Rachel, but he had Mary.

"Well, hello, stranger," Laila called from her seat at the fire.

Chris stood beside her and met Mary's gaze. She smiled. He teleported in front of her and wrapped his arms around her shoulders. She tightened hers round him and closed her eyes against his chest. He leaned his head toward hers, beginning to cry as her face screwed up in remorse. "God, I missed you so much, kid."

"I missed you, too," he barely whispered, embracing one another a moment longer.

"Look at you, you're a man now." Mary smiled, pulled back, and looked at him. "God, you look so much like your dad. So do you." She glanced at me. "But you've always got that hair in your eyes." I laughed as she turned back to Chris. "How are you?"

"I'm good." He wiped his cheeks. "I'm really good."

She cupped his face in her hand and smiled. Her head bobbed in a fast nod. Then, for the first time in my life, I saw Mary break down. Tears bubbled from her eyes, her shaking hands hoisted around his shoulders, and she squeezed tight on the tips of her toes. She laid her head against his chest again as he moved his arms around her upper back. "I'm so sorry."

"It's okay," Chris murmured with closed eyes. "It's okay, I get it."

"Who's that?" Micah appeared beside me.

I jumped, heaving in a gasp. "Jesus Christ."

"Finally got a taste of your own medicine." Laila smiled, running her hand over Micah's hair.

I chuckled, shaking my head. Then Chris pulled back from Mary. She wiped her eyes, and Chris smiled. "C'mon, come meet Micah."

She forced a smile, lowering herself to his height. Micah rested his head against Laila's hip. "Well, hello."

"Hi," Micah said.

"Micah, this is my other mom," Laila said.

Mary's brows wrinkled, more tears forming in her eyes. "You've never called me that before."

Laila raised a brow over her smile. "Should I not call you that?"

Mary smiled. "No. No, please do."

I supposed it wasn't just me who'd managed to let go of the past.

Laila returned her smile. She looked down at Micah and back to Mary. "What do you want him to call you? Gam's taken so you've got to go another direction."

Mary smiled, leaning down so they were at eye level. "Well, that's up to you. What would you like to call me? Grandma? Mary? Granny, maybe?"

He smiled, looking her over. "I can name you anything?"

She laughed. "Within reason."

"Hmm." He thought for a moment. "You's a Angel, huh?"

A slow sigh left Mary's lips. "No, not anymore."

"That won't wowk then." He thought a moment longer. He looked over her and turned his head to the side. "You'we Mommy's mommy, wight?" Mary nodded, and he continued, "How 'bout Mommy two?"

Mary laughed. "I don't think that one will work. How about we just stick to Mary? Can you say Mary?"

"Mawy," he said. "I can say that."

"There you have it then. Mary it is." She smiled. She pulled a little necklace from her pocket. "I didn't have time to get to the store to buy you a toy. But I really wanted to bring you a present, so I found you this."

He opened his palm, and she laid a small rope chain inside. The gem that hung on the rope was a dark stone that looked black but reflected a near purple color when the flames of the fire hit it just right. "This was your grandpa's a really long time ago. He gave it to me, but I think I want you to have it."

"Weally?" he asked.

Mary smiled. "I think he'd like that."

"What is that?" Laila glanced at the gem. "Looks like the same thing Milly's pram is made from."

"It is." Mary stood, meeting Laila's gaze. "Elvan ore. That necklace in particular, at least according to Luka, was centuries old."

Elvan ore.

That's what that shit all over the Fae Realm had been. I didn't know what it meant, or what it was, not really. But that name sounded familiar.

"No shit," she murmured.

"Can I weaw it, Mommy?" Micah asked.

"Sure, kiddo."

CHAPTER FORTY

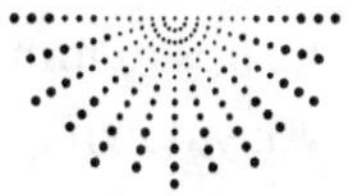

LAILA

Heat from Milly and Micah's sleeping bodies radiated warmth toward mine. I breathed in the soft, baby smell of lavender, eyes drifting over them. Their damp hair against their silky skin, the gentle rise and fall of their chests, and—of course—Tinkerbell curled at their legs.

I laughed. "I think we're going to need a bigger bed."

"We could just slide Micah's right over here and make it a super king." Smiling, Jeremy sat down on the other side of the kids and propped himself on his elbow.

"Might need to custom-make some sheets." I smiled.

"And a plastic sheet," he muttered. "I put the one we used for Milly's birth back on, by the way. Just to be safe. Don't want a repeat of this morning."

It still infuriated me that he was so scared over something so small. But at least he was here. Curled beside me, sleeping soundly. Maybe more peaceful than he'd ever slept in his life.

I bit my lip, letting out a slow sigh. "Yeah, I think it's going to take him a while to see how different we are. But kids adapt quickly, he'll be okay in a few months."

"Hopefully he doesn't remember any of the past three years by this time next year, ya know?"

"I hope," I murmured. My gaze shifted over him for a moment. "But it doesn't matter. As long as he's here, it doesn't matter."

He smiled. "Yeah. You're right."

A yawn escaped my lips, and I rubbed my eyes. "I'm beat though. I'm going to get some sleep. Can you get the light after you brush your teeth?"

"Sure, baby." He touched his lips to mine. "I love you, sleep tight."

"I love you too." I smiled. I lay down and pulled the blankets up to my neck.

The aroma of burning trees and charred skin wafted into my nostrils. Screams soared around me as hot blood splashed against my face. I spat the iron taste from my mouth.

Struggling my knees into the hot sand, I pushed my hips downward against the bloodied, writhing man, fighting with every muscle to keep him still. My gaze rapidly shifted to the men and women wearing thick, dusty black armor around me—almost invisible through the thick smog—instructing in a language I couldn't understand. They grabbed ahold of the man's body and held him down. Bright light illuminated from my palm into the oozing wound in the man's chest.

He sobbed in agony at my hand over his skin. But the blood kept pulsing from the gaping hole. And I shoved my hand into it. I felt the contraction of his abdominal muscles, the warmth of his blood, and the gooey texture of his organs beneath my palm. My fingers grasped ahold of something—perhaps an intestine—pulsing warm liquid. The white light erupted from my palm once more, illuminating within his body like human lamp.

Or maybe not human; I couldn't be sure what the man was.

His screams grew louder than any screech I'd ever heard. But I held onto that organ in my palm with everything I had. I felt the pulse gushing fluid beneath my finger slowly fade before I pulled my palm back to the external wound and let the light seal it shut.

Once I finished, the man expressed something I assumed meant thank you. I smiled, stood, and looked around.

"Véa!" a deep voice called. My head spun around. The men and women who helped hold the man down formed a circle around me. I pushed past them to the sound of his voice. He thrusted one of the guard's aside, grasped my hand, and barked to the people around me.

Jeremy. Not the one lying in bed beside me, but the soul beneath the flesh.

I couldn't mistake those round, vibrant blue eyes in any life.

His long black hair matted with blood and dust hung around his face. I wasn't sure if it was smog from the scene around us or placed there intentionally for aesthetic, but dark gray shadows covered his forehead and framed his eyes. His skin was nearly pink from the bright blue sun in the smoky sky, yet dusty and coated in both wet and dried blood. He wore no armor nor shirt like the others, only a leather garment that wrapped around his hips in the form of a skirt. But his arms and torso were covered in a series of cuts, some large and some small. He held a large sword in his opposite hand, passing it to me before he pulled another from a holster at the back of his hip.

I reached out to heal a cut on his wrist. But he caught my hand and yelled over the clangs of swords and ear-piercing screams. "Nay," and then a bunch of nonsense I couldn't make out. I nodded as he said something else. He kept ahold of my hand and turned.

His fingers stayed tight around mine. He started pulling me through the battleground. But it was unlike anything I'd ever seen.

Fire shot from people's hands, electricity from others, even water in some. Cracks formed along the black sand, then spliced open, swallowing warriors whole and closing as quick as they opened.

But my heart wasn't racing nearly as fast as it would have if this were happening in my own life. Her hands weren't trembling, her stomach wasn't aching.

This was normal to her.

Or me.

Whatever, Véa.

A large, slender hunk of silver glinted before my eyes. I released his hand, ducked, and raised the sword in my palm upward between the man's legs. A deep grunt fell from the man's lips. I ripped the blade back, shower of hot crimson raining down around me. Then Jeremy—or Nix, rather—slid his blade through the man's neck, severing his head from his body.

He turned to me, grasped my shoulder, and looked quickly between my eyes. He said something, which I couldn't repeat if I tried, but the expression told me exactly what he asked. The same face he made every time he said it in this life.

Asking if I was okay.

I nodded. I grabbed ahold of his shoulders and swiftly lifted us above the crowd. His hand gripped my hip as if his life depended on it. Although, I supposed it did. He couldn't exactly fly without me. But hell, I didn't know shit about this life. Maybe he could.

Arrows and other projectiles I don't have names for flew toward us. But he formed a thin film of electricity around us in the shape of a sphere. I yelled something. He yelled back, pointing to the edge of the battlefield. I directed us toward it, moving faster than I'd ever flown in my current life. He gripped my hip so hard; I was sure it'd leave a bruise.

Then we landed in less than a second. Effortlessly, might I add, as though I'd done it a million times.

A man kneeled over a woman, struggling heaving gasps into her lungs. Her salt and pepper hair left her fair skin paper white. She had the same big blue eyes as the man beside me, blinking hard at the red, smoke tainted sky above. A hole of crimson bubbled beneath her hand just beneath her breast covered in a thin, chainmail like bikini top.

There was no denying the resemblance. Those eyes were identical to the man I'd just flown over the field with. She was his mother.

And the moment I saw her, my stomach sunk.

I'd just had my hand inside of a man's gut, and it didn't make me feel the way seeing this woman did.

I knew her. Or rather, Véa knew her. And I cared for her.

He dropped beside her first, taking her hand in his.

But I froze. Just watching the blood bubble beneath her palm as her lips dulled into the pastiness of her cheeks.

An emotion boiled through me. Not fury, not even fear. But... guilt, perhaps.

I didn't know why; I couldn't hear Véa's thoughts. I could only see and feel what she experienced in that moment. But staring down at that woman, my body felt like it was dissolving. Blame, guilt.

Had Véa been responsible for this?

"Véa." He looked up, big blue eyes full of water. His lip quivered. His voice came out as a shaking plea. "Cabrhu."

I swallowed hard, giving a nod. I dropped down beside them, reached up, and touched the woman's clammy cheek. She made what she could of a smile, murmuring something in that language I'd still yet to understand. I laughed softly and gave a nod. I took her palm from her chest and put mine over it.

As the white light radiated to her skin, her dazed eyes widened. A cry like nails on a chalkboard left her lips.

I yelled to the men and women in armor around us. They fell to the ground and grasped her body to the sand. When the wound struggled to heal, I did as I'd done with the last man. My fingers slid into the gap —feeling between her ribs for the source of the blood. When I came across a thumping pulse of slimy fluid, I let my hand light back up.

She kept shaking, instinctively trying to push us off of her as Nix continued holding her face in his bloody hands. Her cries weren't of pure agony, but something else. Betrayal, almost.

Friendly fire, maybe?

No, couldn't be. She had at least ten guards around her. None of her own people would have done it; she was as surrounded as I'd been.

As I kept healing, she struggled through sobs and screams to speak with him. He shook his head again and again, saying 'nay' as if that was the only word he knew.

But the longer I healed, the faster my heart raced. She wasn't healing, not fast enough. Not as fast as the last man had, maybe half the speed.

And then, from above fell a large, silver, precisely aimed sword.

He saw it. I saw it. We both tried to grab it, but it fell too fast.

Straight through her sternum, no more than three inches from my palm inside of her.

An audible gasp left his lips. His jaw fell open, eyes wider than the sky. He shook his head fast.

Her bright blue eyes stared at it for a second. She looked at me. She murmured something that sent a swirl to the pit of my stomach. My throat grew tight as she looked back up to him, words barely leaving her lips.

Then Nix turned to the soldiers around us and screamed a loud, deep command. Most of them took off with swords drawn while a few waited for my direction. I was about to say something when the woman spoke and immediately pulled my attention to her.

"Looks," she said.

Or at least, that's what it sounded like she said.

I yelled something to the man who sat on the other side of her. He grabbed ahold of the sword. Nix nodded to me. He began to sing to her.

If his appearance hadn't been enough evidence for me to realize who that was, his voice was plenty. It was nearly identical to the voice that'd sung me and our children to sleep a thousand times before.

I gestured to the man across from me. He swiftly raised the sword from her chest. I jammed my fingers into the bloody opening, now holding two hands inside the woman's body.

She gasped and gargled, but I kept healing. And he kept singing.

Then, she stopped shaking. She stopped screaming. Blood stopped oozing, but the wounds didn't close.

It hadn't worked. She was gone, and we both knew it. But I kept going because I watched his eyes close, and his brows scrunch down. He was trying to bring her back.

His eyes stayed shut, but his head turned slightly from one side to the other. As if he were searching.

"Nay." He shook his head as his eyes opened. "Nay. Nay, nay, nay."

I couldn't heal a corpse. And evidently, he couldn't bring her back.

Only then did I pull my hands out of the woman's chest. He shook his head, cascades of warm salt water sliding down his smog and blood splattered cheeks. "Nay." A few quiet sobs left his lips. He lifted her body against him, closing his eyes.

Water welled in mine too. My throat was so tight now, it felt like I could barely bring air through it. Swirls spun in the pit of my stomach. I had to press my lips together to keep them from quivering.

I wiped my bloody hands on the tiny shorts that barely covered my ass. I reached my hand out to touch his shoulder.

He looked up, tears pearling from his big blue eyes. Then a quiet murmur left his lips. I placed my hand over hers.

Only then did I notice the vine wrapped around each of our wrists. I wrapped my fingers between hers and murmured a tongue I *did* know a bit of. Elvan. But I only knew it because it was the exact same words Kai had said at his aunt's funeral last year.

From the ground our flesh has come, to the ground our flesh returns. Rest now; and find your place amongst the stars until we meet once more.

The vine at her hand quickly grew, spiraling around her wrist and gradually expanding up her arm. It slid along her shoulder, coiling around her torso. It grew to her other arm, and then either leg. Last, it coiled up her neck and around her face. Before I knew it, her body was wrapped in dark green vines like cloth over a mummy.

Once her body was covered, he gently lowered her to the ground. He leaned down, pressed his lips to her vine covered head, and started to his feet. I stood beside him and put a hand on his sweaty, firm back. His forehead wrinkled, his jaw tightened—fighting the urge to sob— and he gave a nod. He raised his sword, yelled something to the guards, and the two of us charged back into the battlefield.

CHAPTER FORTY-ONE

JEREMY

I squinted through the blue sun, eyes shifting around the massive garden. I waved my hand beneath my arm pit, wiping the other across the sweat beading at my forehead. Along with my body odor, the familiar floral scent I couldn't forget from the Fae Realm wafted into my nostrils.

It wasn't our Realm of Light though, the sun told me that much. After a second or two, I put it together and realized I was on the world we'd taken bits from to form our own ecosystem in the Fae Realm.

Or at least, in a memory from that world.

A voice said something behind me. It sounded a lot like Scottish Gaelic but wasn't quite on the money. It was a bit lighter, it seemed to roll right off the tongue.

But, for the first time, I understood it.

Not just a word or phrase, but each and every syllable. And somehow, it auto translated in my mind. Exactly the way that it did when I heard someone speaking French or Spanish and I had to verbalize it to someone who spoke English.

"Nix," the voice said. I turned and a smile pulled at my lips. He was a burly man with short gray hair and a long flowing beard. His skin was a dark chestnut, heavily tanned, but had no sunspots. His eyes sparkled a soft shade of violet. He stood at least two feet shorter than me but had to have been three times as wide. "Ye aren't a lad no more, are ye?"

I smiled. "And you're just as old as you've always been."

He reached his hand to the back of my neck and pulled my forehead down to touch his. I laughed and patted his back, looking between his eyes with a smile. I took a step back and gestured to the sky. "I've missed it here, you know. I haven't seen a blue sun in far too long."

"This place has missed you." He smiled wider. Then sighed, glancing behind me. "It's gonna miss her too."

I frowned. "She hasn't confirmed yet."

"Aye, but she will. She don't have much of a choice, do she?"

"No. I suppose she doesn't."

He pressed his lips together. He struggled a smile. "You're taking the oath, aren't you?" His purple gaze shifted between mine. "You'll be her watchman?"

"Should she go through with it," I said. "Aye."

He grasped my shoulder, squeezing it firm. "She's yer folk, lad. When you take that oath, don't take it for him. Take it for yer people, just as she's taking this oath for all of ours."

I gave a half laugh. "You sound just like my mum, you know that?"

He didn't smile. His eyes grew firm, serious. "I mean it, Nix. When ye take that vow, ye're not just taking it because she's the queen of your father's land. Ye're taking it because she's the queen of both. Or she will be. Ye keep her safe from all things, even the new folk that'll call her their queen."

Slowly, I hardened my gaze too. I grasped his shoulder just as he grasped mine. It wasn't an intimidating motion. That may have been how one would interpret it in my current life, but there was a familial attachment to the way it was done. It felt almost... Reassuring.

"I'm no child now, Dem," I murmured. "Why do you think I agreed to take the vow? I know what her life means."

His eyes shifted between mine for a long moment. Studying me. He gave a firm nod. He squeezed my shoulder once more. Then dropped it to his side. A smile came to his lips.

I did the same, smiling back. "This doesn't have to be a bad thing, pa. This could be a wonderful change for both worlds."

"I'd have believed that if he hadn't have given her an ultimatum."

Something spun in my stomach. I opened my mouth to speak once more, but the scrape of stone against stone sounded behind me.

Turning, I took in the building that had been behind me. I'd spent so long marveling at the sun and pretty flowers, I hadn't even noticed the castle I stood before.

It stood at least ten levels high, solid black but reflecting purple in the sun's rays. Terraces climbed the rounded towers and sparling walls. Vines and ivies of deep sage and forest greens descended from their railings. Budding hues of blues, pinks, and oranges peeked through the foliage. Despite how depressing a black castle sounds, those touches of nature made it feel so inviting and alive.

But as beautiful as they may have been, they didn't come close to the beauty of the woman pushing open the massive black door with her rounded hip.

Her wide, thick lips were nearly the color of blood. Two vibrant emeralds shined through the brown curls that hung along her blushed, milky cheeks. Those curls had to have doubled the size of her head. Wild, majestic, and gorgeous.

A forest green—entirely sheer—thin-strapped dress fell from her shoulders to the bare soles of her bare feet. Over one shoulder rested a small brown sack tied shut with a hemp like rope. It extenuated the deep curve of her waist into her hips, not hiding a single detail of her physique. Her pale pink nipples pressed firmly against the fabric before her small but perky breasts.

My eyes lingered there a moment too long, stomach flipping.

She didn't seem to care though. She just smiled and met my gaze. "I'm sorry, I'm running a bit behind schedule today."

I smiled, lowering my upper half in a bow. "There's no rush, do gràs. Take all of the time you need."

"Well, that's kind of you, but I'm about ready now. We're just waiting on my brother." She smiled and extended her hand to mine. "Véa."

"Aye, I know who you are." I smiled back and shook her hand in mine. "Nix."

"It's a pleasure to meet you, Nix." She put one hand to her hip, using the other to lift her long brown locks from one side of her head to the other. "So my betrothed couldn't be bothered with the duty of collecting his wife, eh?"

I chuckled. She arched a brow, and I cleared my throat. "My brother doesn't do well with travel."

"Brother." Her gaze narrowed slightly. She tilted her head to the side. "The bastard prince then. Fria's son."

My lips pressed together, giving a nod "Aye. That's me."

"We like this one, Véa." Dem patted my back. "Play nice."

Smiling, she put her hand at her hip. "I wasn't being rude."

"That's quite alright, I am what I am." I smiled and gestured toward the bag over her shoulder. "Do you need help with that?"

"Nay." She made a face. "Why would I?"

I gave a gentle laugh and shook my head.

"Because I'm a woman?" She turned her head to the side with a smile. "So I must be so ill functioned that I ken not to carry my own bag, is that right?"

"Nay, do gràs," I said. "Nay, just being polite."

She smiled and placed her hands at her hips.

Jesus Christ, she was so much like my Laila. That sweet face, that bubbly demeanor, but that harsh attitude, all with a grin across her lips. There was no denying it. And even then, I loved it. It was adorable yet intimidating in the same instant.

She turned to the building and called, "Venark!"

"Aye-yeah!" a man's voice called. "I'm coming!"

"They've both a habit of tardiness," Dem said. "Ye'll get used to it."

A smile pulled at her lips. "He speaks lies, today was the exception."

I laughed. "Of course, do gràs."

"You could have at least left me your flask." A man jogged out the large black door. And there was no denying that man was her brother. The bright green eyes, the dark brown curls that hung just below his ears, the same fair skin. "You won't be needing it where you're going."

"Oh, love, I'll be needing it more than ever," Véa said. She turned to me. "Nix, this is my brother Venark. Venark, this is Nix, my soon to be brother."

That thought sent an unpleasant turn to my stomach.

Mine, Jeremy's. Not Nix's.

"My new colleague, correct?" I asked.

"Aye." Venark put his hands at the hips of his drop-crotch pants and smiled. "Happy to know one of our own already holds a place in your people's army. Might make the transition a bit lighter, don't you think?"

I laughed. "I do hope."

Véa smiled. She reached onto the tips of her toes and leaned toward me. Butterflies flapped in my stomach as her fingertips brushed the blue-black hair that hung in my face behind my ear. A smile edged up her cheeks, fingertips grazing the top. "You ought to pull your hair back and show off your points, love."

I felt my cheeks warm, letting out a quiet laugh as I pulled my hair back to where it'd been. As I did, I felt a sharp peak at its tip. "Best we get prepared for the egress then, eh?"

Damn. Hadn't seen that one coming.

Elvan. I was Elvan in that life.

Judging by the high ceilings and thick, Elvan Ore walls like I'd seen in the Fae Realm, I assumed we were now within the castle. That warm, sticky breeze from outside blew in from the window Véa stood before. She gazed out of the night darkened green fields, hair fluttering in the wind.

And I... I looked at her. More specifically, I looked at her ass. Her round, firm...

I cleared my throat. "You could rest for a while, if you'd like, do gràs. I could have your brother wake you when it's time."

She turned over her shoulder, gave a smile, and shook her head. "I don't think I could sleep if I wanted to."

"No?" I leaned against a table with a smile. "Too excited for the big day?"

Véa let out a huff of a laugh. "Something like that."

I chewed my lip. "You really don't want to do this, do you?"

A slow sigh left her nose. She ran her fingers through her hair, whooshing it from one side to the other. "I... I want peace and safety for my people." She gestured over me. "For *our* people."

"Mm." My gaze turned to the Elvan ore floors beneath my feet. "Well, I know him better than anyone. What do you want to know?"

She leaned against the window. Her arms crossed against her chest. "What's he like?"

"Smart. Very smart. Well-liked by just about every person he meets. Mostly kind, but can be aggressive at times." I looked around in thought for a moment. "He doesn't snore, so that's good." Véa laughed, and a smile pulled at my lips. "He's a good man, do gràs."

"In your entirely subjective opinion, of course." I laughed that time, and she smiled. She fell quiet. After a moment, she turned up to meet my gaze. "Is he a good warrior?"

I chuckled. "In his own way. He does better in courtroom than with a sword."

Her face said she didn't appreciate that. "He doesn't fight with his people?"

"He fights *for* his people," I said. "We all have our parts to play, do gràs."

"And what will mine be then? I am more than a diplomat; I will not watch my people fight battles that I refuse."

My gaze stayed soft. "We do have women in our armies."

"But not queens."

I cleared my throat and rubbed a hand over my mouth. "Because there hasn't been before doesn't mean there won't be now. And I was appointed for a reason. I think he expects you to feel this way."

Watching me carefully a second or two, she then expelled a slow breath. "It won't be an argument then."

"I doubt it. Lux knows your ways, our people's ways. I'm sure he can accept some of them." I looked over her bare physique beneath her dress. My eyes struggled not to catch on her nipples pushed against the fabric. I'd barely classify it as lingerie, even in our day and age. Though technically covered, nothing was hidden. "But your attire probably will not be one of them."

Véa placed her hands on either side of the sill along the window, showing off every inch of her attire. She narrowed her gaze and gave a playful grin. "You don't like my dress?"

"No, I do." I smiled. "But I'm accustomed to both worlds. I hold a greater understanding of the culture than my brother."

Her brow arched. "The affectionate way of saying he'd think me a whore if I arrive in this?"

I laughed. "I wouldn't say that. But... He may ask you to dress a little different."

"I refuse to wear a bodice." She crossed her arms against her chest. "I like to breathe, and I plan to continue to do so."

I chuckled. "I think he'll compromise so long as you're covered. It's not quite as warm as you're used to either, you may appreciate the layers."

She rolled her eyes. She murmured Elvan beneath her breath and shook her head. Her gaze turned back out the window.

"My apologies, do gràs," I said. "Have I offended you?"

"Nay." Her head shook as another slow sigh left her lips. "This is going to be quite an adjustment for me."

"Aye. Aye, an adjustment for everyone."

Véa said nothing for a moment. "Does he plan to take a second wife?"

"I believe he does."

"And I'm expected to share only his bed?" she asked.

I cleared my throat and nodded again.

She scoffed, rolling her eyes. "Yet my dress makes me a whore."

"If it helps at all, you should know that many of us have hopes in this union. Bringing about a new way. Many of the women especially." I felt for the cool, smooth flask in my pocket. I lifted it before me.

Like just about everything else here, it was made from Elvan Ore. I pulled off the cork and took a sip. I have no clue what it was made from, but it was the worst liquor I ever tasted in my life. Stronger than rubbing alcohol.

As I tasted it on my own tastebuds, not Nix's, I grew so annoyed. It was as real as if I were living that moment. I felt that humid breeze coming in from the window, I could smell that honeysuckle in the air, I could taste that liquor. But I didn't know what Nix was thinking, and it was fucking frustrating.

I took a few steps forward and offered it to her. Her green eyes met mine as she grabbed it. "This marriage could make a big difference in our world. A woman as strong as you beside a man as culturally powerful as he." I smiled and raised my shoulders. "Banrig Vèa Matri-aza." *Queen Véa of Heaven.*

She huffed. "I preferred Queen of the Fae folk."

"A merging of peoples means you still will be. The hand of the king, your watchman, is half Elvan. This is... This could be a great thing."

"Mm." She raised a brow, gazing out into the wonders of the green land. She raised the flask to her lips and tilted her head back.

Chug.

Chug.

She lifted the bottle above her mouth and shook the few remaining drops to her tongue. Her gaze flicked back to mine. "If you're Fria's son, you've got more than one." She raised her palm and wiggled her fingers, giving a faint smile.

I laughed, reached into my back pocket, and set another flask in her hand. She smiled, pulled the cork, and took another sip.

"You've got good taste." She wiped her lip and passed it back. She blew out a slow, shaking breath. "I suppose I should try and get some rest after all."

"Aye." I gave a smile. "I'll be here. Sleep well, do gràs."

"Thank you." She looked between my eyes for a moment, returning my smile, gazing over my features. "I have a feeling you and I are going to be good friends, Nix."

"I suppose we'll have to be if it's my job to follow you around, eh?" My smile lifted higher. "Otherwise we'll both be miserable."

"Oh, I'm sure I'll be miserable regardless." Her smile grew a bit teasing. "But it's better to be miserable together than alone, don't you think?"

I laughed. "I'm not miserable."

Still smiling, she huffed. "Goodnight, Nix."

She brushed past me to the door. As it opened, she cleared her throat and turned to meet my gaze with a curious expression. "This may seem like an odd question. But you are older than your brother, no?"

"Aye, I am."

"Then why aren't you king?" Her head tilted. "Why is it your brother who's made the proposition?"

Shrugging, I forced a smile. "Can't give that much power to blood like ours."

Her brows fell further in question. "But it is your birthright."

"On your world. My mother's world." I smiled. "But bastards don't get kingdoms. And I'm not one for kingship either way."

She licked her lips, gaze traveling over me. "That's a shame."

CHAPTER FORTY-TWO

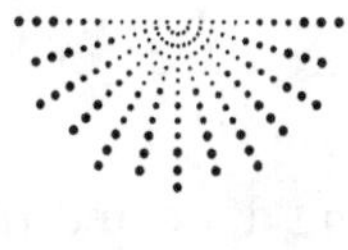

LAILA

Bright light shined in through the white curtains. The smell of the warm cotton sheets mixed with Tink's fur and wisped up my nose. Milly's fingers traced along my upper arm, suckling on the binky behind her lips.

But I just lay there creasing my brows at what the fuck I just witnessed.

A warrior.

That's what Peterson said, he was teaching me to be fearless. To be ready. To be a warrior.

That's what I was at one point. A damn good one, from what I'd seen. So was Jeremy. His mother was killed in a battle. But why was I the one to see that? Wouldn't it have made more sense to show it to him?

Although, his flashbacks seemed to revolve around me. But mine didn't have a pattern. They certainly weren't chronological. The last had been a sex dream, and then of a battlefield. I suppose the first was also a slaughter.

After an hour of silently staring at the ceiling, Jeremy stirred beside me. He wiped his eyes and yawned. He turned to see if I was still sleeping. When he realized that I wasn't, his thoughts echoed in my mind.

Let's go talk on the patio.

Did you remember something? I asked. He nodded. *Me too.*

My wide eyes shifted over the mist settling over the green grass. I gave an ironic laugh, rubbing my hand against my face. "I was the queen of the fairies."

"Well, first. Then you were queen of heaven," he muttered. "And we were fighting a battle you said?"

"Yeah. I was healing some dude and then you came and grabbed me. We flew over the battle to the edge. I didn't understand what the language was, but she looked a lot like you, I think she was your mother. She was bleeding and I was healing her and then a sword just flew into her chest and... She said something. Looks, I think."

He paused. "Lux?"

"Yeah," I said. "Yeah, that was it."

"That's what I called your husband. Lux is light in Latin. And Nix is night." His forehead scrunched up in thought for a moment. "You think he killed my mother?"

"I don't know. But that's definitely what she said."

He ran his hand over his jaw and thought for a moment. "Now I don't feel so bad about fucking his wife."

I chuckled as Tink's fur slid against my calf. I watched her walk down the steps and frolic through the yard for a moment. I turned back up to meet his gaze. "Nix was a Greek goddess, wasn't she?" I asked.

"Nyx," he said. "Had a bunch of kids with Erebus. They either lived in Tartaras or held power over it, the legends argue."

I rubbed my temples. "My head hurts."

"We should try to ignore the mythology for the most part, I think," he muttered. "There might be connections, but they don't line up. Clearly a lot of shit got confused."

"Yeah. Yeah, probably a good idea," I murmured, rerunning through the story he'd just told me. "So I was engaged to your brother, and I was flirting with you."

"I wouldn't say flirting. But... Yeah, I guess you kind of were." He grinned. Then his smile fell. "But you viewed me as the one who should have taken over, I guess. And we had heritage in common, culture. Seemed like he was a lot different."

"Damn." I lowered myself to the patio chair. "Maybe I was a whore."

"Well. Looks like I was a pretty shitty brother too." He brought himself to the seat beside mine. "I get it though. You didn't want to marry him, you just wanted to stop whatever was going on with our people, and I guess he was gonna help with that."

"Gonna force me to marry him to do it too." What was he holding over me exactly? What was so bad that I'd agree to an arranged marriage? I damn sure wouldn't give myself away to some guy in this life.

In fairness, that was why forced marriage shouldn't exist. Not that it makes infidelity okay, but at the same time, consent matters. Coercing someone into marrying you for anything but love is a shitty thing to do.

"It seemed like we were friends, you know," I murmured. "Maybe he was doing something shady, and we found out about it. Maybe that's when we started seeing each other."

"Well, we're getting them a lot lately. Maybe we'll find out soon."

The patio door creaked open.

"What'we you doing?" Micah rubbed his hand against his eye, clutching his stuffed lamb to his chest in the other.

"We're just talking, kiddo." I smiled as I stood. "Are you hungry? Do you want to go have breakfast?"

CHAPTER FORTY-THREE

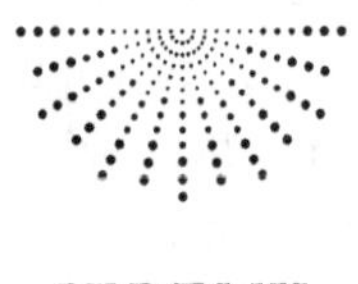

JEREMY

We're here, the text from Connor read.

"What do you think about taking a trip to the park today, baby?" Laila said, wiping spit up from Milly's face.

That seemed like a great idea, actually. If some strange, mystery people were going to be here torturing our captive, I liked the idea of being far away with my kids.

"Yeah, sure. I've got to run down and grab the mail though. I'll be right back. Then we can head out."

"Works for me." She looked at Micah. "What do you think, buddy? There might even be other kids there."

He smiled, lifting his head in a fast nod.

"Alright." I teleported to Laila and pressed my lips to hers. "It's a date."

She grinned.

"Can I come, Daddy?" Micah asked.

"Not this time, kiddo. You've got to get dressed anyway." I smiled and pulled my jacket over my shoulders. "But maybe we'll stop and get ice cream while we're out too."

He smiled, and I kissed Laila once more, saying, *Keep him away from the windows on this side of the house. I don't want him to think anything weird is happening,* into her mind.

Yeah, I know.

I disappeared and reappeared a few hundred yards from where the driveway met the road. I jogged the rest of the way down the path. Before I made it to the gate, I took in those cars. Two black SUVs. Pitch-black windows, like the kind the president would ride in. Connor stood outside of the driver's side of the first.

When I made it to the gate, I clicked in the code, still trying to catch my breath. Damn, I needed to start exercising again. That short of a distance shouldn't have made me so lightheaded.

Connor smiled, adjusting his black jacket around his hips. "How are ya', man?"

"Pretty good. Pretty damn good actually. There's a bunch of food leftover from the party yesterday if you guys want lunch." I smiled as the gates pulled inward. "I'd be happy to join you."

"Oh, I couldn't ask that of you." Connor returned my cunning grin. "I'm sure you're so busy with your son; you've got to use this time off work wisely. We won't have much time for eating anyway."

"Why not the diner when you're finished then?"

"That's alright. We've got plans."

I looked over the car behind his. He wasn't gonna budge. It was pointless to keep trying.

"How many necklaces did you need again?"

"Six," Connor said.

"Six," I murmured. I glanced back at the SUVs. "One of these cars could easily carry six people. Why do you have two?"

He placed his hands at his hips and smiled. "C'mon, man. We went over this, we're on the same side."

"I don't know you, Connor. We may have known each other at one point a thousand years ago, but I don't know *you*." His smile grew. "What? What's so funny?"

"Look, we had a deal, alright? I'm holding up my end. Your son is home, and I'm not taking him. I'm not taking your prisoner either. But don't make me blackmail you into this, man. I don't want to do that to you." I clenched my jaw. He laughed. "Just give me the necklaces, Jeremy."

"I can't even meet them." Annoyance edged my voice. "Can't even see their face."

"That's the deal."

Damn it. That *was* the fucking deal.

I tightened my jaw and reached into my pocket. "Helena's putting up the spell now. Once she does, no one can teleport out of the basement but Adam. Your people have to wait outside until Helena is brought back to our house. Then Adam will give you the clear."

"Just as we discussed," Connor said.

A huff left my nostrils. I placed the group of rope and crystals in his palm. He pulled two out and began to walk toward the second vehicle. When the window rolled down, he looked at me and gave something of a smirk.

The kind of expression one gives a child when they're waiting for Santa to fly over with his reindeer.

Connor reached inside the vehicle to hand them the necklaces. Making out anything identifiable proved impossible, but it was definitely a man's shoulder. A man's hand too, light skinned and speckled with dark brown hair.

The window rolled up. Connor went back to his car and climbed in. I stepped to the side and watched them slowly roll by.

My sixth sense knew they weren't just covert CIA. There had to be a reason they would meet Adam but wouldn't meet us. There was a *reason* they wouldn't meet us. But what the hell could it be? I wanted to believe their intentions were good, but I was still worried.

What if they were stronger than we thought? What if they could break that perimeter Helena had in place? What if they did hurt Adam?

As the second car inched past me, I felt their heavy gazes through the thick black glass. But I felt something else, too. They were blocking their powers; most people wouldn't have been able to feel it. It was barely there; I wouldn't have noticed it unless I was looking for it. They were clearly using the same magic used to disguise Connor and Naomi's energy. Although, far, *far* more powerful.

The way that energy reflected against my own reminded me of the way I felt during a solar eclipse. Kind of airy, slightly disoriented, but also somewhat uplifted. Yet, much different. And still, the strangest feeling of my life. Not necessarily bad. But strange.

They weren't just CIA. They were like us.

But who the hell were they?

I followed behind them up the path. As they drove past the house, I looked at Laila in the window with Milly on her hip. Her brows furrowed as she watched the trucks slowly make their way down the path.

Neither of us liked it. We couldn't trust someone we didn't know. But we had to do what we had to do.

Looking back on it now though, I laugh.

CHAPTER FORTY-FOUR

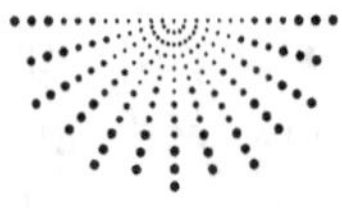

LAILA

Damp, cool wind brushed against my skin. Stray brown hairs fell to my cheeks, the smell of rain and earthworms touching my nose. Gentle speckles of water plopped from the gray clouds above. Jeremy stood behind the kids at the swing set.

From the outside looking in, it may have been a gloomy image. But it was one of the most beautiful I'd ever seen. My stomach danced with butterflies and warmth spread through my body.

It felt so normal. So right. Just a family playing with their kids at a quiet park.

"Woah! Wo-oah!" Micah's eyes widened, gripping either chain of the swing. Smiling, Jeremy pushed him higher. I laughed as I looked at the two of them through the camera. I turned the lens toward Milly kicking her feet in the baby swing.

Jeremy grasped Micah's swing and held it still. "Do you wanna go higher?"

"No, I's scwaed."

"But you're smiling." Jeremy grinned. "I promise I won't let you get hurt."

"Pwomise?" he asked.

"Promise."

Micah's smile got bigger, and he gave a fast nod.

Jeremy grabbed ahold of the swing. He pulled it back until Micah was nearly against his chest. He pushed it forward. Micah's eyes shot open as the kinetic energy hoisted him back into the air. A soft, baby giggle echoed off the trees surrounding the playground.

I laughed, smiling so wide that my jaws hurt. Jeremy's grinning eyes met mine. He lightly tapped Milly forward with one hand and pushed Micah high into the air with the other.

But my phone in my hand began to vibrate. When I looked at it, my heart fell to my stomach. As much as I hated Nastya, I did care for Moriah. And telling her I'd killed her sister wasn't something I looked forward to.

I cleared my throat and looked back to Jeremy. "I have to take this."

"Adam?"

"Moriah."

He licked his lips and gave a nod. I slid the green answer button, walked toward the trees at the edge of the park, and held it to my ear. "Hey."

"Hello, love," Moriah murmured. "Is it true? Is your boy home?"

"He is." I smiled. "I'm looking at him right now."

She exhaled deeply before her breath morphed into a laugh. "Bloody hell, you did it."

I lowered myself to a bench between two trees. "Couldn't have done it without your help. A wolf picked up the scents. We were able to close in on them right before the feds."

She fell quiet for a moment. She cleared her throat. "And my sister?"

I paused. "I'm sorry things turned out the way they did, Moriah. I really am."

"I know, darling," she murmured. There was another long pause. "I just have to ask... Was it painful?"

Slitting a throat sounded like a painful way to go for sure.

"Probably. I didn't actually do it."

"Who did?"

"She did," I muttered. "It was a group sacrifice. Her, Chris, Micah."

"Bloody hell." She gasped. "And Micah's back?"

As much as I liked Moriah, I wasn't about to tell her about Jeremy's newfound ability. I knew what they said about necromancers. That it was black magic, never to be used. That anyone with such ability needed put to death. Hannah had told me about the massacres that wiped out nearly every bloodline with the ability a few centuries ago.

And I did trust Moriah. After all, without her, I wouldn't be looking at that sweet boy on the swing with his daddy.

But I didn't trust people she associated with. I didn't trust the Chambers. And I'd be damned before someone tried to take my husband from me next.

"I healed him just in time," I said. "My sister was there. She got Chris healed too."

"Impressive," Moriah murmured. "I suppose if the sacrifice was not complete, perhaps that means that you stopped it."

I hoped. I really fucking hoped. But something had happened back there.

The flash of Micah's soul leaving his body turned Jeremy's hair white. And when he brought him back, every carcass in the vicinity started rising from the ground.

This wasn't over.

I struggled not to clear the tightness in my throat. "Maybe. Maybe, that's possible. Have there been any signs that you've noticed?"

"No. No, things look calm. Almost too calm. There was a large surge of energy about a week ago, the day you returned, I believe. I heard about a series of small quakes in California but nothing detrimental. Also, a pretty nasty solar flare. But all relatively mild. Most looks normal astrologically speaking, though."

The calm before the storm.

"That's good. Maybe. Maybe you're right. I hope."

"Me too," she muttered.

Desperate for a subject change, I said, "Hey, ya know... Now that things have settled down, maybe we could get that drink some time. Jeremy would probably enjoy a night with the kids."

"Sure," Moriah said. "Sure, in a few weeks or so. I'm sure you'd like to get into a routine with your son."

"Yeah." I smiled, gazing over the three most important people in my world. "Yeah. And I'll keep you updated if anything comes up."

"And I'll do the same."

"Take care, Moriah."

"Likewise, dear."

I managed a smile. I pulled my phone from my ear, ended the call, and slid my phone back into my pocket.

"Awe you weddy to get ice cweam, Mommy?" Micah called as Jeremy scooped him off the swing.

"Yeah, Mommy." Jeremy smiled. "Let's go get some ice cream."

"This is the best thing evew." Micah dug his red spoon back into the banana split.

"Well, you should slow down before you get brain freeze." I took a bite from my chicken wrap. "It's not going anywhere, baby."

"What's a bain feeze?" he asked.

"It's kind of hard to explain," Jeremy said. "It's when you eat something cold real fast, and it numbs the nerves in your mouth. It kind of makes your head feel funny for a minute, but then it goes away."

"Oh." Micah took a bite of the banana.

"Chew real good," I said.

His cheeks scrunched up into his eyes, smiling wide as he chomped up and down on the banana. I laughed and spooned Milly a scoop of ice cream.

This became something of a family tradition for us. Going to the park and getting ice cream together. Usually at Dairy Queen because I had to get my Blizzard. And because, no matter where we were, they all pretty much looked the same. The white Formica tabletops, the aged linoleum, that odd combination of sugar and ice in the air that settled into my lungs.

Chain restaurants get shit for being so similar. Lacking originality, so to speak. And don't get me wrong, I love the unique, nostalgic attributes of my little diner. But there's something to be said for places that give a homey vibe no matter where they're located. They brought the same comfort in my hometown as they did when I visited one in California or Minnesota.

It reminded me of going on road trips with my parents as a kid. I'd be a little homesick, and then we'd go to a Dairy Queen, or a Wendy's, and I'd feel at home. Not because I spent a lot of time at those places at home, but because they felt familiar everywhere they were.

It was like time and space had hardly changed them.

"Daddy," Micah said.

"Micah," Jeremy said.

"Who's Satan?"

Jeremy shrugged. "That answer depends on who you ask. But where'd you hear that word, buddy?"

Well, I was fairly certain we both knew where that had come from.

"Uncle Chwis said it to Aunt Leah. That you wanted Satan at ouw pawty, and he didn't like it." Micah took another bite of his ice cream. "Can I twy one of those, Mommy?" He pointed at the fries on my tray.

As Jeremy sucked his teeth, I passed them toward him and forced a smile. "The person Uncle Chris was talking about isn't the person your dad and I know. A lot of people told stories about him for a long time. When rumors spread, the truth gets twisted. Your Uncle Chris believes what he's heard. But we know Heylel personally."

Micah turned his head to the side. "Heylel?"

"That's what we call him," I said. "Satan kind of has a nasty meaning behind it."

He turned his gaze back to his ice cream. "I like this yellow stuff."

I smiled. That's what I loved about kids. They asked questions, registered what was told to them, then went back to whatever else was on their minds.

Jeremy's phone vibrated on the table. I squinted at it. Adam.

He met my gaze and raised the phone to his ear. "Hey, everything good?" A pause lingered. His shoulders fell in relief, and his head moved in a nod. "Alright. Alright, cool. We'll finish up lunch and come by the house." He paused again. A soft smile came to his lips. "Sounds good. We'll see you soon."

"Everything alright?" I asked.

He smiled. "Everything's great."

CHAPTER FORTY-FIVE

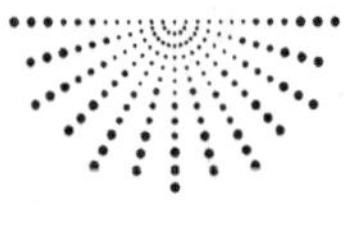

JEREMY

"So he's still down there," I murmured to Adam. "Just like he was."

"Not just like he was. They healed him when they were done, so kind of better condition than we left him." He glanced at the kids in the sunroom. "But they did a number on him, don't worry."

"You remember it?" Laila asked.

"I remember the way he looked." Adam cleared his throat. "And they didn't clean the blood off the floor so that kinda kept the memory alive."

"Do you remember anything else?" I asked.

"Little bit. Yeah... It was... Weird. The feeling that I remember, I mean. Like, somehow, I... I know them. I don't know who they are, I can't remember their voice or what they looked like, but I know them."

"But you don't remember anything about them?"

"Nothing," he said. "They wiped it all, but they let me remember that I trust them. It's not a manipulation thing either, man. I can't explain it. I know the people that were here today. And I felt like they..."

"Like they're family," I murmured. "The way I feel about Heylel."

"Family, yeah, but no. I don't think it's the same thing as it is with Heylel. It wasn't a past lives thing. I *knew* them, dude."

I thought back to that sensation as they drove past. They were definitely like us, but if I'd met them before, I'd recognize that feeling. It made me feel dizzy. No one alive had ever done that.

"Is that all you remember? Trusting them?" Laila asked.

He paused, thinking. "No. No, they had a message for you."

I arched a brow. "A message."

"A long one," he said.

"What was it?" Laila asked.

"That they're 'handling it.'" He made air quotes. "They said that there's nothing you can do that they aren't working on. The phrase they wanted me to emphasize was, 'you have time. Enjoy it.'"

"Can't get much more vague than that," Laila said.

"Well, the advice they wanted me to pass on is pretty specific." Adam rubbed his mouth. He blinked, trying to recall the thought. "They said to work your asses off at Moe's. Don't work yourselves to the point of insanity, but try to bring in as much money as you can. And save the money, be frugal. But don't cash it in for gold."

My head tilted. "No one knows about that plan but us."

"Well, they're CIA, dude. I don't know, they've probably been listening to our conversations for months. We have wire taps all over our houses." Adam glanced at the Google Home on the kitchen counter. "There were a few other things, hang on."

I rubbed my hand against my mouth, waiting.

After a moment, he said, "They said that when you get the money out, have Brody do it at his bank. And make sure the bills are old. As old as he can get, and preferably in big bills."

I heard it, and I'd do it. But I couldn't think of a reason that would make sense. Was it because older bills would be worth more? Was it because new money couldn't be trusted?

The answer was right there in front of me. I don't know why it didn't add up.

"And they said to get a decent stock of essential items. Things that would really matter. Not dumb shit like toilet paper, but plants. A composting toilet. Water cisterns. Solar panels. A greenhouse. And chickens, they specifically said chickens."

Laila made a face. "They want us to doomsday prep."

"There's more, hang on." He thought for a moment. "They said to stand with your agreements in the supernatural community. Give Roland your blood each month as promised, keep your word to protect Moriah. They also said to get on good terms with the Chambers. Spend time with Mèmè and Papy. Go to the meetings, and don't be afraid to voice your opinions, but don't overstep. 'Assert yourselves but earn their respect.' They said you'll know what that means."

My brows fell further. That, I did remotely understand. That's exactly what we'd done when forming alliances with the wolves and vamps worldwide. If the world was ending, we did need the Chambers as allies too. We owed them a meeting now anyway. I didn't like it, but it made sense.

Adam turned to Laila. "And they said to spend time with your mom."

Her mouth fell open a bit. "They said what?"

His eyes shined with worry. "Told me to tell Jen that, too."

Did that mean Rachel was going to die? Last I'd heard, she was in perfect health. She was barely into her fifties, she exercised regularly, and she didn't drink, smoke, or do drugs. But I loved that lady. I made a mental note to tell her to get a check-up.

Laila blinked hard for a moment. She gave a slow nod.

"Was that everything?" I asked.

Adam paused to think. "Yeah. Yeah, that about covers it."

They'd said to enjoy our lives. They'd said to prepare for the worst but enjoy the time we had now. They'd said we *had* time to enjoy.

So for now, that's what I planned to do.

I placed my hand at the small of Laila's back. "Well. Let's do what they said then. Ignorance is bliss, right?"

Laila gave a slow nod.

"Mommy," Micah called from the sunroom. "Can I play outside with Tink?"

Laila smiled. "Sure, buddy."

"I think we've still got a couple gloves and balls in the garage." Adam looked between Micah and Luka. He forced a smile and looked back to me. "Why don't we all go out and play a game?"

I smiled back, moving my head in a gentle nod. "Yeah. Yeah, let's get our jackets on, Micah."

"I'll get Milly's," Laila said.

And we did just that.

Yeah, we were worried. But we needed time. We needed peace. We'd spent too long in misery. We'd spent too long being terrified our son was going to die, or that the world would end, or that we weren't going to make it to the next day.

It was okay to be a little worried.

But we could also enjoy the time we had left.

The story continues in *Flash Back*. Turn the page for a sneak peek, or click the link below to download now:
https://www.amazon.com/gp/product/B096L15NND/

Sign up for Charlie's newsletter and receive a free copy of the Eluding Destiny prequel, *Blood Bar*:
https://liquidmind.media/eluding-destiny-prequel/

If you enjoyed this story, please consider leaving a rating or review on Amazon:
https://www.amazon.com/dp/B0956PTMBX/

Join Charlie's private reader group on Facebook and discuss all things Eluding Destiny and Charlie Nottingham:
https://www.facebook.com/groups/661440911724435/

FLASH BACK CHAPTER ONE

OVER THE LAST FOUR WEEKS - APRIL 30, 2022 - LAILA

At one point, nothing scared me more than becoming a mother. After losing Micah, I thought I'd be a horrible parent. But that was far from the truth. I fucked up the first three years, but I was going to make it right with the following fifteen.

My son and daughter would have good lives. They'd be as close to normal as possible for our kinds. We'd teach them to be good people. That's all that mattered to me. No matter what I had to do, I would shelter them from anything that could hurt them.

Micah had adjusted incredibly well with all things considered. But that isn't to say that every day was a breeze. There were bad ones.

About a week after we brought him home, we realized that he was deathly afraid of the dark. I usually left the wax warmer on in the bathroom at night, but the bulb burned out. I hadn't noticed, neither had Jeremy. But we certainly did when Micah erupted in erratic, uncontrollable sobs around two a.m.

I showed him that he and I always have a source of light—from our glowing eyes to our fiery or illuminated, healing palms. He relaxed a bit after that. But his panic attack still took about two hours to entirely soothe.

We also learned that Micah hated doctors. I wasn't sure if that were a result of Peterson or the hospital where we'd let them cut beneath his skin to remove the implants. Either way. His round of vaccinations the week before may have been the hardest day of my life. Had it not been for Jeremy's ever-present gentle attitude with the kids, I may have become an anti-vaxxer due to simple guilt.

Overall though, we'd gotten into the groove of having two kids. It came effortlessly. I said it before, and I'd say at a million more times over the years. We were built for parenthood. We were good at it, and we loved it.

Then again, I supposed the goddess and god of fertility were supposed to.

It'd been a good month. The first month of my life where I was able to be a wife, a mother to my daughter, and a mother to my son. It sounds so simple when phrased that way. Something most take for granted. But I treasured each and every moment. Then again, some part of me was very aware from the stockpile growing in my basement that I needed to treasure the time while I had it.

I listened to the advice the mystery CIA guys gave Adam. We got the money out of the bank like we were told to, we held our contracts in the supernatural world—we even worked a few quick cases with some allies. They went a lot quicker than they did back in the day.

Jeremy and I scheduled a meeting with the Chambers in France. Small, we told them it had to be small. No more than thirty guests with us included. I didn't trust the people working beneath the Council enough to be further outnumbered than that. They agreed. Reluctantly, anyway.

We also agreed to stay on his grandparent's vineyard for five days the following week. Chris was looking forward to it. So was Hannah. The rest of us were less than ecstatic. She and Chris were well liked by their grandparents. I think Brody held a certain place in their heart too. But the rest of us... not so much.

Regardless, we all needed the trip. Max needed the money. And in all fairness, my kids deserved a chance to at least meet their rich, stuffy grandparents.

And we'd made a deal. One we had to stick to.

The FBI and CIA went radio silent the day after those mystery-people tortured Peterson. I tried calling Tina a few times. She never called back. Jeremy called Connor only to the same end.

But still, we heeded the words they'd left in Adam's mind. I spent more time with Mom. A lot more; we saw her nearly every day. Micah loved the creek behind her house. He said he saw it before, in a dream maybe. That I wore a white dress with pretty flowers on the back.

I'm still not sure how he remembered that. Maybe from seeing memories in Lydia's mind when they were linked? Either way, it brought a smile to my lips. I'd hoped my son would be at our wedding in a little tux, but my hopes usually didn't equate to my reality. At least he was there some way or another.

As instructed, we got some damn chickens. Tink killed two. Luckily, Jeremy found them before Micah. He said we should cut them up and have them for dinner, that we'd have to get used to it if the end of the world was coming. I'd named them; there was no way I could season them and throw them in the oven. But Wyatt and Celena said they were delicious. After that though, we decided to move the coop *outside* the fenced-in section of the yard.

Jeremy threw together an eight-hundred dollar shed from the local department store on the west end of the house. We tossed up some foam insulation, bought heating lamps, and got a series of plants. Bell peppers, tomatoes, cucumbers, lettuce, spinach; the works. Micah and I worked on tending to it together, growing the leaves and fruits before trimming enough for the evening's salad and side dishes. He'd gotten a good handle on earth in that time. Milly even turned a cherry tomato green with a touch. When she did, Micah and I jumped to our feet together, clapping and cheering. She giggled and did it again. It was a life skill they'd both need, regardless of an impending apocalypse.

We invested ten thousand dollars in solar panels. Even at the time, it seemed arbitrary with Jeremy's ability to create energy. But they said it was needed and we had no reason to assume otherwise.

In our garage sat five composting toilets, ready for installation if needed. But for the time being, we enjoyed our septic system.

Thankfully, we had well water with a kick-ass filter. We bought a few cisterns and backup filtration systems to hold onto in case of a serious disaster like a collapsed well. But we didn't hook them up, just held onto them in case we'd need them.

If that wasn't enough already, I went a little doomsday prepper crazy. I pulled some strings with the underground hospital and stockpiled a large supply of broad-spectrum antibiotics. They may expire before they got used, but in an apocalypse, expired is better than nothing. Also, I got a bunch of gowns, gloves, masks, and sterile equipment. Not even for me; I could heal people. Considering the way rubbing alcohol had disappeared during the pandemic, I stocked up on that too. It was the best and least offensive cleaning product available. But I knew that if shit hit the fan, the medical field would probably be as ill-prepared as when the coronavirus hit in 2020. I wanted to be able to help.

Owning a diner made stocking up on food easy without looking odd. I loaded up on tons of canned everything. Canned beans, canned meat, canned pudding, canned nacho cheese, canned vegetables, and tons of canned fruit. Especially fruit that wouldn't survive our climate and I couldn't grow myself in the shed. I got a few quart cans of pineapple because they were Micah and Milly's latest obsessions. Pineapple on pancakes, pineapple on his PB&J, and *definitely* pineapple on his pizza. That insistence sparked a controversy deeper than the fiery political climate.

Moe's made stocking up on necessity items easier as well without clearing out shelves at the stores. Toilet paper, paper towels, hand soap, sanitizer; all the basics. I ordered a few extra boxes each time I placed the usual order.

I feel it important to bear in mind that most of the items I purchased were never intended to be used only by my massive family. I knew that if the end was coming, we'd be on the front lines. People would come to us for help. And we needed to be *able* to help.

We even cleared out a section of trees between our house and the main house. Then the guys made a project of curing the wood. We planned on saving it for lumber. We didn't know if we'd need it. But if the end was coming, we needed a safe place to keep our friends and allies who might need us. Perhaps a makeshift hospital or cabin of sorts. Our houses were large, but the end of the world is the end of the damn world. There were a lot of people out there that would need a safe place to rest their heads, and they couldn't all fit beneath my roof.

Doomsday prepping seemed so silly to me once. Now I was seriously considering digging a fallout shelter a few dozen feet underground. We decided it was too expensive. I considered it though.

It may have seemed a little excessive. But I knew it was coming and now was the time to prepare. Not panic, but prepare.

I'd been given advice once almost four years prior. Leave Jeremy, cash out my inheritance, take my baby, and start over. I didn't listen. I lost the first three years of my son's life. Not to say that I ever wanted to leave Jeremy. I wouldn't have Milly if I had. But sometimes, I still wish I'd taken that advice. Or at least been a bit more cautious than I was throughout my pregnancy. Regardless, I wouldn't make that mistake twice. Someone with more knowledge than me spoke, and I listened.

We warned people as much as we could. Others in the supernatural world, friends, and families. Leah put the word out on the dark web which apparently made it pretty far. She cited the CIA's involvement, which may not have been wise, but it got the attention it needed. We'd even started to see trending stories from major journalists—talking about odd weather changes and intense solar flares. Most weren't taking it seriously, but some did. Stores weren't clearing out, but people were establishing small stockpiles of their own.

Deep down, my core shook. But I needed to stay steadier than stone.

My kids were watching. The other survivors were watching. Leaders in our community were watching. I'd been given an army for a reason, and after seeing the warriors Jeremy and I were in our first life, I understood why.

The races in our world—Guardians, Fae, Wolves, Vampires, Demons—needed to band together. If we were divided, we couldn't fight for our world as one.

And as much as I hated Peterson, he was right.

I made a damn good figurehead.

FLASH BACK CHAPTER TWO

JEREMY

The familiar, homey scent of warm apples touched my nose. My ass was sore against the wooden breakfast nook bench. Soft spring air floated in from the open window behind me. It sent a pleasant chill to my skin. I listened to the kids giggling out there with Laila and Tink and wished I could go out there too.

I loved hanging out outside with them. It was my favorite thing in the world because it was their favorite thing in the world. And I wanted to enjoy it.

"You just have to focus," Hannah said.

"I am focusing," I grumbled.

"Well, not hard enough apparently. You should have been there and back by now. Chop-ch—"

"Maybe if you weren't bitching at me every two seconds." My eyes opened, meeting her blue glare. She placed either hand at her hips and huffed.

"Fine." She plopped into the chair beside the table. "But seriously, put the blindfold on. It helps."

I closed my eyes again. "I don't need a blindfold; my eyes are closed."

It wasn't that I didn't see her point. But the thing was, I didn't care about all of this right now. I just wanted to enjoy my wife and kids. I wanted to bask in the life I'd waited eons for. I finally had it all. My family, a steady income, a beautiful home.

Yeah, I needed to get used to how it felt in the whole afterlife, abyss thing. But I'd been studying. Hannah had given me something of an index with the three fundamental rules of necromancy, and I got it.

Rule number one: We can't save everyone. No matter what, there must be light in the abyss. If we saved every life that passed through, that'd throw off its balance.

Rule number two: Close the door when we leave. Metaphorically, of course, which is what we were working on at the moment. Going there, resting in the abyss for a while—getting accustomed to the peace and silence of it—and returning without bringing any light but my own back.

Rule number three: For every action, there's an equal and opposite reaction. Meaning when we put a life back into its body, death takes another of equal size in its place. That there's a balance to the abyss that can't be knocked off.

But my problem wasn't closing the door when I left. My problem seemed to be opening it. I didn't like it there. It was cold, and dark, and empty. When I had to go to save someone, I did so instantly without much thought and effort. But I didn't want to go there on my own accord. It was the personification of hanging out in a graveyard, and that wasn't my thing.

"Whatever. I'll shut up," Hannah said. "Let me know when it doesn't work and you're ready to listen."

I opened my eyes and glared. "It's not like I'm not trying, dude. But I had no choice the first time I did it. I had to bring her back."

"Should I try stabbing her?" She gestured out the window. "Probably won't get far, but maybe she'll kill me. Then you'll have to bring me back."

"Can't we just bank on it kicking in when I need it?"

"You know what you sound like?" Hannah asked. "Laila pregnant with Micah."

"That isn't fair. She didn't know—"

"And neither do we." My baby sister looked a lot more like a woman in that moment, wide, serious eyes shifting between mine. "That's why we have to do this. You have to know what you're doing. This isn't amateur hour anymore, Jeremy. The end of the world might be coming, and you need to know what you're doing to keep your people safe. You were a god once; you need to live up to what that entails."

I huffed. A god. Yeah, that may have been what people called me, but that was never how I envisioned myself.

"No, I need to know what our plan was two thousand years ago." I rubbed my temples. "We need to know whether to retreat or stand our ground. We need to know what this is going to look like. Nuclear? Natural disaster? Can we form an alliance with these people?"

"We don't even know anything's coming for sure," Hannah said. "But I know that no matter what, you need to know what you're doing with this."

I turned my gaze out the patio door. Micah's little light-up shoes glowed blue and green as Laila chased him through the yard. With each flash of those bulbs on his feet, I remembered that massive flare of white light just as blood shot like a fountain from his neck.

A knot solidified in my throat, and I shook my head. "You weren't there, Han. Something happened. It turned my hair gray." I gestured to the streaks that hung around my face. "Then some mystery CIA agents that may or may not be allies of ours from thousands of years ago tell us that we need to stock up and grow a garden and get chickens." I shook my head again. "No, it's already started. It's just a matter of time before we see it."

She fell quiet, looking out the window with me.

That image is forever imprinted in my mind. The three most important people in my world chasing one another through the early spring, wildflower-covered field off my family home's kitchen. Milly's little white dress flowing in the wind, Laila's long brown hair flying in her smiling face, Micah's bubbly baby laugh. Like something out of a 1950's movie. I could practically hear the opera singing in the background.

Still so young. Still so innocent, really. But a wonderful memory.

"When are you..." Hannah cleared her throat. "I just mean... Do you have plans?" She glanced at the basement door. "For him, I mean?"

I clenched my jaw. "Laila and I have been working up a list of things to ask him. We were hoping we'd have remembered more by now. Then we'd have more to go on."

"You haven't had any more dreams?" she asked.

"No, I've had a few. But they've been more like flashes. Seeing her walk by in some place I think is a castle. Fighting in battles and shit. We made one hell of a team on a battlefield—she healed; I held their souls in their body. We saved a lot of lives."

"And no conversations in these little flashes?"

"Not really." A good portion of them were us fucking. "Nothing worth asking Peterson."

"I think we should start asking the questions we do have though," Hannah muttered. "Kai and I can watch the kids for a few hours back at the house. Give you guys some space to... You know."

It wasn't that I was excited to torture Peterson. But I was excited to get the information we needed. I was even more excited to see what he'd look like as a corpse.

Laila and I had pushed him to the backs of our minds since we got Micah back. He'd taken so much time with our son already, we couldn't let him take any more. But Micah had adjusted well. He was doing great. And so were we.

Which was why I wasn't excited for this. We knew it was Laila he'd answer questions for. And it wasn't going to be easy for her to face that man.

"Yeah, probably a good idea. I'm going back to work when we get back from France so that'd be a good thing to cross off the list first. And the survivors want a date for the execution. So we need to get to work." I ran my fingers through my hair, letting out a deep sigh. "I'll talk to Laila when she comes in. Text me when you're free before we go."

"Pretty much whenever. I'm on spring break," Hannah said. "But we really need to work on this too, Jeremy. The biggest concern with this apocalypse is too many people dying at once. We don't know what will happen if so many souls are stuck there at the same time."

"I know, Hannah. But there's a lot on my plate right now and I'm a little overwhelmed." I ran my hand over my mouth. "I'm going to work on it, alright? But there's a lot going on. Let me get through this trip. We'll work on it around my schedule at the diner."

"Alright. We'll start working on it after the trip. But study the notes I've given you, okay? Those were Mom's rules. And they're good ones to follow."

"Yeah, I have the notecards at the house. I'll study."

"I'm serious. You need to memorize—"

"I know, Hannah. Jesus."

Her face said she didn't appreciate my tone.

I closed my eyes and rubbed my hands against them. "I'm sorry. I'm not trying to be a dick, alright? I'm just stressed out."

Hannah looked over me carefully for a moment. She continued. "Are you okay?"

A loaded question, and I knew what she was asking. If I planned on sticking a needle in my arm. But that wasn't it. I just didn't want to think about this shit. I wanted to enjoy my life. When I was happy, drugs were the last thing on my mind. And right about then, that's what I was. Happy. Life was good. I wanted to focus on that joy.

I didn't want to think about what I knew was coming.

"Yeah, I'm fine. I'm stressed, but I'm fine. I'm not relapsing in the foreseeable future if that's what you're asking. And yes, I'm still clean."

"That's not really why I asked," Hannah muttered. "This is about Mémé and Papy, isn't it?"

Yeah, I guessed it was.

I knew we had to make friends and play nice with the leaders of the supernatural community. If the world was going to end, we needed them behind us. But races aren't supposed to mix. People didn't like that I married a hybrid and that our children were massively powerful creatures. And for the most part, I didn't care.

But my grandparent's opinions were different. Not that they

mattered to me. They didn't. I could handle any shitty comments they made. But my kids weren't even three and one yet. Micah wouldn't understand why they treated him like a pariah. And he didn't deserve to. He was perfect, I didn't want them filling him with insecurities over something as arbitrary as his DNA.

"He called my marriage blasphemous. I can only keep my mouth shut for so long. And Laila's picked up a little French from me working with the kids, she's not one to bite her tongue either."

"The Chambers are going to be bending over backwards to kiss your ass. I doubt Mémé and Papy are going to be any different. You guys are a big deal in our world."

I raked my hand through my hair. "Yeah. Yeah, I hope. But if they say something shitty about my kids, I'm leaving."

"I agree. But let's hope that isn't the case."

Intrigued by *Flash Back*? Click the link below to download now!
https://www.amazon.com/gp/product/B096L15NND/

ALSO BY CHARLIE NOTTINGHAM

The Eluding Destiny Series

Eluding Destiny

The Horrors That Created Us

Aftershocks

The Precipice

Land of Light

The Quiet Army

Sacred Sins

Flash Back

The Shift

Lost to Time

Gods Among Us

The Cover Up

Blank Slate

Eluding Destiny Prequels

The Last Beginning

Blood Bar

Raven's Cry Series

(MMFM Paranormal Romance)

Raven's Cry

Raven's Song

Celena's Story Duology

(Completed—paranormal romance, urban fantasy)

New Normal: Celena's Story Part 1

Reprisal: Celena's Story Part 2

Origins of the Gods

(Completed Trilogy—fantasy romance, more information on the origins of the Fae and Angels, how life began on earth, where Guardians came from, and— most importantly—a badass forbidden romance)

Origins

The Thrones of Ore and Ice

Creation

Stand Alone Novels

Curse of the Gods: The Bridge Between Origins of the Gods and the Eluding Destiny Series

Sign up for Charlie's newsletter and receive a free copy of the Eluding Destiny prequel, Blood Bar:

https://liquidmind.media/eluding-destiny-prequel/

ABOUT THE AUTHOR

Charlie is a... Okay, talking about myself in third person is weird.

Nice to meet you! My name's Charlie Nottingham, and my whole world revolves around fantasy. When I'm not writing a new book, I'm either hanging out with my dogs, talking with my fans online, or reading some amazing urban fantasy, paranormal romance, or fantasy romance series (always a series, never a stand-alone, because I hate to fall for a character and never see them again). Or re-watching some Buffy or Supernatural. (They never get old!)